COWBOY HEART

for my cowboy,
who has a heart
as big as all outdoors
and who is always
in my heart

X o P
L

COWBOY HEART

A Novel

JoAnn Guidry

To order additional copies of this book, contact:
Xlibris Corporation
1-888-7-XLIBRIS
www.Xlibris.com
Orders@Xlibris.com

THIS BOOK IS DEDICATED TO EVERYONE WHO
BELIEVED IN A CAJUN AND HER COWBOY.

1

In a blur, the two cowboys and the steer were into the arena.One. Two. Scott, the header, throws his rope; good one down low at the base of the horns. He dallies the rope around his saddle horn as his horse, Marlboro, turns the steer to the left. One. Two. Ben, the heeler, tosses his rope and it slides perfectly beneath the steer's hind legs. Ben dallies and his horse, Cherokee, holds his ground. The two horses are facing the steer, the ropes are taut and the clock stops at 4.5 seconds. The crowd roars its approval.

"Yes, folks, let's hear it for the roping team of four-time world all-around cowboy Ben Matthews and partner Scott Barnes!" the announcer says. "They will be the ones to beat in tomorrow's finals of the Waco State Rodeo!"

Jim Reynolds turned the corner, spotting Ben and Scott behind the chutes and surrounded by a large group of cowboys and cowgirls. And it was plain to see that it was Ben who was the center of attention. Still a star. In this thirty years as a rodeo official, Reynolds had seen a lot of cowboys come and go. He had witnessed the great ones like Larry Mahan and Tom Ferguson become six-time world all-round champion cowboys. And five years ago, he had watched as a roughstock-riding sensation by the name of Ben Matthews began a legendary career.

Ben seemed born to the role. A third-generation south Texas cowboy from a prominent ranching family, he had been a high school and University of Texas all-around champion. The rodeo world had eagerly awaited the day that he turned pro, and Ben more than lived up to everyone's expectations.

He dominated the ever-dangerous events of bronc and bull riding like no one had since Mahan. On his way to winning four consecutive all-around champion cowboy titles, Ben also became a great spokesperson for the sport of rodeo. With his good-looks, killer Texas cowboy smile and easy-going manner, he was a publicist's delight. The women loved him, men liked and respected him, and young boys wanted to grow up to be him.

Then two seconds away from his fifth all-around title, Ben's storybook existence was shattered. Reynolds had been there that day at the National Finals in Las Vegas. It had been one of the worst bull-riding wrecks he had ever seen. And as he watched them load Ben's bloodied and broken body into the ambulance, he had already begun to mourn the loss.

But to his and everyone's astonishment, not only did Ben survive—he came back to compete again. The bull left his mark, though. Ben now had a long scar down the left side of his face, and he walked with a limp. And the damage the bull had inflicted on his body forced him to switch to team roping. But the star was back as though he had never been gone. Only a little more than a year after Reynolds was sure that bull had killed Ben, another championship title was within his grasp. It was truly a remarkable and courageous comeback.

Now Reynolds wondered if he'd be able to summon enough courage to do what had to be done. The last of the buckle-bunnies scurried away with an autograph; Scott ambled off with another cowboy, and Ben headed toward the stable area. Taking a deep breath, Reynolds started after him.

"Ben, I need you to come with me," Reynolds said, wrapping an arm around Ben's shoulders as he caught up to him.

"If it's about last night, we left more than enough money to cover the damages," Ben said lightheartedly. "We were just having a good time and got a little carried away."

"Come on, son," Reynolds said quietly, steering Ben around.

When they reached the arena office, Reynolds opened the door, motioned for Ben to enter and then closed the door behind them. Ben found himself face to face with two Texas state troopers. Damn. It had been just a usual barroom brawl, and nobody had gotten seriously hurt. What the hell were these guys here for?

"Ben Matthews?" the taller, older one asked.

"Yes, sir, I'm Ben Matthews. What's the problem?"

"I'm sorry to have to tell you that there's been an accident," the state trooper quietly began. "The driver of an 18-wheeler fell asleep at the wheel and struck your father's truck on the interstate about twenty miles from here. The gas tank exploded on impact, and the vehicle caught fire. I'm sorry. No one survived."

There was a tremendous roaring in Ben's head. He stood there, trying to catch his breath. "Are...are you sure...it was my family?" he heard himself ask weakly.

The other trooper, the younger one, nodded. "Yes, sir, I'm afraid so. On impact, the truck's license plate was knocked loose. It's how we tracked you down."

Ben felt his knees buckling, and he was sure he was going to throw up. Then someone was on each side of him, guiding him into a chair. And then he felt nothing.

They had left Waco an hour ago. Scott periodically glanced over at his friend as he drove the royal blue and silver pickup pulling the matching two-horse trailer back to San Antonio. The Matthews Ranch was just north of that south Texas city, located in the fertile central Texas hill country. Ben sat slouched in the front seat, his head resting against the back of it with his hat partially covering his face. Scott was sure he wasn't sleeping, not that he didn't need to. For the past two days, Ben hadn't eaten or slept and had only spoken when he absolutely had to, and that had been little.

Scott Barnes had known Ben all his life, and he had never seen him like this. Not even after that bull had nearly killed him. But no one had been nearly killed this time. This time, Ben's family had been killed—had burned to death—in a senseless, random accident.

Thomas and Sara Matthews had driven up to Austin to pick up Chris; they had all wanted to be there for Ben's next step toward another championship. Ben's recovery had been a long, frustrating ordeal for all of them. But together they had gotten through it. It had been Chris who had pointed out to his big brother that although bulls and broncs were out, there was no reason Ben couldn't compete in team roping.

Scott had been the natural choice for a partner since the Matthews had always considered him a part of the family. An only child, his father had died when he was ten, and although his mother later remarried, he never felt close to his step-father. His mother later sold their small spread that bordered the Matthews Ranch, and they moved into San Antonio. But Scott remained close to Ben's family and practically grew up on the Matthews Ranch, spending more time there than in the city.

Since he was a year younger than Ben and three years older than Chris, Sara Matthews called Scott the middle son they never had. And with his reddish brown hair and hazel eyes, he looked more like Chris' brother than Ben did. Ben had inherited his father's looks. He was tall and lean with striking dark blue eyes and the wavy, black hair of his father's youth.

Scott blinked to clear his blurry vision, feeling the warmth of tears in his eyes. Ben wouldn't like him crying. Ben was a lot like his father in that way, too. He didn't always think it necessary to voice his feelings, but they always showed in his eyes. And for the last two days, Scott had seen so much pain in his friend's eyes that he didn't know how Ben hadn't broken down.

Ben had always been there for him, as much a big brother to him as a friend. And now he felt so damned helpless; there just didn't seem to be anything he could do to help him get through this. Although Ben was physically next to him in the truck, it seemed to Scott that he had willed himself somewhere else. And Scott was worried he'd never come back.

Four hours later, Scott and Ben unloaded the horses, bedding them down in the Matthews Ranch's main barn. Ben still hadn't said a word; he just silently stepped out of the truck when it rolled to a stop and just as silently unloaded Cherokee. Scott followed suit, leading Marlboro into an adjoining stall. It was 8 p.m. and no one else was around.

Once the horses were watered and fed, the two men climbed back into the truck and Scott drove past the Matthews' house; Ben's house was on the far side of the ranch. Once again the vehicle came to a stop and, in silence, the two men got out, retrieving their suitcases from the compartments on each side of the trailer. Scott followed his friend into the unlocked, comfortable ranch house that had been built with Ben's rodeo earnings. Wordlessly, Ben went down the hallway and disappeared into his bedroom, the door closing firmly behind him. With a sigh, Scott veered off into the bedroom he often used when he was on the ranch.

A couple of hours later, something woke Scott from a light, fitful sleep. He lay there listening for a moment, deciding he might as well get up. Reaching over, he grabbed his jeans and a T-shirt from his still opened suitcase on the floor.

Padding down the hallway in his bare feet, he flipped on the light switch as he turned toward the kitchen. But just enough light spilled over for him to make out Ben sitting on the couch in the den. Scott changed directions and headed toward his friend.

Ben wasn't alone; there was a half-empty bottle of Jack Daniel's on the coffee table and a half-filled glass in his hand. Scott walked over to the bar, got himself a glass and then joined his friend. Sitting in the chair next to the couch, Scott leaned over and poured himself a full glass of the only whiskey Thomas Matthews said was worth drinking. He settled back into the overstuffed chair and took a generous drink, savoring the whiskey as it slid down his throat.

"It's my fault," Ben said flatly.

The sound of Ben's voice startled Scott; he hadn't realized how accustomed he had become to the silence. "What?"

"It's my fault," Ben repeated in exactly the same monotone.

Scott moved to the edge of the chair. "No, Ben, it was an accident. A terrible accident..."

"That wouldn't have happened if they hadn't been coming to see me in a damned rodeo."

"Please don't do this to yourself. It was an accident that could have happened anytime, anywhere."

Ben was relentless. "But it happened twenty miles from a damned rodeo I had no business being in."

"What are you talking about? Your family has been coming to see you in rodeos since you were in high school. This time was no different."

"Yes, it was, and you know it," Ben snapped. "After that damned bull, I should have given it up. I should have just settled down on the ranch and given the damned rodeo up." He stopped as something caught in his throat. Quickly, he got to his feet and hurried back to his bedroom.

Wiping away the steam from the bathroom mirror, Ben made himself look at the stranger glaring back at him. He traced the scar that ran down the length of the left side of his face, cheekbone to jaw. Dropping his hand down to his left rib cage, he felt the deep, jagged scars that ran down to his hip. There were scars on his left leg, too. Beneath them were pins and plates that held his leg and hip in place.

Turning away, Ben slipped on the blue bathrobe and walked slowly from the bathroom to the bed. He lowered himself onto it and sat there, staring at the three metal boxes on the dresser. Those three boxes held what remained of his family; cremation had completed what the fiery accident had begun.

This couldn't be real. This had to be a nightmare he just couldn't wake up from. His father, mother and brother could not have been killed in an accident twenty miles from the rodeo grounds. No goodbyes. No final "I love yous." Just "Sorry, Mr. Matthews, there's been an accident." And they were gone; their lives were over.

This was all wrong. He should be the one who was gone. His life should have ended on that arena floor in Las Vegas. Ben caught his breath, shuddering as the memories tumbled over each other in his head. It was Chris who had saved him.

When he'd regained consciousness three days later, the first thing he became aware of was George Strait singing "Amarillo By Morning," his classic homage to the rodeo cowboy. And then when his vision began to clear, the first thing he'd seen was Chris grinning at him.

"I knew if anything was going to wake you up, it was going to be George," Chris matter-of-factly said, obviously quite pleased with himself.

Ben later found out that it had taken some talking and pleading on Chris' part to convince the doctors to allow him to bring the tape player into the intensive care unit. But Chris was a very persuasive twenty-two-year old, who was also a pre-med student at the University of Texas. He was a great believer in the research which theorized that comatose patients were thought to be able to hear and feel things, although they couldn't respond. His conscious brother was all the proof he needed to give Strait credit for proving the theory valid.

But at the time, Ben hadn't been so sure he wanted to be conscious.

His head was pounding and the left side of his face hurt like hell; his chest felt like he was in a vise. When he focused his eyes ahead, all he saw was what he assumed was his left leg in an ankle to hip cast, propped up in a metal frame at a 45-degree angle.

"I hope...someone killed...that damned bull," he rasped. His throat was still raw from the respirator tube that had only been removed that morning.

"We'll have barbecued steaks when you get home," Chris replied, still grinning from ear to ear.

The next morning the doctor told Ben how lucky he had been. The bull's kick that had hit him in the head had fortunately been more a glancing blow than a direct one. He had only a hairline fracture and hadn't suffered any brain damage. Although he'd have a scar where the bull's hoof had raked down the side of his face, none of his facial muscles and nerves had been severed.

And while the four broken ribs and resultant punctured left lung would make breathing painful for awhile, one of those ribs could have just as easily have punctured his heart—which had been bruised, as had his left kidney. His spleen had ruptured, and he had nearly bled to death. But human beings, the doctor told him, could get along just fine without a spleen. He'd just have to guard against infections.

True, his left hip and leg had suffered multiple fractures, but some well-placed pins, plates and a cast did the trick. Sure, he'd have a limp, later arthritis, and eventually would need a hip replacement. But, short term, he'd be fine after some physical therapy. Not fine enough to ride bulls and broncs again, but fine enough to lead a normal life. All in all, he'd been a very lucky young man.

When the doctor finally left, Ben and his family remained silent. Thomas Matthews was a good man of few words, who preferred to keep his emotions in check. Tall and lean with a full head of silver hair at the age of 50, Thomas Matthews—and he answered only to Thomas, not Tom—had always believed "doin' means more than sayin.'" He patted Ben on the right shoulder, making fleeting eye contact, then left the room.

Sara Matthews, from whom Chris had gotten his chestnut hair, wiped away the tears coming from her hazel eyes, then bent over and kissed her eldest son on the forehead. "You get some rest, honey," she said softly, squeezing his hand and then she, too, left.

Ben glanced over at his kid brother, who was standing by the window looking out into the night. He was so glad that Chris, who was a fair cowboy in his own right, had always wanted more and had a career as a doctor ahead of him. Because then he wouldn't ever have to lie half-broken in a hospital bed, scared and wondering how the hell he was going to go on with the rest of his life. He had known that the day would come when his rodeo career would be over, but he hadn't planned on it ending like this.

It was as though Chris had heard him thinking. Slowly, he turned around and walked to the bed. "It's going to be all right, Ben," he said quietly, placing his hand on his brother's arm. "You're my big brother and there isn't anything you can't do. No bull is going to get the best of you. I promise, it's going to be all right."

The Texas spring morning broke clear and cool. After lingering in the bunkhouse longer than usual, the ranch hands reluctantly began tending to their chores. But there was no sense of urgency in their manner as they struggled to deal with death's reality. One by one, they made their way to Ben's house to pay their respects. Ben wasn't up to any visitors, Scott told them. They nodded in understanding, shook his hand, and left.

Scott was relieved when Lisa appeared at the kitchen door. He had long been in need of comfort himself.

He hugged her tightly. "I'm so glad you're finally here."

Lisa kissed him on the cheek. "You're exhausted," she said softly, pushing away stray strands of hair from his forehead.

"It's been pretty rough."

"How's Ben?"

"Not good."

Lisa slowly opened the door when Ben didn't respond to the knock or her calling out his name. She stood there in the doorway, her big, brown eyes brimming over with tears. Ben stood up in time to wrap his arms around her as she came to him. He rested his chin on her head, her auburn hair so soft on his skin.

Ben had loved Lisa Stanton for as long as he could remember, even when she was a pesky tomboy challenging him to horse races across the prairie. Everyone, including him, always figured they'd be married by now and have a passel of kids.

But their choice of colleges had slowed down their relationship. In addition to being a hell of a barrel racer, Lisa was a talented artist and had received an art scholarship to a prestigious East coast school. The University of Texas at Austin was as far away as Ben cared to go. The two stayed in touch with letters and phone calls, planning to meet in San Antonio during school breaks. Then graduation further altered their plans; Ben began his professional rodeo career and Lisa left to study in Europe.

For the next four years, she would come back to San Antonio from Thanksgiving through New Year's Day. She and Ben would be inseparable, and she had been there for his first four all-around titles. Then that fifth year, she decided not to come home, and Ben thought she was probably involved with someone else. She would never say if she was, but promised she would be there when he won his record-tying sixth title.

There had been little communication between them after that. And Ben dared anyone to contact her after his accident; he couldn't bear the thought of her seeing him the way he was. Then suddenly six months ago, she had come back to San Antonio and opened her own art gallery. Ben was almost fully recovered by then, and they immediately resumed their relationship as though no time had passed between them. And at the moment, she felt so good in his arms that he never wanted to let her go. Maybe the nightmare was over. Maybe he would wake up now.

"Oh, Ben," Lisa said, reaching up and cupping his face in her hands. She kissed him gently, sorry that she had been in New York for an art show when she had gotten the tragic news.

When their lips parted, she looked up into his deep blue eyes, surprised by the lack of tears there. They were full of anguish and rimmed in red from exhaustion, but they were no tears. She decided he was still in shock, still denying what had happened.

She finished snapping the last three buttons on his dark blue Western shirt. "People are already at the house. We need to get going," she said quietly, wondering how they were going to get through the day.

Scott and Lisa took turns keeping a close eye on Ben during the south Texas open-house memorial service. Ranchers had come from all parts; the Matthews family had been well-known and well-liked. Zombielike, Ben accepted condolences, limply shaking hands and halfheartedly returning hugs.

First chance he got, Scott pulled Lisa aside and told her how Ben blamed himself for what had happened. "I'm worried about him, Lisa," he whispered as they stood in the hallway. "It's like he's just shut down."

Lisa wiped away a tear. "I know," she said. "But he'll come out of it. And when he does, he's going to need us. We're all he has left."

Scott leaned back against the wall. "This just doesn't seem real. I can't believe they're gone," he mumbled, feeling the tears streaming down his face. "I want to be strong for Ben, but it hurts so much."

"It's okay." She extended her arms to him and the two embraced. "It's better to let it out. Sooner or later, Ben will, too."

Lisa led Ben into the bedroom, closing the door behind them. She gently pushed him onto the bed and pulled off his boots, lifting his legs so that they were resting on the mattress. Walking around to the opposite side, she slipped off her own shoes and climbed in beside him. She cuddled up next to him, draping her arm across him and resting her head on his chest. And she silently prayed for the man she loved.

She woke with a sigh, feeling the warm sunlight streaming in through the window. Lisa knew even before she rolled over that Ben wasn't there. And then when she sat up, she saw the three metal boxes were gone from the dresser.

Ben loped Cherokee across the wide-open pastureland that his father had raised white-faced Hereford cattle on for thirty years. The feel of the big bay horse beneath him, the sun and the wind on his face were the first things that had felt right in days. The huge oak tree soon came into his view, a lone sentinel on the prairie. That tree had always been there. It was where he and Chris had come as kids to escape chores and dream about what they were going to be when they grew up—a champion rodeo cowboy and a doctor.

On cue, Cherokee eased into a walk and then finally stopped under the tree. Dismounting, Ben stepped back and removed the small shovel and the three boxes from the saddlebags. He took off his hat and perched it on the saddle horn. Kneeling down under the tree, he set the boxes on the ground and then started digging.

It took him only a few minutes to scoop out a three-foot hole in the rich, almost black, soil. One by one, he opened the boxes and slowly emptied the ashes into the hole. When the last box was empty, he sat back on his haunches, hands on his thighs, and stared at the mound of ashes. That was all that remained of his family, of the three people he loved and who had loved him more than anyone else in the world.

It hurt so much. He wanted the pain to go away, but it wouldn't. He wanted to cry, but he couldn't. He was afraid if he did, he wouldn't stop. That if he'd let himself fall apart, he'd never recover.

Lisa watched from atop one of the ranch horses. She had brought it to a stop on the slight ridge just before the pasture where the tree stood. That tree held a lot of memories. She, Ben, Chris and Scott had played cowboys and Indians under that tree. Ben had kissed her for the first time under that tree, two awkward teenagers trying to sort out all those strange new feelings.

She waited as Ben shoveled the dirt into the hole. She had decided not to intrude; he would have asked her to come with him if that was what he'd wanted. She was sorry he hadn't. Turning the horse around, she galloped back to the ranch.

Dusk was settling in when Ben finally returned. Lisa heard the kitchen door shut, and then his approaching footsteps.

"Are you hungry? There's plenty of food that everyone brought over," she said, as he limped past the couch where she sat and to the bar.

"No, thanks." He poured himself half a glass of whiskey and took a swallow.

Lisa laid the book she'd been reading on the couch and went to him. "I'm sorry I wasn't here for you when this happened," she said, reaching up and gently fingering the scar on the left side of his face. "But I'm here now. Please, Ben, don't shut me out. I love you. You don't have to go through this alone."

She stared up into his eyes, hoping to see some sign that she was getting through to him. Relief swept over her when he pulled her to him and hugged her tightly. Maybe. Just maybe, she could keep him from slipping away from her.

The following week, Ben went through the motions of participating in the daily ranch routine. Spring branding season was just about over and then the cattle would be left to graze through the summer. Scott and Lisa had decided to stay on the ranch for awhile. Scott usually helped out during this time of the year anyhow, and Lisa was only a phone call away from her gallery staff.

Ben continued to be silent and distant. Even out with the ranch crew, he tended to keep to himself. Scott would often catch him just staring off into the horizon, as though looking for what he had lost. No one had gone back into the Matthews' house since the memorial service. One morning while they were saddling the horses, Scott came upon Ben standing in the barn doorway, gazing out at it in the pre-dawn light. But that was as close as he got.

What really worried Lisa and Scott was that neither of them had seen Ben cry. The grief was evident in his eyes and etched in his haggard face, but it was as though he refused to allow himself any relief from it.

Lisa turned off the bathroom light and climbed into bed, snuggling up against Ben. He draped his arm around her; it was as responsive as he had been since the accident. She slid up on his chest, bending over him and kissing him deeply. Ben returned the kiss, and she felt his arms wrapping around her. Lowering her head, she kissed his chin, his neck, his chest and then the scars along the left side of his rib cage.

Ben loved the feel of Lisa's body against his. He loved her and he wanted her now as much as he had ever in his life. He wanted her to take away all of the pain. But he knew she couldn't.

"Lisa..." he whispered.

She had felt his body grow tense beneath her. She stopped trying to arouse him and looked up at him.

"I'm sorry...I can't," he said regretfully.

She gently caressed his face. "It's okay," she assured him. "I love you," she said, kissing him and then sliding back down into the crook of his arm.

They had just finished supper, and Scott was trying to make small talk with Ben, who had pushed his food around his plate more than he'd eaten it. Lisa had begun clearing off the kitchen table.

"I think I'm going to go away for awhile," Ben announced quietly.

Scott looked at him in surprise from across the table; Lisa reseated herself between the two men.

"Where would you go?" Lisa asked.

"I talked to Clay Tyler, and he said I'm welcomed to a cabin at the Bar T," Ben replied, referring to a family friend who owned a ranch outside of Jackson, Wyoming.

There was silence among the three friends. Scott and Lisa glanced at each other in concern.

"I have to get away from here," Ben said. "I see them...I hear them...everywhere." He paused for a moment, then added, "And you two...are smothering me. I know you mean well. I know you want to help me, but we can't go on like this."

Lisa reached over and took Ben's hand in hers. "We're here because we want to be."

Ben sighed. "I know that and I appreciate it. But you can't babysit me forever. I have to get through this on my own. And I can't do it here."

2

Ben had been smiling for miles now, ever since the magnificent Tetons had come into view. He turned up the volume on the radio-cassette deck; George Strait was singing "Fool Hearted Memory" from one of his greatest hits tapes. Reaching over, he turned up the volume, and then drummed his fingers on the steering wheel to the beat of the whiskey-drinking, cheating song. What Merle Haggard had been to his father, Strait was to him—kindred spirits who could sing what they were feeling.

Ben felt especially close to Strait because he, too, was a south Texas cowboy and a team roper. He'd met the singer on the rodeo circuit when he was still performing in Texas honky-tonks. And even though Strait was now a country western megastar, they'd maintained a casual friendship.

Turning off the main road, Ben was glad the Bar T Ranch was only another twenty miles. It was going to be good to see the Tylers again.

Clay Tyler was a longtime family friend, and the Matthews boys had spent many summers at the Bar T. While Tyler raised a few head of cattle, his main occupation was rodeo stock contractor. Tyler bred and raised some of the meanest, best-bucking broncs a cowboy ever wanted to sit on. Ben had won both of his saddlebronc titles on Bar T stock. In fact, the last time Ben had been up to the ranch three years ago was to look at some of Tyler's bucking stock. As a side income, Tyler turned his place into a dude ranch for the summer. Ben found it humorous that the guests, mostly from the East and Midwest, paid Tyler to let them play cowboy for a week. He and Chris had always gotten a few laughs at the expense of those dudes.

Ben steered the truck off the main highway and onto the packed dirt road. He and Chris had had some great adventures on the Bar T. With a sigh, he wondered if he hadn't made a mistake coming here. There would be memories to deal with here, too. But he had to get away from the ranch, and this was the first place that had come to mind. As Strait was singing "Right Or Wrong," the barns and corrals of the Bar T appeared amid the pines and the aspens.

The minute Ben stepped stiffly out of the truck in front of the main house, Clay Tyler wrapped him up in a bear hug.

"Gawdamnit, Ben, it's good to see you," Tyler said, slapping him on the back with both hands.

Ben felt like the six-four, 300-pound man had just squeezed and beaten all the air out of his body. He could only imagine what Tyler did to people he didn't like.

"For gracious sakes, Clay, let the boy catch his breath." Martha Tyler had come to the rescue, tugging on her husband to no avail. On his own, Tyler eased, but didn't release, his hold on Ben. "I'm so sorry, son," he whispered in his ear and then stepped back. "Me and Martha sure had some good times with your folks. And that Chris, well, you couldn't have asked for a finer young man."

Martha slipped between the two men and kissed Ben on the left cheek. "Come on, Ben, I've got supper waiting for you," she said warmly, taking him by the arm and leading him into the two-story log house.

Ben was surprised how cold it was when he stepped out of the cabin the next morning. He had forgotten that frosty summer mornings were commonplace here in the middle range of the Rockies. And now he knew why he was limping more than usual; he'd have to borrow a jacket from one of the ranch wranglers.

An hour and a half-pot of strong coffee later, Tyler and Ben headed for the barn. The wranglers had just finished bringing in the horses and were sorting them into the various feeding pens.

"So when do your first dudes arrive?" Ben asked with a chuckle as they strolled into the barn.

"Tomorrow. Laugh all you want, but they pay for winter feeding."

"Yeah, I know, Mr. Clay. They're a necessary evil," Ben replied as he slowly became aware of someone staring at him. He realized that several of the college-aged wranglers, who came up every summer to work at the Bar T, were eyeing him.

"All right, boys, come here and listen up," Tyler ordered, and the six young men quickly filed in. "This here is Ben Matthews. Yes, *the* Ben Matthews—the four-time world all-around cowboy," he said as their eyes grew wider. "Now, he's here for some rest and relaxation, so I don't want you boys bothering him. Now get on back to work."

The young cowboys did as they were told, although with whispers and backward glances as Ben and Tyler turned away and continued through the barn.

"I've got a special project for you, Ben," Tyler said matter-of-factly as they exited the far end of the barn. He motioned toward a corral built up against the mountain.

Its lone occupant was a blood-bay paint horse, who was contentedly grazing. His deep reddish brown coat was highlighted by large irregular white patterns on his neck, withers and haunches; his mane and tail were black, as were his front legs, while his hind legs had white stockings up to his hocks. Between his wide-set eyes was a broad star that tapered down into a white stripe all the way down to between his nostrils. At 15.2 hands, he weighed a muscular 1,200 pounds.

Ben grinned. "That ain't no bronc."

"He is a fine animal, ain't he?" Tyler commented as the horse casually lifted his head, studied them for a moment and then strolled over to the fence.

"Well, hey, pretty boy," Ben greeted, letting the horse sniff his extended hand before patting him. "Still a stud, huh?"

"Yeah, I couldn't bring myself to cut him," Tyler answered. "He's green broke, but he's as smart as he is pretty. And I think he'll make one hell of a ranch horse. But he needs some special attention, if you know what I mean."

Ben glanced at Tyler and then slipped between the corral railings. "Got all the buck out of him?" he asked as he walked around the animal, who cocked his head to the side and eyed him.

"Never did buck much. But when he does, ain't nobody here been able to stay on him," Tyler answered. "It'd be a shame to see a horse like this go to waste, don't ya think?"

Ben looked over at Tyler from where he now stood next to the horse's right shoulder. "I don't ride broncs anymore, Mr. Clay."

"I know that, Ben," Tyler said quietly. "But like you said, this ain't no bronc. Just one smart horse and none of my boys have been able to outsmart him yet."

Ben moved toward the horse's head, and the animal craned his neck to nuzzle him. "What's his name?"

"The Sundance Kid. We just call him Sundance," Tyler replied with a wide, knowing grin.

Ben lugged a Western saddle, a bosal headstall and a Louis L'Amour paperback out to the paint horse's corral. He ignored the horse, who was curiously watching him, entered the corral and plopped the saddle down on the ground. He lowered himself down and propped himself up against the saddle, then stretched his legs out in front of him and began to read.

Sundance stood there, his majestic head held high and his intelligent eyes peering at Ben through his too-long black forelock. After a few minutes, he lowered his head and resumed grazing.

Ben just kept reading the book, periodically glancing at the horse from beneath the brim of his hat.

Fifteen minutes later, the horse was grazing just within Ben's reach. But he made no movement toward the animal. Finally, curiosity got the best of Sundance and the walked right up to Ben, sniffing the book in his hand.

"You can read it when I'm done," Ben said quietly, but still made no motions toward the horse.

With a snort, Sundance wheeled and trotted off back to the center of the corral and then turned to face Ben. Still, Ben ignored him. After a few minutes of just standing there, the horse dropped his head and began grazing again. A few chapters later, Ben collected himself, the riding gear and left the corral without a word to the horse. But he could feel the animal's eyes on him as he walked toward the barn.

The next day, Ben went through the same ritual. And this time when Sundance approached him, he put his nose right up against Ben's face, sniffed him and then gently nuzzled his shoulder. Casually, Ben reached up, patted the horse and then returned to reading. Once again, Sundance snorted indignantly and trotted back across the corral.

On the third day when Ben emerged from the barn, Sundance was waiting for him at the gate.

"I hope you keep in mind that this was your idea," Ben said matter-of-factly as he slowly tightened the girth.

Gathering up the soft round-rope reins, Ben slowly eased himself into the saddle with the thought of bailing off at the first sign of trouble. The last thing he needed was to injure himself again. Sundance stood perfectly still. Ben waited a few moments and then cued him forward; the horse immediately responded, and they moved to the perimeter of the corral.

From just inside the barn's back entrance, Tyler watched as Ben methodically put the horse through the various gaits, stopped him, backed him and then loped him in perfect figure eights.

Tyler smiled; Thomas Matthews had always said his eldest son was the best damned natural horseman he'd ever seen.

When Ben came in for lunch, Martha Tyler told him Lisa had called again. That was the third time in the past two days. "You can use the phone in Clay's office," she said warmly, handing Ben a glass of iced tea. "When you're done, come on out to the back porch. I'll set our lunch out there."

In her own subtle way, Mrs. Martha was telling him he had better return Lisa's call. Ben took a long swallow of the tea and then headed for the office.

Lisa answered on the third ring and Ben heard the relief in her voice. "Really, I'm fine," he assured her. "I can't believe I'd forgotten how beautiful it is here."

"I miss you, Ben."

"I miss you, too," he returned. "Is Scott behaving himself?"

"Yes, we went riding yesterday afternoon. I rode Cherokee. I hope that was okay?"

"Sure. I don't want him getting fat and lazy while I'm gone. You ride him anytime you want."

"How long are you going to be up there, Ben?"

There was a sudden silence, and Ben shifted uncomfortably in the chair. "I don't know," he answered truthfully.

Silence again. "What if I came up for a few days?"

"No," Ben blurted out and wished he hadn't. "I'm sorry. I didn't mean to say it like that."

"But you did mean you don't want me to come up there?"

"Lisa, please." Ben sighed; he had heard the hurt in her voice. "This isn't about me and you. I meant it when I said I have to get through this on my own."

"Why, Ben? Why do you feel like no one—not me, not Scott—no one can help you get through this?"

"Because you can't, damnit," he said, and again was sorry his anger was getting the best of him. "Listen, I'm going to ride up into the mountains by myself for a few days. Maybe I'll be in a better mood when I get back."

Lisa sighed in resignation. "Okay. You be careful. I love you, Ben."

"I love you, too," he conceded. "Tell Scott not to work the crew too hard. I'll talk to you soon. Bye."

Ben gave Sundance his head and let him feel his way up the steep mountain trail. "That's it, boy, you're doing fine," he said, giving the horse an encouraging pat on his neck.

Tyler hadn't been too sure it was such a great idea for him to go up in the mountains alone on a greenbroke horse. But Ben had convinced him he'd be fine and it would be great schooling for Sundance. Grudgingly, Tyler had given in only after he promised he'd be back in three days.

"Let's take a breather," Ben said, feeling the horse laboring beneath him as the elevation had gradually increased. He turned the horse sideways on the trail so he could catch his breath.

Ben glanced back down the trail; the Bar T was long out of sight. The ranch sat in a valley at about 8,000 feet and the lake where they were headed was at 10,500 at the edge of an alpine meadow. To get to it, they were going to have to traverse rocky inclines, pine forests and ice-cold streams. Soon, there would be no distinct trail to follow and he would have to pay attention to tree markers, use a compass and the sun.

"Come on, pretty boy." Ben urged Sundance forward. "I wanna be fishing by lunchtime."

The sight of the crystal blue lake, glistening from the sunlight bouncing off it, took Ben's breath away. It was framed by the meadow's yellow and lavender wild flowers and by the pine trees tall enough to pierce the baby blue sky. Ben's first inclination was to cue Sundance into a gallop across the lush, green meadow. But he knew the horse was tired from his first trip up the mountain. He was content now to walk the horse toward the cabin that was just becoming visible among the trees. Overhead, a red-tailed hawk announced their arrival.

Ben was sure Sundance sighed in relief when he slid the saddle off him. "Yeah, you just had it too easy before I came along," he said, chuckling, then led the horse down to the lake.

Sundance needed no prompting, lowering his head to drink from the untainted lake. Ben loosely held the lead rope as he gazed out across the water; the snow-covered mountains in the distance completed the picture-perfect scene. If this wasn't paradise, then he didn't know what was.

He unsnapped the lead rope from the halter, certain that the horse wouldn't run off. Once free, Sundance trotted a few feet away from the lake, then dropped to his knees and rolled in the grass.

"I think you have the right idea, Sundance," Ben said, laughing. Taking off his hat as he sat down, he then pulled his boots and socks off and dipped his feet in the lake. The icy water sent shivers up his legs, but he resisted the urge to yank them out. It felt good to feel something else besides the dull aching that had been with him since Waco. His feet were growing numb from the cold when he finally pulled them out and onto the grass. He glanced over at Sundance, who was now grazing hungrily.

Ben lay back in the grass and smiled at the two hawks circling overhead. He folded his arms across his chest, thinking how great the sun felt on his face. It was his last thought before he drifted off into a deep, restful sleep for the first time in weeks.

Lisa loved riding Cherokee, not only because he was a great horse, but when she was on him she felt close to Ben. "Race you to the tree?" she challenged Scott, who was riding alongside her.

Scott's reply was to kick his horse into an instant gallop; he knew even with a head start, there was no way Marlboro could outrun Cherokee. And he was right. His lead was short-lived as Lisa rode the powerful bay horse with the blaze face past him halfway to the tree. Even at that, he suspected she'd held Cherokee back—something Ben wouldn't have done.

After arriving at the oak tree, they took off the bridles and saddles so the horses could graze. Lisa handed Scott a sandwich from her saddlebags, while he sipped water from the canteen. They sat down under the oak tree, each remembering the good times they had had there as kids.

"Ben buried their ashes right over there," Lisa said quietly, pointing to a spot where new grass had sprouted.

Scott stared at the area. "He never said a word to me about what he had done with them."

"Don't feel bad. He didn't tell me either," she said and then told him about the morning she had followed Ben out to the tree. "I don't understand why he's being so hard on himself—why he's shutting us out."

Scott leaned back against the tree. "Ben has never been the same since that bull nearly killed him," he said quietly. "And now this...it's too much for him—for anybody—to have to deal with."

"I asked him once to tell me about his accident," Lisa recalled. "He got very angry and told me—ordered me—never to ask him about it again."

"I'm not surprised. Once it was over, it became a subject no one wanted to talk about," Scott replied, taking another drink from the canteen.

"You were there, Scott. Maybe if you tell me about it, I'll be able to understand what's happening to him now. Maybe if I know, I'll be able to help him through this."

Scott sighed and looked away. Yes, he had been there when it had happened and all through Ben's nearly year-long recovery. The whole ordeal was something he didn't like to remember, and he understood why Ben didn't want to talk about it. He didn't know if he had the right to tell Lisa.

"I promise, Scott, I'll never let Ben know you told me." She reached out, touching his arm.

He had never been able to resist Lisa; he'd had a crush on her all his life, but he had always known it was Ben she loved. And now she was asking him to do something Ben wouldn't do for her, and he couldn't let the opportunity pass.

"Going into the bull riding, Ben and Clint Logan were tied," Scott began, and in that instant, he was back a year and half ago at the National Finals Rodeo in Las Vegas. "Logan had had a hell of a ride and Ben knew he was going to have to have a personal best to beat him. It was going to be his fifth consecutive title and put him only one away from tying Mahan and Ferguson.

"You know how much that had always meant to Ben. And now with it so close, he was even talking about breaking the record and winning seven titles. Hell, all of us believed he was going to do just that.

"He drew a pretty good bull and he had a good shot at getting the kind of ride he needed to win." Scott paused suddenly as in his mind's eye he saw that chute opening. "But Ben decided to shorten his odds. A jump outta the chute, he started spurring that bull."

Lisa heard herself take a breath and felt her stomach grow queasy. Maybe she didn't really want to know after all.

Scott shook his head. "That bull went insane. I don't know how Ben stayed on, but he did. And what a ride it was. It would have won it for him easy." He paused again as the scene played itself out in his mind. "I had never seen a bull spin so hard and so high...and when he came down, his legs couldn't take the impact, and a ton of angry animal came crashing down with Ben.

"He almost got himself clear—almost." Scott stopped, taking a breath. "Chris went crazy. I literally had to wrap my arms around him to keep him from jumping in that arena before the clowns could get the bull away from Ben. I know it all happened in seconds, but it was like watching a slow-motion silent movie."

Lisa squeezed his arm. "Take your time."

"When that bull got to his feet, he didn't run off like they usually do," Scott quietly went on. "He just kept spinning and kicking. He just ignored those clowns and kept after Ben. The best

Ben could do was try to drag himself away. Until that last kick—
the one that caught him in the head—then he went limp.

"That's when I let Chris go. And I just knew Ben was dead."

Lisa felt the tears trickling down her face.

"Chris and I got to him before the paramedics did," Scott
continued. "He was lying face down in the dirt; the left side of his
face was split open and there was blood everywhere. His left leg
from his hip down was twisted in ways it shouldn't have been. His
shirt was soaked in blood where I knew one of those kicks had
bashed in ribs.

"There was no way he wasn't bleeding internally. And if his
back was broken, then I hoped he really was dead."

"Oh, I shouldn't have made you go through this," Lisa cried,
hugging him tightly as they sat side by side.

Scott knew he shouldn't, but he liked the feel of Lisa next to
him. "If I was thinking Ben was better off dead than broken in
pieces, Chris was thinking just the opposite," he continued. "He
wasn't about to let his brother die. The minute we got to Ben, he
grabbed his hand and started talking to him. He kept saying he
wasn't going to let him leave him, that he was there and that Ben
had to hang on.

"I swear, Lisa, I'll always believe Ben was almost gone when we
got to him, and Chris willed him back," he said, looking at her.
"He rode with him in the ambulance and as soon as he was in the
intensive care unit after surgery, Chris was there. Him and those
George Strait tapes."

"What?" Lisa asked in puzzlement.

"Ben had slipped into a coma. The doctors were optimistic
he'd come out of it; they just didn't know when," Scott explained.
"Well, that wasn't good enough for Chris. He convinced the doctors to let him play Ben's favorite Strait tapes while he sat there
holding his hand. Lo and behold, three days later Ben woke up to
'Amarillo By Morning'."

The two of them were surprised by the sound of their voices,
laughing lightly.

Lisa hugged Scott. "Thank you. I know how hard it was for you to remember and tell me all of this."

"I guess I hadn't realized how I had been carrying what had happened around with me," he said, feeling a sense of relief. "I always wanted to tell Ben how scared I was that day. And how grateful I was he was alive.

"But once he got home after two months in the Vegas hospital, we all just focused on his recovery. Even though Ben was mad as hell about it, Chris had decided to take a leave of absence from school. Thank goodness he did. Chris and Mrs. Sara were the only ones who could handle him day after day. For the next eight months—until he could get back on a horse—he was a sonofabitch."

Lisa chuckled. "Kinda makes me glad I wasn't here," she said, then added, "Did he withdraw like he's done now?"

"He would have these tremendous mood swings. Either he didn't say a word or he was so angry, you were afraid to even be around him," Scott answered. "But considering what he had been through and how long his recovery was taking, you couldn't blame him.

"The best thing that happened was Chris suggesting Ben and I becoming team roping partners. Once he had that to focus on, he was almost back to his old self. But now this...I just don't know if he's going to be able to handle this, Lisa."

Ben reeled in the third trout he had caught in less than an hour. It was another picture-perfect Wyoming day: not a cloud in the sky and 75 degrees. He was dressed comfortably in jeans, a grey sweat shirt and sneakers. Sundance had not been impressed by this fishing business, wandering over twice to nudge Ben. He finally promised the horse an afternoon ride.

Sitting down, Ben worked the hook carefully out of the fish's mouth and then dropped it in the pail of water with the others. Satisfied he had plenty for lunch, he laid the fishing rod down and gazed across the water. All morning he had been struggling with memories of the last time he had been at the lake.

It had been the summer after he graduated from UT and before Chris' senior year in high school. With his pro rodeo career to
soon start in earnest and Chris looking ahead to college, they had
decided to spend the summer together at the Bar T.

And what a great summer it had been. They rode nearly all
day long except for Sundays. Sometimes they took the ranch guests
on rides, and other times they just went off on their own. On
Saturday nights, the two of them and the ranch wranglers partici-
pated in the rodeo in Jackson. Of course, the Matthews brothers
won more than their share of the competition.

Ben smiled as he remembered how Chris had fallen head over
heels in love with that little cowgirl from Cheyenne. It was the
summer Chris lost his virginity. That little cowgirl could get him
to do anything she wanted, and she had wanted Chris the minute
she saw him. And, of course, Chris had gotten his heart broken
when the summer, and the romance, ended. He had given Chris
the big brother speech about all those fillies out there in the world
just waiting for him. Chris recovered in short order, though he
never adopted his big brother's "love 'em and leave 'em" philosophy.

Chris had always been a sensitive soul, another trait inherited
from their mother. While he tended to ride roughshod over people
without really meaning to hurt them, Chris was always concerned
about the other person's feelings. Chris used to tell him all the
time that he needed to remember not everyone had been *"blessed
by the gods"* like he had. But Chris also told him that he knew he
could always count on his big brother, and when he needed strength
to draw on, he knew where to turn.

But he had known for a long time now that it had been Chris'
strength that had gotten him through those dark days after his
accident. While his body and spirit recovered, he had depended
on Chris to keep him from giving up. Chris wouldn't allow him to
wallow in self-pity, telling him he was still the same person he had
been before the accident. Maybe he was going to have to make
some adjustments now that his body was less than perfect, but it

didn't mean his life was over. His life wasn't going to be any less than it had been before, just different.

And he had slowly started to believe Chris, to be grateful he'd had the opportunity to win four all-around titles. No one could ever take that away from him. But he still felt like there was a void where his dream of breaking the record had been. And he couldn't imagine his life without the rodeo. That's when Chris came up with the idea of him and Scott becoming team roping partners. That competition involved riding and roping with speed and precision; his broken body could handle that. Right away, he was thinking world titles.

Life was good again. Lisa came back into his life and he was still a hell of a rodeo cowboy. Until Waco. Until he lost what really mattered the most in his life. Not the rodeo, not world all-around titles, but his family.

If only he had realized that before Waco. Then he would have been content to give up the rodeo and stay on the ranch. And then they wouldn't have been driving to Waco that day. His parents would have been home; Chris would have been in Austin. They would all be alive.

Ben took a deep breath, trying to ease the tightness in his chest. All his life, there had never been anything he couldn't do, couldn't overcome. But this—this trying to accept that his family was gone...

He suddenly jumped to his feet, grabbing the rod and pail as he hurried to the cabin. "Come on, Sundance."

Taking only a minute to exchange sneakers for boots, Ben hauled the riding gear outside and quickly saddled the anxious horse.

Ten minutes later, Ben urged Sundance into a smooth lope across the meadow. Giving him some heel in his flanks, Ben asked for more speed and got it instantly. Ben focused on the pounding of the horse's hooves on the ground, the sound of his breathing and the blur of the scenery as they galloped across the top of the mountain. The tightness in his chest began to ease.

As they came to the edge of the meadow, Ben picked an opening in the trees and urged Sundance into the forest. He let the horse slow to a trot, taking a deep breath of the sweet pine scent.

Both rider and horse were having such a good time that neither saw the rabbit until it was too late. It had darted out right in front of Sundance and then was suddenly trapped between his front legs. The horse half-reared and wheeled to the left, slamming Ben into a tree. His hip and thigh absorbed the brunt of the impact, and he heard himself cry out in pain.

In reflex, Ben shifted his weight to the right as the horse snorted and sidestepped away from the tree. The movement sent waves of pain through Ben's left leg, and he could feel himself sliding off the horse. No, he had to stay on. The memory of being trapped beneath that bull flooded his mind. Grabbing a handful of mane, he pulled himself back up into the saddle as Sundance still pranced. When his left foot settled back into the stirrup, it sent a jolt of pain searing up his left side. He thought he was going to pass out as he fell forward on the horse's neck. No, he couldn't do that either.

"Easy, Sundance...easy," Ben said between clenched teeth, still holding on to the horse's mane, while he patted him on his right shoulder. "Easy now...easy."

As the horse came to a gradual standstill, Ben could feel his sides heaving beneath him. He slowly straightened up in the saddle, and then saw the trampled rabbit. Damn.

His left leg was throbbing now, and he knew it wouldn't be long before it would start to swell. Damn. What if he had broken it again? He couldn't stand to be laid up again—especially not now. But first he had to get back to the Bar T.

Very carefully, Ben shifted his weight over to his right side; Sundance moved beneath him. "We're going to take this nice and slow," he said, turning the horse back in the direction they had come.

This time they walked across the meadow. Ben glanced at the cabin as they ambled by, thinking about the fish he wouldn't have for lunch. There was no point stopping at the cabin for his gear; if he got off the horse, he knew he wouldn't be able to get back on. He sat back against the cantle, concentrating on keeping all his weight off his left leg. It was easy to do on this fairly level ground, but Ben knew the hard part was going to be when they started down the mountain—down those uneven rocky trails. He made himself stop thinking about it and cursed that damned rabbit.

It had taken them twice as long to come down the mountain as it had to go up, the opposite of what was normal. Ben had sung every country western song he knew twice. Anything to keep his mind off what had quickly become agonizing pain. No matter how slowly or carefully Sundance picked his way down the mountain, Ben had felt every rock he stepped on, every shift in the ground's surface.

He had almost passed out more than once, so he'd purposely shift his weight to the left to use the resulting new stab of pain to keep him conscious. Perspiration leaked down his temples, and the sweat shirt was damp against his chest. He wondered if he was just imagining the Bar T's barn rooftop.

The minute Tyler saw how Ben was sitting on that paint horse coming down the mountain, he knew something was seriously wrong.

Ben lay flat on his back on the doctor's examining table. They had had to cut his left pants leg to get his blue jeans off him; his leg had swelled until it pushed against the denim. The doctor had given him a shot for the pain, and as he drifted off, he'd heard Tyler telling the doctor about the bull and his injuries. He'd been vaguely aware of the doctor and a nurse then taking him for X-rays. That was the last thing he remembered until he woke up on the examining table.

"Well, Mr. Matthews, you're a lucky man," Dr. Stan Morgan said as he entered the room.

Ben looked up at him, wishing doctors would quit telling him how lucky he was whenever he was lying flat on his back.

The doctor popped the X-ray sheets into the row of viewers attached to the wall. "My, my, someone did a hell of a great job putting you back together," he said in admiration as all of the metal in Ben's leg and hip showed clearly on the illuminated screens. "You're real lucky you didn't break or dislodge anything. But there is some severe trauma and deep bruising."

"Which means?" Ben asked, not looking at the X-rays.

"Which means, cowboy, you're grounded for at least two weeks," Dr. Morgan said matter-of-factly. "No riding. Just plenty of rest and keeping that leg elevated. I'll send you back to the ranch with crutches, but I want you off your feet as much as possible. You get a blood clot in that leg and you're in serious trouble."

Ben propped himself up on his elbows. "Can I go now?"

"Sure. I'll send Angie in with some clothes," the doctor said, moving toward the door. "And I'll give Clay your pain medication."

"I'll pass on the pills."

The doctor shook his head. "You cowboys always have to act so tough," Morgan said as he stood with his hand on the doorknob. "But I'm telling you that you were damn lucky you didn't lose that leg when you first busted it up. Now don't be stupid and let some doctor's fine work go to waste. Make it easy on yourself and take the medication," he ordered and then left.

Ben lay there for a few minutes, trying to figure out how to sit up without hurting himself. As he rolled over to the right, the sheet that had been covering him from the waist down fell to the floor just as the nurse walked in. She carried sweat pants and sneakers. Ben, clad only in the grey sweat shirt and navy blue briefs, smiled sheepishly at the small blond woman.

"Relax, cowboy, I'm the one who cut your blue jeans off," she said as she shut the door behind her and approached the table. "Let's get you dressed before you start getting any ideas that you turn me on."

"Shy filly, aren't ya?" Ben shot back as he let her help him sit up.

"Life's too short to be shy," she quipped, unfolding the pants.

"You won't be able to get into jeans for awhile, so this is your wardrobe, cowboy."

"I've been through this before. You're Angie?"

"That's me," she said with a small, quick smile. "And you're Ben Matthews, some hotshot champion rodeo cowboy." She reached to help him pull the pants over his left leg.

Ben ignored her comment about who he was and picked up the sneakers. "Guess I'll have to ask you to put these on for me."

"You have an odd way of asking for help." She took the shoes from his hands. "Guess champion cowboys are used to telling people what to do."

He looked into her hazel eyes and smiled his Texas cowboy smile. "Would you please put them on for me, Angie?"

She felt her heart skip a beat. He was so good looking. And damnit, he knew it. She forced her gaze away from those dark blue eyes and that killer smile. "That's more like it," she said coolly, bending down to slip the sneakers on his bare feet.

After Ben had hobbled out of the examining room on crutches with a parting, "Thanks, it's been fun," Angie took a closer look at his X-rays. She had overheard Clay Tyler telling Dr. Morgan about the bull-riding accident. Now as she studied the X-rays, remembered the scars on his face and leg, she was suddenly sorry she had made the snide comments about him being a hotshot champion cowboy. It was just that good-looking men always made her nervous. But now she realized that Ben Matthews had been humbled by something much more formidable than a smart-mouthed nurse.

For two days, Ben was the perfect patient. He stayed in his cabin, reading while lying in bed or sitting in the overstuffed chair with his leg propped up. He ate everything Mrs. Martha brought him, and he even took the prescribed medication. It wasn't that the pain was unbearable, but the pills provided sleep void of dreams.

With whiskey off limits while his leg healed, the pills would have to do.

"Wish I got fed as good as you," Tyler greeted as he entered the cabin on the third morning, balancing a tray of food with one hand.

"Hmm, seems to me you're not missing out on too many meals," Ben returned as Tyler set the tray across his lap and then sat down in the chair. "Is Sundance behaving himself?"

Tyler accepted the strip of bacon Ben offered. "I swear that horse feels bad about what happened. He's just been moping around and is off his feed a little. I knew better than to let you off alone on a greenbroke horse."

Ben swallowed the mouthful of scrambled eggs. "It wasn't his fault that rabbit picked the wrong time to cross the trail. And, besides, he calmed down almost right away and got me down the mountain. You were right. He is one smart horse, and he is going to make a hell of a ranch horse."

"Glad you feel that way," Tyler said, getting to his feet. "Because he's yours now."

Ben grinned. "I'll have to borrow a trailer to take him back to Texas."

"That can be arranged," Tyler said, heading for the door. "I'll come by later and drive you out to visit him. Maybe that'll pick his head up a little."

Ben found himself smiling as Tyler shut the door behind him. It wasn't just Sundance's well-being that concerned the owner of the Bar T. Ben knew he was very fortunate to have Clay and Martha Tyler looking out for him. And, thinking of friends, he knew he needed to call Lisa and Scott. But he had no intentions of telling them about his little mishap; they'd be on their way before he could hang up the phone.

Moving the tray aside, Ben carefully maneuvered himself to a sitting position on the side of the bed. Gingerly, he massaged his left leg. The swelling was going down, leaving splotches of purple and blue bruises. But, all in all, he was pleased with the progress. After two days of lounging around, a shower and shave were due.

Twenty minutes later, Ben hopped out of the steamy bathroom with only a towel wrapped around his waist; he had forgotten to bring clean clothes in with him. He was reaching for the sweat shirt on the chair when he realized he wasn't alone. Angie was standing just inside the doorway.

"Damn," he said, balancing himself against the chair. "You seem to have a knack for catching me half-naked. Ever hear of knockin'?"

Angie tried not to stare at his lean, hard cowboy body, but knew she was. "I did, but obviously you couldn't hear me. I was just going to leave these here for you," she said, referring to the two sets of sweats in her hands. "But then you had to make your grand entrance."

Ben smiled at her. She was pretty—not knock you off your horse gorgeous like Lisa—but pretty just the same. "Sure. The truth is you just wanted to have another look."

"My, my, if your leg is as healthy as your ego, you won't be needing these any longer," she said, walking to the bed and putting the clothes down.

"Actually, it's doing pretty good," he said as he opened the towel so she could see his left thigh. "What's your professional opinion?"

She knew he was teasing her, and without hesitation she approached him. "Hmm, you're right. It looks much better," she said, extending her hand and very carefully touching his leg with her fingertips.

"So I'll be just fine, right?"

She straightened up and found herself staring at the scars down his left side. That bull had really put this man through hell. "Dr. Morgan will have to be the one to tell you that," she said, clearing her throat. "I really need to get back to the office."

Ben watched her walk toward the door, liking the way her five-foot-four body filled out her jeans. "Do you like horses?"

She pivoted, placing her hands on her hips. "It would be hard to live in Wyoming and not like horses."

"Quick, aren't ya?" he said, grinning. "Give me a minute to dress and then you can drive me to the barn. I'll show you the prettiest horse you've ever seen."

"There you go again, telling people what to do."

He gave her that same Texas cowboy smile he had in the doctor's office. "Would you like to see the prettiest horse you'll ever set eyes on?"

Her heart fluttered like before. "Yes, I would."

Sundance nickered at the sound of Ben's voice and trotted across the corral. "Well, guess you really did miss me, pretty boy," Ben greeted as the horse nudged him. "So what do ya think?"

"Oh, my, he is beautiful." Angie reached out to pet him; Sundance sniffed her, and then let her touch him.

"Hmm, I think he likes you," Ben said, shifting his weight on the crutches. "Do you ride?"

"Yes, but I'm sure not up to your champion rodeo cowboy standards."

"I'm sure you do just fine. And, besides, which one of us is on crutches?" He grinned and they both laughed. "Tell you what. Once I'm walking on my own power, I'll take you up into the mountains. Sorta thank you for the sweats."

Angie smiled at him. "It's a deal, cowboy."

Scott answered the phone in the kitchen on the third ring, pleased at the sound of his friend's voice. "Mr. Clay working you hard?"

"The problem is Mrs. Martha. If she doesn't stop feeding me, I'm going to be one fat cowboy."

Scott laughed. "Well, everything here is just fine. Hot as hell, but we've been gettin' enough rain."

"Good," Ben said, wondering why he was having so much trouble talking to someone had known all of his life. "I really appreciate you taking care of things for me, Scott."

"Considering all you've done for me, it doesn't hardly seem like enough," Scott said, then quietly added, "How are you doin', Ben?"

There it was again—that tightness in his chest. "I'm doin' okay," Ben managed, then quickly said, "Do you know where Lisa is? There wasn't any answer at her place."

Scott had turned around at the sound of the kitchen door opening. "Well, actually, she just walked in," he said. "You take care, Ben," he added, then handed the phone to Lisa.

They exchanged small talk for a few minutes, and then Lisa asked him the inevitable question. "When are you coming home, Ben?"

He sat back in the chair. "I'm thinking of staying the rest of the summer."

Lisa knew from the sound of his voice that he had already made up his mind. "And I suppose you still don't want me to come up?"

She was hurt; Ben knew that when she was hurt, she didn't waste any words and got right to the point. "I'm still trying to sort things out. And I still think it's best if I do it on my own."

There was a moment of silence. "I wish you didn't feel that way, but obviously there's nothing I can say or do to change your mind," Lisa said, sadness tinging her voice. "I love you."

Ben was afraid he wasn't going to be able to catch his breath; the tightness was threatening to smother him. "I know," he whispered.

3

Ben and Angie sat next to each other on the rock outcropping, silently admiring the vista before them. It was the third time in less than two weeks that Ben had taken her up the mountains to show her some of his favorite places.

He had been more relaxed around her than he had felt around anyone in a long time. Maybe it had something to do with them not having a history. It seemed a relief to him to be around someone who hadn't known him before his accident. And someone who knew nothing of what had happened twenty miles outside of Waco.

"We actually met before. But I know you don't remember," Angie suddenly said, turning to face him.

Her words brought him out of his musings. "What?"

"I said we met once before."

"When?"

"Seven years ago my family and I came to the Bar T for vacation. It was my brother's high school graduation present," she explained, grinning at the puzzlement on his face. "Of course, I looked a little different then. I weighed about thirty pounds more, had mousy brown hair and plain brown eyes. And you and your brother had eyes only for the pretty little cowgirls struttin' around the ranch."

Ben couldn't help himself; he purposely eyed her up and down. "Late bloomer, huh?"

She laughed. "Something like that," she said. "It was the first time my family had been out of Rockford, Illinois. I just couldn't believe a place like this really existed. And that there were real cowboys like you and your brother. Of course, all the girls thought you two were gods on horseback."

Now it was Ben's turn to laugh, but he felt a twinge of uneasiness at her references to Chris. He hoped she wouldn't ask about him. "So, how did a mousy little girl from Rockford, Illinois, wind up living in Jackson, Wyoming?"

"Once I got home, I could never get this place out of my mind." She paused, glancing at the valley below. "If places like this really existed, then I started thinking anything was possible."

"How so?"

"All my life I had felt like there was this other person inside of me," she said, looking back at Ben. "Sorta another version of Angela Wilcox, daughter of an accountant and a homemaker, sister to a mathematical genius. But she was trapped in a little glass box inside me. She could see out, but she couldn't escape. Until I came here.

"I went on to nursing school in Chicago. But the day I graduated I packed up my car and drove here. I lost weight, dyed my hair, got colored contact lenses and became Angie."

"It must have been hard, leaving your family and friends," Ben said. "That took a lot of courage to just pick up and start a new life."

Angie shook her head. "It wasn't that hard, really. I mean I love my family, of course, but I always felt like I didn't belong where I was, like I had been misplaced at birth," she said. "But I guess it's difficult for someone like you to understand what that feels like."

"What makes you say that?"

"Well, I bet you've always had a strong sense of who you were and what you were going to do with your life," she said matter-of-factly.

"And look at you—the perfect poster boy for what a cowboy should look like. Talk about blessed by the gods."

Angie's last words hit Ben like a slap in the face; he felt his stomach knot up.

"Are you all right?" Angie asked in concern as Ben suddenly looked ill.

"Um, I'm fine," he replied, looking away from her as he scrambled to his feet. "We'd better head back."

Angie urged her horse into a trot to keep up with Ben and Sundance. "Geez, tell a guy you wear colored contacts and he leaves you stranded on a mountain top."

Ben slowed Sundance to a walk; he loved this woman's sense of humor. "Sorry, I just remembered something I promised Mr. Clay I'd do for him today."

"Must be really important."

"Well, I take my promises seriously. And Mr. Clay and Mrs. Martha have been real good to me."

"I appreciate your loyalty," she said. "You never did say why you were up here. There must be plenty to do at your family's ranch in Texas. And isn't this the middle of rodeo season?"

Ben gave Sundance a little heel. "Just needed a change of scenery," he said as he moved out ahead of her once again.

She had seen that look of distress overtake him again. And, deciding that she'd better mind her own business, settled in behind him for the rest of the trip back to the Bar T.

Ben rested his head back against the chair as the third straight glass of whiskey slid down his throat. He had skipped supper, giving an excuse of a headache. He refilled the glass and took a swallow. *"Blessed by the gods."* He still couldn't believe Angie had spoken those words—the very phrase Chris always used to describe him and the relative ease with which he succeeded at everything.

"Damn, Ben, you were blessed by the gods. Everything comes easy for you. The rest of us mere mortals actually have to work hard to get what we want out of life. So try to be a little more patient with us."

He drained the glass and immediately refilled it. He didn't feel so blessed these days, more like abandoned by the gods.

Angie eased her foot off the gas pedal, realizing she was going too fast again on the packed dirt road back to town. Good way to flip her vintage red Mustang. But she couldn't get Ben Matthews off her mind. And it wasn't just that she was physically attracted to him. Because with a good-looking man like that, it was an automatic response.

But he had surprised her. The more time she spent with him the more intrigued she was, and the more she liked him. There was actually a person behind that perfect rodeo cowboy facade. She had even sensed a sadness about him, and then today, she had seen it.

The other trait that surprised her about him was his sense of humor—something generally lacking in handsome men. Not that he wasn't aware of his physical attributes and didn't know how to use them. Especially those dark blue eyes and that damn Texas cowboy smile. But he operated more with a sense of playfulness rather than arrogance. He was an intelligent man who appreciated the challenge of the chase. Of course, she suspected he hadn't known defeat too many times—if ever—when it came to women.

She probably should do the smart thing and get out now while her pride was still intact. That's what Angela Wilcox of Rockford, Illinois, would do. She grinned. But Angie of Jackson, Wyoming, had other plans. She suddenly steered to the left, made a U-turn and sped back to the Bar T.

Ben didn't know why, but he wasn't surprised when the door opened and Angie came in, grinning at him. "I can't believe you just walked in on me and I'm fully dressed."

"Well, we can remedy that," Angie said slyly as she approached the chair and sat sideways in his lap. She immediately started pulling at his shirt's pearl snaps.

"Hmm, you weren't kidding about this not being shy business," Ben said, keeping his hands where they rested on the chair's arms.

She pulled his shirt out of his jeans and then kissed him hard; the taste of whiskey filled her mouth. She felt him start to return the kiss, but then he pulled away.

"Angie..." Ben halfheartedly protested, feeling her small, soft hands working their way down his chest.

"I know there's someone in Texas you're going to marry," she said as she unhooked his belt buckle. "I don't want to marry you. You'd be hell to live with," she added, slowly unzipping his jeans and then kissed him again.

This time, Ben returned the kiss as he embraced her, liking the feel of her small, full breasts pressed against him. He suddenly realized she didn't have a bra on.

Angie saw the puzzled look on his face. "I took it off in the car. One less thing to worry about."

He chuckled. "I guess that means you're sure you want to do this, huh?" he asked, bringing his right hand around and fingering the top button on her blouse.

"Stop worrying so much," she said in feigned exasperation. "I'm not a virgin, I'm on the pill and I promise I won't fall in love with you."

Ben laughed again. "Sounds like a deal I can't refuse," he conceded, now hurriedly unbuttoning her blouse.

Ben rolled over only to find himself alone in bed. Where Angie should have been, there was only a sheet of Bar T stationery. Propping himself up on his right elbow, he read the note: *Had to get to the office early. After you tossed and turned most of the night, I didn't have the heart to wake you. Talk to you later. P.S. Hell of a ride, cowboy!!!*

Ben fell back against the pillow. Angie was a special person and it had been a hell of a night. So why did he feel like such a jerk? Damn. He knew why. Lisa. Since she had come back into his life, he had been faithful to her. And for someone who rather liked his love 'em-leave 'em lifestyle, that had taken some getting used to. But he had because he knew Lisa really was the only woman he had ever truly loved.

So why had he done it? He hadn't been that drunk. Okay, so Angie made it easy. That wasn't fair. The only thing she was guilty of was bad timing. Whatever it took—whiskey or sex—he was willing to do anything to stop thinking about Waco. But he most certainly had no right to use Angie that way.

Angrily, he threw his legs over the side of the bed and limped to the bathroom. Maybe an ice-cold shower would clear his head.

When Angie returned to Ben's cabin late that afternoon, she found it empty. He was probably at the barn.

"Ben headed out this morning. Said to tell you he'd be back in a couple of days or so," Tyler told her as they stood outside the barn.

"Hmm, he didn't say anything last night about going up by himself," she said, almost half to herself.

Tyler saw the genuine concern on her face. "I don't think Ben wanted to be around here for the Fourth of July hoopla."

Now she was really confused. "Why not?"

Tyler sighed. "I should have known he wouldn't have said a word about it to you. I swear I see more and more of Thomas Matthews in that boy everyday," he said, shaking his head. "Ben's folks and his brother, Chris, were killed in a highway accident about six weeks ago."

Ben sat nearly on the very spot on the lake's bank he had more than three weeks ago. All the Fourth of July celebration talk at the breakfast table had sent him hurrying to the barn. He was not in the mood to celebrate anything.

He had just packed up his gear, saddled up Sundance and headed out with no particular destination in mind. But he was not surprised he had ended up back at the lake. Despite what had happened before, he was still drawn to this place.

Ben glanced back at Sundance, whose main concern appeared to be eating as much of the lush grass as he could. As he admired the striking animal, Ben wondered what Chris would think of Sundance. *"Damn, Ben, you finally found a horse as flashy and cocky as you."*

Ben started to laugh, but something caught in his throat. Damn. He tried to get to his feet, but the tightness in his chest made him double over as he fought to catch his breath. Slowly, he sank to his knees and sat back on his haunches. He tried to choke back the tears, but he felt them sliding down his face.

His father would be so angry with him for this. It was not how Thomas Matthews had taught his eldest son to deal with life. *"When something bad happens to you, Son, you just put it in its place and go on with it."*

That's how he had handled what that bull had done to him. Or at least had tried to; he had never told anyone about the nightmares. But where the hell was he supposed to put this? There was nothing but emptiness inside him, nothing but pain.

"I'm...sorry..." Ben cried, wrapping his arms around himself as he rocked slowly back and forth. "I'm...so sorry, Dad...I'm sorry," he sobbed as the grief finally overwhelmed him.

Angie sat in her car in front of her house. She didn't remember driving back from the Bar T, and she didn't know how long she had been sitting there. She was still numb from what Clay Tyler had told her.

But now she knew she had been right about the sadness in Ben's eyes. She had thought it was because he was still dealing with what that bull had done to him. As a nurse, she knew that often psychological healing continued long after the body had mended. And in the time she figured had elapsed since his bull-riding accident, there was no way Ben had fully come to terms with the trauma. Then he'd lost his family.

And there she had been yesterday morning, rambling on about that summer long ago—about Ben and his brother. The man was trying to cope with his grief—that's why he had come to the Bar T—and there she was stirring up painful memories. Wherever he was up in the mountains, she hoped he was finding some peace.

Ben lay on the bunk in the lake cabin, listening to the rain falling steadily on the roof. He thought it was late afternoon, but he wasn't sure. And he didn't care. Whoever had said crying made you feel better had lied. All he felt was shame for having disappointed his father, for not controlling his feelings like he'd been taught by the man he had worshiped. It was the same kind of shame he had felt after that bull. He had failed his father then, too. Not that he'd ever said that to him; he'd never said a word about the accident. It had happened; it was over, and life went on.

He remembered the day he'd finally returned home from the hospital. He'd sat there on the side of his bed, staring at the ghostly white withered thing that was supposed to be his leg. When his mother came in with fresh clothes, he'd been fighting back tears. Without a word, she'd sat down and taken him in her arms. For those few minutes, he was her little boy again, and it was okay to cry.

His mother was gone now. Because of him, that wonderful, loving woman was gone. He rolled over and buried his face in the pillow.

There it was again. Ben pulled the brightly-colored Indian blanket over his head, trying to muffle that damned noise. He just wanted to sleep forever. There it was again. What the hell...Ben threw the blanket off. Damn. It was Sundance, neighing loudly and insistently. Maybe a bear was after him.

He flung open the door. The noonday sun made everything a golden blur. He used his hand to shield his eyes until the yellow spots faded. There was Sundance, right up to the porch, nickering and tossing his head. Delighted that he'd roused Ben, the horse did a pirouette.

"Damn, Sundance, you're worse than a naggin' woman," Ben said, relieved the horse was all right.

The horse impatiently pawed at the ground and nickered at him again.

"All right, all right. At least give me a chance to go to the bathroom," Ben said, turning to go back inside.

When Ben came back out ten minutes later, boots on and toting the saddle, Sundance was standing sideways up against the porch. The horse's bare back stirred up childhood memories of playing renegade Indians with Chris, hoopin' and hollerin' as they rode bareback across the prairie. Ben dropped the saddle, then took off his boots and socks.

He put his hands on the horse's withers, boosted himself off the porch and onto Sundance's back. Grabbing a handful of mane, he cued him forward.

While the eager horse walked briskly around the meadow, Ben shifted his weight until he found the most comfortable position for his left leg. Sundance was prancing impatiently now, and Ben finally gave him the signal to lope. This time, they were staying in the meadow and out of the trees.

Angie couldn't dash out of her house and jump into the car fast enough after Mrs. Martha called. After five days of worrying about him, Ben was finally back.

But halfway to the ranch, she started wondering what she was going to say to him. Or if she should say anything at all. She wanted at least to apologize for upsetting him. Hell, she wanted to do a lot more than that. She wanted to put her arms around him and tell him how sorry she was that life was treating him so unfairly. And she wanted to hold him as long as he would let her.

From where he sat on the cabin's porch, Ben saw the red Mustang coming up the narrow dirt road. That little woman must have ESP. He took a sip of the whiskey and then balanced the glass on the arm of the rocking chair.

"It's a good thing I outgrew my inferiority complex a long time ago," she quipped as she stepped onto the porch. "I don't think I ever sent anyone running off into the mountains before. I didn't think I had been that rough on you," she said, bending over and kissing him.

"See? It worked. You missed me," Ben said when their lips parted and she sat down cross legged on the porch. "Want a drink?"

She shook her head. "Did you and Sundance have a good time?"

"Yeah, you know how we cowboys are about our horses," he said, stretching his long legs out in front of him and crossing them at the ankles. "You can take away our whiskey and even our women, but don't mess with our horses."

Angie laughed. "Bet you were riding before you could even walk."

"Almost. I had my first pony when I was two. My mother has this great picture..." Ben caught himself too late, and in that same instant he saw something in her eyes.

He felt like a trap door had just opened up beneath his feet. Damn. She knew about Waco. He wanted to run, but all he could manage was to look away. The last thing he wanted or needed was to see pity in her eyes.

Angie wanted to try to comfort him. But she was afraid that if she moved, he would bolt like a spooked horse.

"You going through the terrible twos, now that's a frightening picture," she said with an exaggerated shudder. "I can imagine the hell you gave your mother when you were a kid."

Her words surprised Ben. He had braced himself for the obligatory "I'm sorry" speech. Then he was equally surprised by the sound of his own voice. "Dad always said it was a good thing Chris and I were so different because Mother would have left him if she'd had to raise another one like me," he said quietly, still avoiding any eye contact with Angie. "But the truth was, she was tougher than all of us."

Angie was relieved he was responding to her. "Yes, there's no doubt who's the strongest of the sexes. You men would be lost without us," she said, snickering and then realized she'd said something wrong. He tensed up and pain rippled across his face.

Ben looked away. Lost. That's exactly how he felt. Concentrating on keeping his hand from shaking, he drank the last of the whiskey and then put the glass down on the wooden floor. He got up and stepped off the porch.

Angie watched him stride out across the yard. She had screwed up. He was just going to walk away and never say another word to her. Suddenly he stopped and turned to face her.

"You were right what you said about me that day in the mountains," he said, willing himself to look at her and keep his emotions in check. "I always knew who I was—eldest son of Thomas and Sara Matthews, Chris' big brother and all-around champion cowboy."

He paused, taking a breath as he clenched his hands into fists at his sides."All that is gone now. And I don't know who the hell I am anymore."

Angie's heart ached for him, but she knew she had to keep her distance. "I'm not going to say I know how you feel, because I don't," she said gently. "I can't even imagine what it must feel like to have gone through the terrible things you have. My body hasn't been broken and put back together again—and my family is safe in Rockford. But I do know that you're holding yourself together a lot better than you realize.

"In fact, your strength is intimidating. That's how I felt when I met you—despite the fact that you were a patient in considerable pain. Normally, I respond with compassion to my patients. But with you, I thought I was going to have to resort to hand-to-hand combat."

Again Ben was taken aback. "Yeah, I guess I do sorta come on strong sometimes," he admitted, relaxing his hands at his sides. "It's just my competitive nature."

"No kidding," Angie said, then quietly added, "But the thing is you're probably harder on yourself than you are on anybody else. And that's scary. Because there's no way you're going to get through this, Ben, if you don't ease up on yourself."

He wanted to tell her that he wished he could. But everything that had happened was his fault—and he didn't know how he was going to live with that. But he couldn't say the words and, instead, he slowly walked back to the porch, sitting down a few feet from her.

Angie eyed him and she could feel him withdrawing. This was one tough man. She hoped that woman in Texas really loved him, because he was determined to put himself through hell.

"Hey," she quietly called to him, and he turned to look at her. "I could really use a hug."

He managed a small smile, gesturing with his arm. She hurried to slide under his arm and tightly wrapped both of hers around him. She hoped he could feel how much she cared.

Ben pulled her closer, grateful for the comfort. Maybe there was hope. Maybe he was somehow going to be able to pick up the pieces of his life. Maybe.

Two days later, Angie met Ben as planned at the barn to go riding. But only Sundance was saddled up and in the corral. Maybe he felt like he needed to be alone again.

"Okay, cowgirl, it's time you rode a real horse," Ben said, coming up behind her and ushering her into the corral.

She tried to dig her boot heels into the ground. "No way. He's too much horse for me."

"You'll be just fine," he said, taking hold of her by the waist and lifting her onto the saddle. Sundance craned his neck around and looked right at her. "Don't mind him. He's just trying to spook ya."

"It's working," she said nervously as Ben adjusted the stirrups to fit her much shorter legs.

Ben moved to the center of the arena. "Okay, move him out," he ordered and she gave him a pleading look. "Come on, you can do it."

She took a deep breath and then gave the horse a little leg pressure. Sundance responded, smoothly moving out to the perimeter of the corral.

"Relax, relax," Ben said as he watched them circle the corral twice. "That's better. Now pick up the pace a little. Easy, just trot."

"Now quit sittin' on him and ride him. You two have to be doin' this together. That's it. That's better."

Angie felt herself beginning to relax. Ben was right. Sundance felt different beneath her than any horse she had ever ridden, not that there had been that many. But there was a definite difference. And the more she listened to Ben's instructions, the more she began to enjoy the horse.

"Okay, do some figure eights around me."

She cast him a 'you've got to be kidding' look, but did what he said anyhow.

"All right. Now lope him and just do a bigger pattern."

Angie took a deep breath. This horse was something else. Kind of like a sports car on four legs. She found herself imagining what a wondrous experience it would be to gallop this horse across a meadow.

Ben grinned. "Okay, Annie Oakley, you can take a breather."

Scott handed Lisa her drink and then sat down with his in the chair. It was the third time that week she had come over for supper.

And each time, Scott found himself liking not having to share her with Ben.

"It's been three weeks and not a word from Ben." Lisa sat on the couch, stirring her bourbon and ice with her fingers. "I'm beginning to wonder if he even cares about me anymore."

"You know better than that," Scott replied. "It's just Ben has a lot of pride. Hell, all of us men do. It's why he wouldn't let us contact you in Europe after his accident. He didn't want you to see him down then, and he doesn't now, either."

"But if you love someone, you should trust them enough to let them see you at your worst." She paused and sipped her drink. "I need him to love me enough to trust me during good and bad times."

"He'll come around. You're just going to have to be a little more patient."

She took another swallow of the bourbon. "I don't know what I'd do without you to talk to. I really appreciate your friendship."

"My pleasure, ma'am," he said, toasting her with his drink.

"It's strange how differently people handle their grief," she mused. "Ben turned away from us, the two people closest to him. And yet, the two of us have found comfort by being together. How do you explain that?"

He shook his head. "I don't know what to say to make you feel better. I wish I did."

Lisa could feel the warmth of tears in her eyes. "I just want him to put his arms around me and tell me it's going to be all right," she cried softly.

Scott didn't even have to think about it; he went to her and wrapped his arms around her as she sobbed. "It will be all right, Lisa."

After a few minutes, he could feel her composing herself, and he started to slowly pull away. To his surprise, she hugged him tighter and when he looked down at her, she kissed him. Not in that friendly way they always had, but passionately.

Then it was as though a jolt of electricity passed between them. She pulled away and he let go. They sat there, somewhat stunned and ashamed by what had just happened. Suddenly, Lisa sprang from the couch and ran out of the room.

Scott was numb. He heard the back door slamming and then, moments later, the sound of Lisa's Corvette speeding away. What in the hell had happened? He knew—he had always known—it was Ben who Lisa loved. He'd never even thought he had a chance with her.

That kiss had meant nothing. She was hurt and lonely. It was a reaction to him comforting her and nothing more. It could be nothing more.

For the next two days, Scott would pick up the phone only to slam it down again. And twice when he had answered it, there had been a disconnecting click. He didn't know how he'd react if he answered the phone and heard Ben's voice.

Scott sat at the kitchen table, trying to make himself eat a turkey sandwich. He looked up at the sound of the back door opening.

"Can I come in?" Lisa asked sheepishly.

"Of course," he answered, and she sat down across from him.

"I've been doing a lot of thinking about what happened..."

"Don't worry about it. It's forgotten."

She looked at him. "What if I said I didn't want to forget about it? What if I said I had been wanting to do that for a long time?"

Scott was dumbfounded. He stared into those beautiful golden brown eyes of hers, hoping to see she was lying to him.

"Things started to make sense to me after you told me that Ben has been different since his accident," Lisa said. "I thought things were not the quite the same between us because we'd been apart so long. And, with time, it would be like it was before.

"But after you told me what that bull did to him, then I knew it was more than just the time we had been apart. I knew something had happened inside him. And how could he have not come through that unchanged? Nobody could have."

Scott stared unblinkingly at her. "He still loves you."

"I'm not so sure anymore," Lisa said. "I think we just slipped right back into what had been a very comfortable relationship for us both. Actually, for everybody—Mr. Thomas, Mrs. Sara, Chris, you. When didn't everyone think of me and Ben together?"

Scott sat forward, resting his elbows on the table. "I'm a little confused. Are you saying Ben doesn't love you like he did before his accident, or that you don't love him because he's changed?"

She hesitated for a moment, glancing down at the table and then back at Scott. "Both."

"I don't believe that, Lisa. Once Ben is back..."

"Then it will be over. I can't love a man who can shut me out like he has," she said sadly. "And if he loved me, he wouldn't have been able to do it. He would have needed my love to help him get through this."

"You're just hurt and angry with him right now."

She nodded. "Yes, I am. But I don't blame him," she said. "I know he went to Wyoming because he felt he had to. I know he didn't do it to hurt me.

"But I need someone who can share his pain, as well as his joy. I need someone who will stand by me and let me stand by him no matter what happens. I need someone like you, Scott."

He sat back in the chair. "You're not being fair to Ben," he said, trying to ignore what she had implied. "I remember what it was like when my father died. No matter how close you and I were to the Matthews, they were Ben's family. He's the one who lost his father, mother and brother all at once. We can't even begin to know the kind of grief he's going through.

"And, yes, I do believe that bull took something out of Ben. But not the best part of him. He's still the Ben Matthews who has always been my friend. I love him like a brother. So how do you think it makes me feel for you to sit there and tell me that kiss meant something?"

Lisa blinked back her tears. "Just like it makes me feel. Scared."

They sat in silence, overwhelmed by the flood of uncomfortable feelings.

Scott leaned forward, spreading his hands out in front of him. "What are we going to do?"

Ever so slowly, Lisa reached out and took Scott's hands in hers. "I don't know."

Angie couldn't believe how anxious she was to get to the Bar T. It had been four days since Ben first put her on Sundance's back. Everyday they'd gone riding, she on Sundance while Ben used a ranch horse. They never spoke again about his family. Mostly they talked about horses; he told her great stories about horses he'd had, while he continued to give her riding lessons. He told her the most important thing she needed to remember about horses was that in the best of them, there was something that belonged to no one. And if she respected that spirit in them, they would always give her something special back.

And yesterday when she finally got to gallop Sundance across a meadow, she understood. It took her breath away.

Angie parked her car alongside Ben's truck. Hurriedly, she strode through the barn and to Sundance's corral. "Isn't it a gorgeous day?"

"Yes, it is." Ben led Sundance up to the gate. "I've been having a little chat with this fella. He tells me you've become a pretty fair cowgirl."

"Is that so?"

"Yep, and he thinks you two will get along just fine," Ben said, unlatching the gate and leading the horse out.

Angie looked at him, puzzled. "Is this a test or something? I have to go out on a ride by myself?"

"No, that's never a good idea," Ben cautioned. "Remember

what happened to me when I went off alone. And I'm a champion cowboy," he added with a grin.

"Then what are you talking about?"

Ben put the lead rope in her hands and held it there. "I want you to have Sundance."

Her eyes grew wide. "Oh, Ben, I–uh–I don't know what to say."

He laughed. "That's a change," he teased and then bent down to kiss her.

As he pulled away, he let go of her hand and she felt her heart sink. "You're leaving, aren't you?"

He nodded. Angie looked away, fighting the sudden tears.

"Hey," Ben quietly said. "I sure could use a hug."

The tears spilled onto her face as they embraced. She didn't want to let him go. Then too soon, she felt him releasing his hold on her and gently pulling away.

"You take good care of her, Sundance." Ben gave the horse one last pat and the animal nudged him. "And, you, Angie of Jackson, Wyoming, you have a hell of a life," he ordered, flashing his Texas cowboy smile.

Angie stared into those incredible blue eyes, wondering if he'd ever be free of the pain that still burned in them. "You bet I will, cowboy," she whispered, smiling and wishing she could will him to stay.

But in the next moment, he was walking away from her. As she watched him disappear into the barn, she wondered if he knew she had broken her promise. She had fallen in love with him.

4

When Ben crossed the New Mexico state line into Texas, he was doing his best to harmonize with Strait on "The Chair." Although he doubted he'd being doing a duet with George anytime soon. Just because they were both south Texas cowboys sure didn't mean he could sing like Strait. He turned up the volume so Strait's voice drowned him out.

Ever since he'd seen the mileage marker for San Angelo, he hadn't been able to get Clint Logan off his mind. They'd always been friendly competitors, and Logan had finished second to him those two years before his accident. Then that day while he was being rushed to the hospital, Logan was finally winning his first all-around title. That bull had changed both their lives that day.

Ben hadn't talked to Logan since then. But he had heard that he had hit hard times and wasn't competing anymore. It always seemed odd that Logan's career had taken a downturn after he finally won the all-around. He'd always wondered what had happened.

Maybe he should give Logan a call and pay a visit to his San Angelo ranch. After all, he wasn't on a time schedule to get back to San Antonio; he hadn't even called Scott and Lisa to tell them he was coming home.

Ben drove through the open gate with the Rocking L Ranch sign above it. While not as impressive as the Matthews Ranch, it was a nice, working spread that just needed some maintenance. As Ben parked his truck in front of the adobe house, Logan came out to greet him. He looked like hell. His sandy blond hair was way too long, and he had apparently given up shaving some time ago. His light blue eyes were bloodshot, and he was at least fifteen pounds heavier than Ben remembered him.

"Good to see ya, Ben," Logan said, extending his hand as he eyed the scar on Ben's face. "Come on in and we'll have a drink."

"That sounds good to me." Ben followed him into the house. Once inside, he couldn't help but notice the place looked messy. Not dirty, just messy the way a house looks without a woman around to pick up after a man. Ben was puzzled; Logan had a wife and two kids.

"Beer okay?" Logan asked as they entered the kitchen.

Ben nodded as he scanned the room; the sink was overflowing with dishes, and there were several uncovered pots on the stove. He knew if he didn't have a maid come in once a week, this was what his house would look like.

"So, you've been up at the Bar T, huh?" Logan asked after they had sat down at the table. "How's Clay Tyler doing? Still raising those mean broncs?"

"Him and Mrs. Martha are doing fine. And his broncs will be giving cowboys hell for a long time to come."

The two men laughed and then each took a drink.

"I hear you and Scott Barnes are team roping."

Ben nodded. He didn't see any point in telling Logan there would be no more rodeos for him. He hadn't come to talk about his career.

"I came to see you in the hospital in Vegas," Logan said, glancing at Ben then back down at the beer can. "But then when I saw you in that bed—saw the way you looked—I...uh...I couldn't go in the room."

Ben took a swallow of beer and sat back in the chair. "I never liked seeing one of us hurt either. It made me think if it could happen to him, it could happen to me."

Logan looked at him. "I had wanted to beat you so bad for so long. But I didn't want to win the way I did," he said then drained the can. "Want another?"

Ben shook his head as he watched Logan go to the refrigerator and retrieve another beer.

"And it was like no one recognized my title," Logan continued, reseating himself. "All that everybody would say was that was the year Ben Matthews got hurt. Not the year Clint Logan won the all-around.

"That ate away at me. I felt like I had to prove to everybody—including myself—that I could win it outright. But the next year, the harder I tried, the worst my luck got.

"I drank too much. My wife left me and took the kids. Then I broke my arm in Houston. That was it for me. I just didn't have the heart for it anymore."

Ben sighed. "I'm sorry. I didn't know," he said. "But you did win the title. No one can ever take that away from you. It's in the books—you have the gold buckle."

"But I never had the respect you did."

Ben eyed Logan. "I respected you," he said. "Because of you, I always knew I had to do my best and more. You're a damned good cowboy, Clint. Too good to be sitting here and not out there showing 'em how it's supposed to be done.

"My all-around days are over. That's a fact. But yours don't have to be."

They shook hands at the door and Ben headed for his truck. Logan watched him limp away, wondering what had made Ben come to see him. Whatever the reason, he would always be grateful to him for it. He suddenly remembered something and couldn't believe he hadn't said a word about it.

"Ben," Logan called out, and as he turned to face him, added, "I'm sorry about your family."

Ben acknowledged with a slight nod, then hurriedly climbed into his truck. He was suddenly anxious to get home.

Scott and Lisa lay together on the couch; both were feeling somewhat guilty for being so comfortable in each other's arms. They had tried to stay apart until Ben came back, but that had only made them miserable.

"I can't pretend anymore," Lisa said suddenly, rising to her knees on the couch.

"What are you doing?" Scott asked in disbelief as she began unbuttoning her blouse.

"Come on, Scott," she said, slipping the blouse off and dropping it to the floor. "I know you want to as much as I do."

Scott couldn't help but stare. She was beautiful. Her full breasts filled the French cut blacklace bra; her torso tapered down to that perfect tiny waist. She lowered herself down on him and kissed him; her long auburn hair cascading over his face.

"Lisa...please..." he pleaded, trying to sit up. "We have to talk to Ben."

She held him down. "I don't want to talk about Ben," she said as she started unbuttoning his shirt. "All he cares about is himself. I have needs, too. We both do."

He took hold of her wrist. "This is wrong, Lisa."

"No, it's not," she said, grinning mischievously. Then she started tickling him; he'd always been ticklish.

It was 10 p.m. when Ben parked his truck next to Lisa's Corvette; he was delighted she was at the ranch. After three days of driving, he was bone-weary and glad he was finally home. As usual, he entered the house through the back door and, in reflex, hung his hat on the rack. He dropped his suitcase next to the kitchen table as he crossed the room.

The sound of Scott and Lisa laughing made Ben smile.

He'd really missed both of them. He headed down the hall toward the living room.

Ben couldn't believe what he was seeing. No. That couldn't be Lisa and Scott together on the couch. No. That couldn't be Lisa only in her bra and jeans, on top of Scott.

From the corner of his eye, Scott saw movement and was suddenly aware someone else was in the room. Grabbing Lisa by the arms, he forcefully sat both of them up.

"Hey..." Lisa protested. Then she saw Ben standing there.

Scott, his shirt now completely unbuttoned, let his hands fall away from Lisa as nausea washed over him. Ben's eyes bored into him. Scott wanted to say something, but suddenly he had no voice.

Ben silently stepped forward, bending down to pick up Lisa's blouse. He glared at her as he let it drop in her lap. "I want you two out of my house—and off my ranch—now," he said, his voice thick with barely controlled anger, and then turned away.

"Ben, wait," Lisa said, jumping to her feet and hurrying after him; she grabbed his arm. Jerking free, Ben pivoted and took hold of her by both forearms as he stared into her eyes. Lisa had never seen him like this; his eyes were cold and grey. She felt the sting of tears; he was hurting her. Silently, he released her and then turned away again. She watched him limp down the hallway to his bedroom. Seconds later, the door slammed shut.

In the darkness, Ben slowly lowered himself onto the bed. His heart finally started beating again. It pounded so furiously now that he had to grip the sides of the bed to steady himself.

Lisa sat at the kitchen table, nursing her third cup of coffee. Sooner or later, Ben was going to have to come out of his bedroom. Scott had pleaded with her to leave with him. He told her he had seen Ben that angry before; the last time was just before he beat the hell out of a cowboy who had suckerpunched Chris. It had taken three of them to pull him off that poor bastard.

She had told Scott that Ben would never physically hurt her.

She didn't tell him about the fear she had felt last night as those cold, grey eyes bored into her. But she had to stay and try to explain. She had to make him understand what had happened since he had been gone.

In exhaustion, Scott had finally given up and left. Poor Scott. She would never forget the look of devastation on his face at the sight of Ben. She realized now she should never have pushed the issue; her physical needs had gotten the best of her. Lisa heard footfalls and looked up to see Ben coming down the hall. He still had on the same clothes as last night, but the brown and green plaid shirt was pulled out of his jeans and he was barefooted. He looked awful.

When Ben saw Lisa, his first impulse was to go back to his bedroom. Damn. This was his house. He strode to the stove without looking at her. He could feel the anger welling in him.

"I told you to leave. I suggest you do it now," he said as he poured himself a cup of coffee and then headed out of the kitchen.

"Ben, we have to talk," Lisa said, following him at a safe distance into the living room.

He sat down in the chair and took a sip of coffee. "Funny, I don't have anything to say to you," he said. "I think what I saw last night says it all."

"First of all, what you saw was my fault, not Scott's."

"He didn't seem to be complaining."

"Everything is so messed up," she said in frustration, dropping down to the couch. "If you just wouldn't have gone to Wyoming."

Ben took a deep breath; he needed to keep his anger under control. "Out of sight, out of mind, huh?" he said with a snicker. "So, how long did it take you? A day? Two? Was I even out of San Antonio?"

That hurt. But she was determined not to cry in front of him. "Please, Ben, it wasn't like that and you know it. And nothing more than what you saw happened between me and Scott."

Looking her square in the eyes, he said, "I don't know anything, Lisa. Nothing makes sense anymore."

For just a moment, she saw the pain in his eyes and she wanted to go to him. But then his eyes grew grey and he looked away from her.

"Since I've been back, I kept feeling things weren't quite right between us," Lisa said quietly, hoping he would listen to what she had to say. "There seemed to be a place in you I couldn't touch—a place you kept me out of," she paused, being careful not to reveal she knew about that place because of Scott's detailed account of his accident.

"And then—after Waco—it became a wall. I tried, but I couldn't get through it or around it. You just closed yourself off and shut me and Scott out," she said sadly, wishing he would look at her. He didn't.

"You never even cried in front of us, Ben."

Lisa's last words scraped against a raw place in him. He wanted to tell her he had finally cried. That in the mountains he had cried like the lost child he had felt like since Waco. But he didn't say any of those words. She had betrayed him and he wanted to stay angry with her.

"Look at you. You're still shutting me out," she said in exasperation.

Ben methodically placed the coffee cup on the lamp table next to the chair and turned to look at her. "If there are magic words that will change everything that's happened, just tell me what they are, Lisa. And I'll be more than happy to say them," he said. "If not, I don't see much point to this conversation."

Lisa blinked at the tears burning in her eyes. "You just won't do it, will you? You refuse to admit that you're a mere human being like the rest of us.

"No, you're the great Ben Matthews—star of the rodeo and star with the women. And you don't really need anybody, do you?" she asked, getting to her feet, pacing a few feet, and then faced him again.

"Well, did you ever think that maybe me and Scott needed you? I know they were your family, but we loved them, too.

We needed you to help us get through our grief. You've always been the strongest one of us." She paused to once again keep her emotions in check.

"But you left and so we did the best we could to comfort each other. And then we realized there was something between us we had denied for a long time. It just happened, Ben."

He clutched the chair's arms, digging his fingernails into the fabric. "I always knew Scott had a crush on you as big as Texas," he conceded, then coldly added, "But I never thought you would take advantage of it—especially not under the circumstances. Me or Scott, I guess it didn't make much difference to you as long as you got what you needed."

Lisa flinched. "Damnit, I loved you," she whispered. "I still do. But somewhere along the way, our love stopped growing—and we just didn't know it. Then when I started having these feelings for Scott, I had to face the truth."

"And just what is the truth, Lisa?"

"I think I love him, Ben," she answered and waited for him to explode, but he didn't.

Instead, he slowly rose from the chair. "Hmm, you think you love Scott, huh?" he asked as he approached her.

Lisa found herself backing up as Ben neared her. She hadn't forgotten how he had hurt her last night, but he didn't seem angry. He just kept walking toward her, and she thought he was almost smiling. She suddenly had no place to go; he had backed her up against the wall.

Methodically, Ben placed his hands against the wall on each side of Lisa's head. He pressed his body against hers and then kissed her hard, almost too hard.

She tried weakly to resist him, but felt herself physically responding. And when she did, he stopped kissing her and she was staring into those same cold, grey eyes she had last night.

"Just a little something to remember me by," Ben whispered icily, still pressed against her with his face only inches from hers. "I'm going to take a shower. You'd better be gone when I'm done."

As he slowly pulled away from her, Lisa felt relief flooding her body. But it wasn't until he had long disappeared down the hallway that she even dared to take a breath.

When Ben came into the kitchen for the second time that morning, Lisa wasn't there. She had wisely taken his warning seriously.

He slowly sat down and drank the too-hot coffee. Not quite the homecoming he had envisioned. Thanks to Angie, Sundance and the Tylers, he had actually been feeling fairly good when he left Wyoming. As he drove home, he had even thought maybe it was time he and Lisa got married. And Scott. He knew his father had left Scott part of the ranch; he had thought of asking him to become equal partners with him.

Well, at least he could stop feeling guilty about his and Angie's one night together. Damn. Now he wished he had allowed himself more nights with Angie.

He put the coffee cup down and ran his right hand through his still damp hair. When was this nightmare going to be over? Any peace he had found in Wyoming had been shattered when he'd walked into the living room last night. Right now, he wanted to jump in his truck and run back to Wyoming, back to Angie and Sundance. But he knew that wasn't the answer. He wasn't any good to anyone the way he was.

Maybe Lisa was right. Maybe he really didn't know how to need someone enough to let them all the way in. Maybe what had been left of him, after that bull, had died in Waco.

Ben suddenly got to his feet, grabbing his hat as he hurried out the back door. If nothing else, he still had the ranch and he needed to make sure he didn't lose that, too.

Lisa handed the waiter the menu and then waited until he was out of hearing range. "You were right about Ben. His anger scares the hell out of me."

Scott sighed. "He has every right to be angry." He looked across the restaurant table at her. "He shouldn't have found out about us the way he did."

"All right, all right. I'm sorry. It was my fault and I told him that," she admitted, adding, "But it didn't seem to make much of a difference. It was like I was talking to a stranger."

He took a sip of water. "I'll wait a couple of days before I try to talk to him. Maybe he'll be more willing to listen then."

"I wouldn't count on it." She considered telling him how Ben had both frightened and humiliated her, but decided against it. She knew Scott was going to have to deal with Ben in his own way.

It was three days later when Scott finally decided to risk a confrontation with Ben. He had just driven through the front gate when Pete Jenkins drove by on his way out.

"Good to see ya, Scott," Jenkins, who had been the Matthews Ranch foreman for twenty years, greeted as they stopped their trucks alongside each other.

"Hey, Pete. Do you know where Ben is?"

"Sure do. He's up at the main barn, stacking hay. There's enough for a full crew, but he won't let anybody help him." Jenkins wondered what had happened between Ben, Scott and Lisa. "He's been that way since he got back. Rides Cherokee first thing in the morning and then does the work of three men the rest of the day. Guess it keeps him from thinking."

Scott nodded. "See ya later, Pete," he said as the two trucks headed off in different directions.

The minute he stepped out of his truck, Scott could hear the country western music blaring from the barn. The oppressive August heat hung heavy in the air, and he wished they'd get an afternoon thunderstorm.

Scott walked around the truck that had been backed into the barn's double-door entrance; its flatbed trailer was loaded with hay bales. Ben, dressed in a sleeveless, faded orange University of

Texas T-shirt and very worn jeans, was busily hauling hay from the flatbed and stacking it at the back of the barn. While Ben had always been lean and fit, Scott thought he was looking a little gaunt. Probably wasn't eating or sleeping much. He reached into the cab of the truck and turned off the radio.

Ben glanced back at the sudden silence. When he saw Scott, he looked away and resumed working.

"Did you find the way I kept the books okay?" Scott asked, walking toward the far end of the trailer. "I tried to keep the supplies we ordered down to just what we really needed."

Ben didn't respond and just kept stacking the hay. Sweat trickled down his face and soaked the T-shirt.

"Chris' roommate sent his stuff from Austin. I put the boxes in the house."

Ben paused for just a moment, then continued stacking.

"What do you want to do about the land your father left me?"

This time Ben stopped and straightened up. "Do what you want with it. It's yours. Dad wanted you to have it," he said, pulling the gloves off his hands.

He climbed down from the flatbed, and Scott watched him go to the cab of the truck and retrieve a water jug and a towel. After he took several gulps, he poured some of the water on his head and then wiped his face as it dripped down.

"We can't just leave things the way they are between us, Ben. At least give me a chance to explain."

Ben took another drink, and then put the jug and towel back in the truck. "Don't worry about it. Lisa explained everything," he said, sitting down on a hay bale.

"You have to believe me. I was totally surprised when Lisa told me how she felt," Scott said, moving forward a few steps. "I didn't want to believe it."

"You were surprised? Well then, you can just imagine how surprised I was," Ben said calmly. "But I guess sometimes people aren't always what they seem. I sure found that out the hard way, didn't I? But that's the draw. Sometimes you get a good ride and sometimes you get a bad ride." He got to his feet and then walked away.

"Don't do this. Don't act like it's nothing," Scott called out to him. "I know it was wrong. I know I hurt you. I'm so sorry."

Ben slowly turned on his heels. "You're sorry? Well now, that makes what happened okay, huh?" he said, the anger seeping into his voice. "My family takes you in. I treat you no differently than Chris. And this is how you show your gratitude?

"I come back to find you and Lisa all over each other like two horny teenagers—and all you can say is you're sorry? And what? I'm supposed to give you and Lisa my blessings?" He glared at him. "Go to hell, Scott. And take Lisa with you," he said angrily, turning away.

"Ben, please..." Scott pleaded, reaching out to stop him. The minute he touched Ben's arm, he knew he had made a serious mistake.

Anger overwhelmed Ben. With both hands, he grabbed Scott by his shirt collar and slammed him into the side of the truck. The force of the blow knocked the wind out of Scott. When he took a deep breath, pain quickly spread throughout his back as he was pinned against the truck's door.

Ben couldn't believe how angry he was; he really wanted to hurt Scott. He tried to control his rapid, ragged breathing. "I trusted you," he said between clenched teeth.

Scott felt tears burning his eyes. "I'm sorry, Ben," he said. "Please forgive me. I can't lose Chris and then you, too."

Just as quickly as it had overcome him, Ben felt the anger leave him. It was as though all of his strength went with it, and he was suddenly exhausted.

He slowly released his hold on Scott and backed away. "Get the hell out of here," he said hoarsely. "Just get the hell out of here and leave me alone," he muttered as he staggered away. "Just leave me alone."

That night Ben decided to get falling-down drunk. He sat there in the semi-darkness of the living room, pouring himself a drink from his second Jack Daniel's fifth. As he fell back against the couch, he wondered how in the hell he had ended up so alone. Damn. How had this happened? His family, Scott, Lisa—all gone. No. This couldn't be real. He put the glass down on the table and awkwardly pushed himself up to his feet.

The truck lurched to a stop, and Ben almost fell out of it when he leaned too hard against the door. He stumbled up the rock walkway to the unlocked front door and entered the house he had grown up in. He moved with familiarity through the entryway, flicking on the light switch as he entered the large living room. The two lamps, one on each side of the chocolate brown couch, came on.

Ben was suddenly sober. He stood there, unable to go any farther. Everything was in its place; frozen in time waiting for the occupants of the house to return. His mother's knitting basket was on the floor next to her rocking chair, the one with the well-worn green cushions. His father's carving knife and the last L'Amour western he had been reading were on the lamp table next to his tan recliner. He listened to the steady ticking of the grandfather clock to the left of the fireplace.

He didn't want to, but his gaze strayed up to the vintage Winchester rifle he had bought for his father last Christmas. It was displayed above the stone fireplace in a gun rack his father had carved himself. Below that, all the length and width of the solid oak mantle, were the family pictures his mother so proudly displayed. There was hardly a part of his and Chris' childhoods that wasn't depicted in those pictures.

The tightness in his chest was back; he thought he had gotten rid of it in Wyoming. But he didn't fight it like before; he didn't seem to have the strength to stop the tears he could feel coming.

As he scanned the room that held so many memories, he shivered. While everything was in its place, the room didn't feel right. It felt cold and empty. He now saw the boxes Scott had told him about, the ones that held Chris' belongings from Austin. They were neatly stacked against the far wall.

Ben took a deep breath. It was real. His family was gone. He couldn't bear the truth; he could feel it crushing him. And it was his fault. No matter what he did—drinking, working to exhaustion, being angry with Scott and Lisa—nothing could free him of that guilt.

Scott flinched as Lisa gently rubbed the liniment on his sore, bruised back.

"He could have really hurt you," she said as she ran her hands over the large discolored area between his shoulder blades. "Please stay away from him."

He shook his head. "You know I can't do that." He reached for his shirt. "Of all people, you should understand that."

Lisa helped him put on his shirt. "I do understand. The three of us have been friends all of our lives, and there's a part of me that will always love Ben. But so much has changed. I just don't know if he will ever accept things the way they are now."

Scott looked at her. "I have to believe he will. I have to believe we can somehow save our friendship."

She kissed him on the cheek. "You're a good man, Scott Barnes."

The flames were everywhere; the heat of the fire made his eyes water. He wanted to run away. But he couldn't. He could hear his father, mother and Chris calling his name, begging him to help them. But every time he took a step forward, a new wall of fire erupted in front of him. And still he could hear their screams.

Ben jolted up to a sitting position in the bed; cold sweat poured down his face and his heart thumped against his chest. He struggled to catch his breath. Slowly, ever so slowly, he began to regain his senses. Damn. He swung his legs over the side of the bed. If he'd ever needed a drink, he needed one now.

It was the third straight night that the nightmare had tormented him. He used both hands to splash cold water on his face and then pressed down on the counter top to steady himself. He tried to focus on the sound of the running water and not on their screams that lingered in his mind.

Shutting off the faucet, he grabbed the towel and hesitantly returned to the bed; he left the bathroom light on.

He didn't know what the point was of going back to bed; he might as well just give up sleeping. Hell, he might as well just give up—period. If this was what the rest of his life was going to be like, he didn't see much point in going on.

As he wiped his face with the towel, he remembered another time not too long ago when he doubted life was worth living. Chris had just brought him back from a therapy session; his leg hurt like hell, and he just didn't see any way it was ever going to be sound enough for him to ride again. He could accept no more broncs and bulls, but the idea that he might not be able to ride again at all was too much to bear.

And that's when Chris told him what the doctors had suggested should wait until he was fully recovered. They said sometimes the news set patients back. But Chris thought the time was right and so he told him what even their parents and Scott didn't know.

"You went into cardiac arrest just as we got to the hospital. As they rushed you into the emergency room, I got shoved aside. But they were so focused on you that no one noticed I was still in the room. They had to hit you three times with the electroshock paddles. But you came back.

"You've been through hell and back, Ben. I know—I was there. I was holding your hand when you died. And I was standing right there when you came back. I felt you come back.

"So don't tell me you're going to quit. Because my brother doesn't know how to give up."

The sound of Chris' voice comforted Ben. He cried softly and even dared to close his eyes.

Jake's Saloon was crowded, smoky and noisy. And that was just fine with Ben. He had started coming to the popular bar between the ranch and San Antonio nearly every night during the past week.

During the day at the ranch, there was always plenty to do: fence lines to check and mend, barns to paint, cattle to tend. But once darkness came, the walls of his house closed in on him. And it took too long to get drunk at home. He needed the distractions of the bar—the music, the people, the noise—to keep him from thinking, from feeling, until the whiskey took effect.

Billy Joe Parker plopped himself down in the chair. "Hey, Ben, how ya doin'?"

"Just fine, Billy Joe." He refilled his glass with whiskey.

"Me, too." Billy Joe grinned, cocking his hat to the side as he leaned back in the chair; he was definitely feeling no pain. "So, you and Scott gonna rope in Fort Worth next week?"

Ben took a long swallow of the whiskey. "No."

"Me neither. Gotta take a load of ponies to Louisiana and then Florida."

"Still doin' that, huh?"

"Yeah, those racetrack trainers love my ponies," Billy Joe said. "They use 'em to take those racehorses to the track. And mostly, those trainers just like to set on 'em while they watch their horses work. As long as they pay top dollar for 'em, they can do what they want with 'em."

Ben thought for a moment. "Want some company this trip?"

"Who? You?"

"Yeah, I've never been to a racetrack. And things are quiet at the ranch."

"Hell, I'd love some company," Billy Joe said, slapping his hand on his knee. "It's a long-ass drive from here to Miami."

5

It was somewhere in Alabama that the pounding in Ben's head finally eased. Damn. Those Cajuns sure knew how to have a good time. Or as they said, "Let's pass a good time, cher." He couldn't remember when he had eaten such spicy food, drunk so much beer, and laughed so hard. His feet still hurt from doing the two-step to that toe-tapping Cajun fiddle music; it was why he decided to put on sneakers instead of boots to drive. It had been a hell of a three days in Lafayette, Louisiana.

Ben glanced back at Billy Joe, snoring away in the backseat of the cab-and-a-half truck. He had practically carried him out of the hotel room that morning and dumped him in the backseat. He had figured if he didn't get them on the road, they'd never get to Florida. Billy Joe never had been one to hurry out of a place when he was having a good time.

Of course, he hadn't been so sure he wanted to leave earlier that morning. He'd woke up in bed with two dark-haired, dark-eyed Cajun women. But thanks to the beer, he had no recollection of how all three of them had ended up together. That was one of the things he hated about getting drunk on beer. At least with whiskey, he remembered what he'd done; hurt like hell, but he remembered.

Damn. Two Cajun women. He was one worn-out cowboy. He had virtually crawled out of bed and stumbled to the bathroom, where he promptly threw up. That was the other thing he hated about getting beer drunk; it always made him sick. He hadn't felt much better after a cold shower, but at least he was awake.

After he had collected Billy Joe and gotten a thermos of coffee to go from the hotel restaurant, he drove over to Acadiana Downs. They had boarded the horses and parked the stock trailer at the Cajun country racetrack. Martin Boudreaux, one of the trainers who had bought a pony horse, helped him hook up the trailer and load the eight horses bound for Miami. All the time, Billy Joe snored away in the backseat.

Ben took a swallow of the lukewarm coffee from the paper cup. What the hell was he doing driving Billy Joe Parker's rig to Florida? He needed to be careful about decisions he made with a fifth of Jack Daniel's in him. But that same sense of restlessness— of wanting to run away—that had sent him to Wyoming had gotten hold of him again. And that night in Jake's Saloon as Billy Joe told him of his trip, it suddenly seemed like the out he had been looking for.

The whole Scott and Lisa situation had really shaken him up. Not only that it had happened, but that he'd gotten so angry with both of them. He'd always had a temper, and he knew it had gotten worse since that bull. But he had never before unleashed his anger on someone he loved.

There had been pure fear in Lisa's eyes when he'd backed her up against that wall. And there had been real pain in Scott's eyes when he had thrown him against the truck. How could he have done that? How could he have made the woman he had loved all his life afraid of him? How could he have physically hurt a man he considered as much a brother as a friend?

But he had done those very things to Scott and Lisa. And that was one of the reasons why he knew he needed to get away again. That and the fiery nightmare. It was driving him crazy. Just when he thought it was gone and he'd actually get a decent night's sleep, it came again with a vengeance. Sometimes, even in the day, he'd hear his parents' and Chris' screams in his mind.

And so here he was, driving Billy Joe Parker's rig to Florida.

His father had always said that cities were where people who didn't know any better lived, and Ben had always agreed with him. As he scanned the sprawling Miami skyline, he was once again puzzled by the appeal of city life. San Antonio and Austin were bearable; Fort Worth and Dallas were only tolerable for a rodeo. So what the hell was he doing in Miami?

Ben glanced over at Billy Joe, who he had to admit was doing a hell of a job maneuvering the rig through the freeway traffic. Billy Joe had taken over the driving when they had left Ocala that morning, and now he was glad he'd driven the day before. They were headed for Canton Race Track, one of three tracks in the Miami area; the other two were Gardner Park and Hallandale Park. He was having a hard time envisioning horses co-existing with all this city madness. But Billy Joe had told him that Thoroughbred breeding and racing were major businesses in Florida. He'd only gotten a glimpse of the Thoroughbred farms in Ocala; they had boarded the horses there overnight, and then headed out at 4 a.m. for Miami. Billy Joe had suddenly become anxious to sell his stock.

As Ben followed Billy Joe through the barns on the Canton backside, he felt like a kid at the circus for the first time. Yes, indeed, there were horses here in the middle of Miami. Everywhere he looked, high-strung, prancing Thoroughbreds were being ridden or led. He was amazed by the size of them and by the lack of size of the people handling them. Little men and women weighing hardly more than 100 pounds were trying to control 1,200 pounds of horse, bred to be nearly uncontrollable.

"Loose horse! Loose horse!" someone warned just as a riderless Thoroughbred came galloping right at Ben.

Without hesitation, Ben stood his ground. "Whoa, easy now," he said quietly as the horse tucked his hind legs and skidded to a stop. Ben reached out and took firm hold of the reins. "Easy now. You're okay," he assured the animal.

Billy Joe laughed and cocked his hat back. "Anybody but you would have just gotten his ass run over."

"Well, I'm damned glad he didn't," Dan Cooper said as he walked past Billy Joe and toward Ben. "And since he's wearing a cowboy hat, I assume he's with you, Billy Joe."

"Yep, Dan Cooper meet Ben Matthews."

"Considering you just caught one of my best horses, I'm mighty glad to make your acquaintance, Ben," Cooper said as he shook Ben's free hand, and then relieved him of the horse.

"How'd he get loose?" Ben asked.

"Dumped his rider. He has this nasty habit of wheeling at the gap," Cooper answered as they headed for his barn two down from where they were. "That's why I'm awful glad Billy Joe finally showed up. My pony horse died two months ago, and I've been without one since."

"Dan is from Beaumont and started training horses at Acadiana Downs more than twenty years ago," Billy Joe explained as they walked into Cooper's shedrow.

"Thanks, Billy Joe, for reminding me how long I've been trying to make a living training these useless longnecks," he said, handing the horse over to a groom. "Cool him down real good."

"Don't let him fool ya, Ben," Billy Joe said as they followed Cooper into his tackroom office. "Dan is a hell of a trainer and makes a damn fine living. Better than most rodeo cowboys do."

Cooper handed Ben a mug of coffee, looking up at him. "That's where I know your name from. You won the all-around a couple of times, didn't you?"

Ben only nodded in reply as he turned away to look at the winner's circle pictures lining the walls.

"A couple? Four straight years," Billy Joe answered for him. "Best damned roughstock rider since Mahan. And a hell of a roper, too."

Cooper sensed Ben was uncomfortable with the praise. "So, Billy Joe, how much are you going to rip me off for that pony horse?"

Billy Joe laughed. "Once you set eyes on him, you'll pay me whatever I want," he said, leading the way out of the office.

Ben followed a few steps behind Billy Joe and Cooper, glancing in at each stall as they ambled down the shedrow. He suddenly stopped; the striking chestnut Thoroughbred had to be all of seventeen hands tall, and he practically filled up the stall. When Ben stepped closer to the door, the horse pinned his ears and lunged at him. Ben quickly stepped back; he had never had a horse react to him quite that way.

"It's your hat," Cooper explained, pointing to his own hatless head of grey-flecked brown hair. He and Billy Joe had backtracked when they realized Ben had fallen behind.

"What?"

"It's your hat. Most Thoroughbreds spook easy, and a cowboy hat is definitely spook material," Cooper said. "I quit wearing mine a long time ago."

Ben slowly took off his hat and held it out for the horse to inspect. Cautiously, the animal extended his head out over the stall door and sniffed the hat. With a snort, he nonchalantly retreated and resumed eating his hay.

Ben chuckled. "Smart horse," he said, thinking of Cherokee and Sundance.

"Yeah, and fast, too," Cooper said. "His name is Time For Bucks and he's in a $100,000 stakes race tomorrow. Are you guys gonna stay for a couple of days?"

"Absolutely," Billy Joe answered as they moved away from the horse's stall. "There are a few south Florida ladies I plan to reacquaint myself with."

The next morning while Billy Joe shopped his ponies around, Ben spent time with Cooper. As they watched the horses galloping

on the track from the trainer's viewing stand, Ben found himself
asking question after question.

"Why do the riders stand up like that in the stirrups?"

"Keeps the weight off the horse's back, lets him stride out
more and gives the rider more leverage for control."

"Why don't the jockeys exercise the horses they ride?"

"Some do, but mostly when they're just starting out. A jock
will come out and get on a stakes horse for you. But mostly they
make their living riding in the afternoons and don't want to take a
chance getting hurt exercising in the morning. Besides, there's
plenty of exercise riders to go around."

"Are Thoroughbreds that different from Quarter horses?"

"In a lot of ways, yes. And then again, a horse is a horse. You
know how competitive a good cow pony can get? Well, Thoroughbreds are competitive that way about racing. And the good ones
know when they've won and when they've lost. Just like a good
cow pony knows when he's bested that cow."

"So, do you miss Texas?"

"Yeah. But I love the racetrack. There's a real feeling of family
on the backside. Kinda like on the rodeo circuit. And since not
everyone was cut out to be an all-around champion like you, it's
not a bad living for a good ol' Texas cowboy."

Time For Bucks was in the ninth race that afternoon. Ben
watched him strutting around the saddling paddock; it was all his
groom could do to keep him from dragging him around. His red
coat shone like a new copper penny, and the muscles of his powerful, fit body rippled with each step. There was no doubt about it;
Cooper had him ready to run.

When the gates opened, Time For Bucks was bumped hard by
the horse to his left and immediately the jockey had to take him
back. The rest of the field quickly drew away. From his grandstand

seat, Ben watched as the jockey skillfully steadied the horse and then began to chase after the field on the backside. As they came into the final turn for home, they had caught up and were in the middle of the pack. But midway down the stretch, Ben realized the horse was boxed in and had no place to go.

It seemed to Ben that, on his own, Time For Bucks dropped back out of the pack and swung three-horses wide to the outside. Ben figured the race was lost. But that big red horse pinned his ears flat on his head and shifted into another gear. The jockey was hand-riding him high on his neck as they bore down on the leaders. With only one stride left to the wire, Time For Bucks got his head out in front.

Ben, Billy Joe and Cooper went crazy, cheering and slapping each other on the back. As he watched Time For Bucks come prancing proudly back toward the winner's circle and a smiling Cooper lead him in, Ben knew why his fellow Texan had fallen in love with the racetrack life. Whether it was rodeoing or racing, winning was winning. And it was intoxicating and addictive.

That night when he and Billy Joe returned to the hotel after a celebratory supper with Cooper and his wife, Ben was still replaying Time For Buck's race in his mind. Just like he used to with every winning bronc and bull ride.

"Mm,mm, look at all those pretty fillies," Billy Joe said with a grin as they stood just outside the hotel lounge.

"Think I'll just get a drink to go and call it a night."

Billy Joe looked at him in surprise. "You sick or something?"

"Just tired."

"Then by all means, you get a good night's sleep. I'll take up the slack with the ladies," Billy Joe said with a chuckle as he moseyed on into the lounge and right up to a table occupied by two women.

A quick shower later, Ben leaned back against the bed's headboard and sipped the Jack Daniel's he had brought up to the room.

Billy Joe probably wouldn't have believed him if he had told him he was looking forward to a good night's sleep more than being with a woman. But sleep had become a rare commodity for him these past months. And since he and Billy Joe had been on the road, he hadn't had any nightmares. Granted, he had stayed drunk those three days in Lafayette. But that had not been the case here in Miami, and he had slept undisturbed for two nights; he was hoping for the same tonight.

The next morning, Ben was at Cooper's barn by six; he wanted to watch the horses train one more time. As he walked down the shedrow toward Time For Bucks' stall, he took off his hat.

"Hey, big guy, you ran a hell of a race," Ben said as the horse finished off his grain breakfast and then came over to the front of the stall. "Bet you even know you won that race, don't ya?" he said as he pushed the horse's forelock away from the perfect white-diamond marking on his forehead.

Time For Bucks nickered and tossed his head. Ben laughed; Cooper was right—horses were horses.

When he and Billy Joe pulled into Ocala that night, Ben was still thinking about that race and how much he had enjoyed the whole racetrack experience. As he settled in for another good night's sleep, he thought about Angie and how she had moved to Wyoming to start a new life. As much as he loved Wyoming, he knew he couldn't live there year-round. Thanks to his leg, the long, harsh winters would render him a cripple for more than half the year. But Miami had even milder winters than San Antonio. True, it was a damned city. But it was a city where horses were trained and raced all year long.

Ben slowed down enough to drop his suitcase by the kitchen table on his way to the phone.

"Cooper Racing Stable."

"Hi, Dan, it's Ben Matthews. I wanted you to know how much I enjoyed our visit and you taking the time to answer all my questions."

"My pleasure. It was nice to have another good old Texas cowboy around, and especially one who wasn't trying to sell me something."

Ben laughed at Cooper's reference to Billy Joe. "How would you feel about taking on an assistant? One you didn't have to pay and one who might even buy a couple of racehorses."

Cooper chuckled. "I thought I saw that racetrack bug get a hold of you," he said. "But training Thoroughbreds is a full-time occupation. I don't think you'd be able to do it and rodeo, too."

"My rodeo days are over," Ben said deliberately. "And I'd really like a chance to try my hand at training racehorses. Do you think we can work something out?"

"Sure, Ben. After all, we Texas cowboys need to look out for each other."

"Thanks. Give me a week or so to take care of things here and then I'll head back to Miami."

Cooper put the phone down and leaned back in the chair. He had liked Ben right away and sensed he was a hell of a horseman. It just seemed to him that Ben was still too young to give up the rodeo; it was as addictive a lifestyle as the racetrack, and you just didn't decide one day to retire. He wondered if Ben's limp and that scar on his face had something to do with it. Cooper pulled out the middle desk drawer and retrieved a black phone book. Maybe he'd give his old friend, Jim Reynolds, a call. He was a longtime pro rodeo official, and if anyone knew the story on Ben Matthews, he would.

It was a full-moon south Texas night. Ben folded his hands behind his head as he lay in the sleeping bag beneath the oak tree. As he stared up into the star-filled sky, he could hear Cherokee quietly grazing nearby.

He'd been unpacking his suitcase and mentally sorting out all the details he needed to take care of when the anxiety set in. He had only been home a half hour, and already the fiery nightmare was back on his mind. Leaving his half-full suitcase on the bed, he'd hurried out of the house. Twenty minutes later, he and Cherokee were headed for the oak tree. Somehow he'd known he wouldn't have the nightmare there.

But now other thoughts were making him uneasy. Was he really going to leave Texas and the ranch, the only home he had ever known? And if that was what he was fixing to do, what would his father think about it? Would he understand? Would he forgive him? Three generations of Matthews had worked the ranch, and now he was the last of the line.

Ben sat up and leaned back against the tree. If that bull had taught him anything, it had been fear. And right now, he didn't know what scared him more—staying or leaving.

"Who was that on the phone?" Lisa asked as Scott rejoined her on the couch.

"Pete Jenkins," he answered, putting his arm around her. "Ben is back. But Pete said he headed out on Cherokee late this afternoon and never came back."

Lisa sighed. "Remember when we camped out like that when we were kids?"

Scott smiled momentarily at the memories. "Seems like another lifetime ago now, doesn't it?"

"Yes, but I want us to be happy now, too," she said, turning to face him. "We need to work at that together—and let Ben go on with his life."

He looked into her golden brown eyes. "But I can't just leave him alone. I can't just turn my back on him."

"I know that and I love you for it," she said gently, taking his hands in hers.. "But I want you to think about something. When Ben and I talked that morning after he came back from Wyoming, he never once said he loved me or asked me not to leave him. I think he knew too much had happened for us to go on together. I think he knew he was going to have to be on his own for awhile."

"What are you saying? Our friendship is over and I'm just supposed to forget about him?"

She squeezed his hands."You were right when you told me the best of Ben survived that bull," she said, trying to comfort him. "You need to remember that and remember how strong he really is. He's going to be all right, Scott."

He hugged her tightly and prayed she was right.

Walter Hancock peered at Ben over the rims of his glasses; they were pushed down halfway on his hawkish nose and his full head of silver hair reminded Ben of his father. Hancock had been the Matthews family's lawyer as long as Ben could remember.

"Now, let me see if I understand all it is you think you want to do," Hancock drawled, glancing down at his notes on the yellow legal pad. "You want to lease the ranch and all of its assets to the University of Texas, specifically the agriculture department, for a dollar a year. The only property not included are the two houses, which will remained locked and unoccupied. Necessary housing or facilities may be built with your approval.

"The UT rodeo team is to have free lifetime use of the ranch facilities and stock. You and the school will divide all profits equally, and your share is to be put into your account here.

"Under no circumstances is the ranch ever to be sold. After your death, the ranch would then be owned solely by UT, but will always be known as the Matthews Ranch."

Ben nodded when Hancock paused.

"And when the wrongful death insurance settlement from the trucking company comes in, those millions of dollars are to be used to establish UT scholarship funds in the names of Thomas, Sara and Chris Matthews. Their purpose will be to assist needy sons and daughters of ranchers obtain a college education," Hancock concluded.

Again Ben nodded. "I think that takes care of everything.

I'd like you to draw up the legal papers as soon as possible," he said. "I told the UT people we'd finalize everything as quickly as we could."

Hancock sat back in the high-backed leather chair. "And you're going to be where and doing what?"

"In Miami, Florida, training Thoroughbred racehorses," Ben said matter-of-factly, getting to his feet.

"What about Scott Barnes? Is he going to include his inherited part of the ranch in this deal?"

Ben paused for a moment at the door, keeping his back to the lawyer. "You'll have to ask him about that," he replied quietly, and then left.

Ben let Cherokee settle into that smooth fast walk of his; he was suddenly not in a hurry to get back. All the legal papers had been signed three days ago and the UT people would officially take over the ranch next week. As soon as he'd gotten back from Hancock's office, he'd saddled up and ridden out. And for the past three days, he'd tried to cover as much of the ranch as possible. It was as though he was afraid it would fade from his memory once he was in Miami. Yet he knew it would always be a part of him. And maybe one day, he'd be able to come back and not be overwhelmed by the pain he now felt.

He was going to have to leave Cherokee, too. It would be unfair to confine the horse to the racetrack life in Miami. Pony horses lived in stalls and never got to roam free in wide-open pastureland. Cherokee was the product of three generations of Matthews-bred Quarter horses; he had been bred to be a ranch and rodeo horse, not a racetrack pony horse.

Chuckling to himself, Ben remembered how Cherokee had bucked like hell for a week when he broke him just before his accident. But when he had been ready to get back on a horse for the first time eight months later, it was Cherokee that he chose. There had never been any doubt in his mind that he could trust the horse.

It would be hard to leave Cherokee behind, but he knew it was the right thing to do. He had spoken at length about Cherokee with the UT rodeo coach and knew the horse would be in good hands. A lot of young cowboys and cowgirls would learn much on Cherokee's back.

Ben led the horse through the opened gate just like he had so many times before. "You probably won't even miss me," he said as he unbuckled and then slipped off the halter. "Well, go on. Your buddies are waiting for ya."

Instead of galloping off as usual to join the herd, Cherokee just stood there. Ben could swear that horse was looking right at him. Then Cherokee nudged him.

"Ah, come on, Cherokee, you wouldn't like where I'm going," he said, patting the horse on the neck. "Now, go on and get out of here," he ordered, slapping him on the shoulder. Slowly, the horse turned and trotted off.

Latching the gate behind him, Ben collected his saddle and bridle. The custom-made saddle, a college graduation present from his father, was coming with him. He put it in the back of the truck and then walked around to the cab, retrieving his keys from the ignition switch.

As Ben walked toward his parents' house, he tried not to think about how they and Chris would feel about him leaving the ranch. He just kept telling himself it was what he had to do. He slid the key into the front door's lock, turned it and heard the quiet click.

When Ben came out of his house with the last box, Scott was standing beside his truck.

"It's true. You're leaving," Scott said in disbelief. He had been in shock since Hancock had called him. "How can you do this?"

Ben didn't answer him as he put the box down in the last open space in the truck's bed and then snapped down the vinyl covering. He walked back to the kitchen door and locked it.

"Weren't you even going to say good-bye?"

Ben looked at him. "I figured you and Lisa would just be glad I was gone," he said quietly.

"That's not how we feel and you know it," Scott said. "You don't have to do this. This is your home. Lisa and I will move."

Ben shook his head. "I wish it was that simple," he said sadly. "I keep hearing Dad telling me to just get on with my life. And damn, I've tried. But I finally realized that what my life used to be, doesn't exist anymore."

Scott felt sick to his stomach. "That's not true."

"Yes, it is."

The two men stood there in the sudden silence, each reliving their friendship's lifetime of memories. Ben stifled the emotions that threatened to overwhelm him; it hurt too much to care about Scott, Lisa or anything. He made himself move.

Scott stepped sideways, blocking Ben from reaching for the truck's door handle. Ben avoided his gaze as Scott slowly extended his right hand. Ben thought about it for a moment, and then decided the least he could do was shake his hand. But the minute he took hold of it, Scott pulled him toward him and wrapped his arms around him. It took all Ben's strength not to return the gesture; his arms remained at his sides. He could feel Scott trembling against him as he clutched him tightly, and he knew he was crying.

Ben took a deep breath; his own eyes were stinging from the tears he fought back. "Scott...please," he whispered. "You have to let me go."

Scott felt his heart breaking. He knew Ben was right. It hurt like hell, but he knew Ben was right. Ever so slowly, he released his hold on him and backed away. Wearily, Ben climbed into the truck; the emotions had drained him. Silently, and careful not to look back at Scott, he started up the truck and drove away.

Scott stared at the road long after the truck had disappeared. As the tears streamed down his face, he had this terrible feeling he was never going to see Ben again.

6

Ben's racetrack education began in earnest as soon as he was back in Miami. A whole new world had opened up before him, and he was an eager student. There was so much to learn.

There was the difference between a sprinter—horses which ran best at the shorter distances of six to seven furlongs—and a miler and a stayer, those which fared better at competition over a mile. Not only were they trained differently, but they were bred differently. Ben had grown up with Quarter horses, and now he had to learn Thoroughbred bloodlines.

Then there was the condition book, a two-week slate of races available to run in, which was written by the track's racing secretary. It determined how a trainer readied a horse, depending on what races were in each condition book. And Ben had always thought a race was a race. Wrong. There were classes of races: claiming, allowance, handicap, stakes and graded stakes. And then each class had its own sub-class. Racing had its own democratic way of determining a horse's ability and providing a type of race for it to run in.

In addition to the different kinds of races, there were also races with conditions of age, sex and how many races a horse had or had not won. Horses that had never won a race were called maidens and mostly ran in maiden races. Once they won a race, then they could run in non-winners of two races with certain weight allowances for age and sex.

Then you had to consider distance (short/long), surface (dirt/turf), post position (inside/outside), equipment (blinkers/tongue ties/special bits) and of course, jockeys (honest, good hands, good seat).

Every night Ben went back to his high-rise hotel room across from the racetrack with his head spinning from all this new knowledge. He was grateful that horses had always been part of his life and he hadn't had to start from scratch. He knew about conformation, nutrition, basic equine health and competitive conditioning. That knowledge just had to be adapted to Thoroughbreds.

While the racetrack life had long days which started at 5 a.m. and finished late at night on race days, it was an easier lifestyle than ranching and rodeoing. Ben found himself looking forward to each day, to being around the horses and absorbing as much knowledge from Cooper as he could. He was anxious to buy a couple of his own and put to use what he was learning.

There were even days he didn't think about Waco. About that bull. And at night, he slept free of nightmares.

"I did a little rodeoing in my younger days," Cooper said to Ben as he cut up his steak. "Of course, I wasn't in your class. Just did a little roping and steer wrestling. But I sure did have my share of good times."

Ben managed to chuckle, although he really didn't want to talk about the rodeo. "Yeah, well, no matter what, rodeo cowboys always find a way to have a good time."

"Made a lot of good friends, too," Cooper added. "In fact, I talked to Jim Reynolds not too long ago. He had nothing but good things to say about you, both professionally and personally."

Ben stared down at the food on his plate; he had suddenly lost his appetite. "He's a good man and always was a fair judge," he said quietly, not looking up at Cooper.

"Jim said it took a lot of heart for you to come back to the rodeo after what that bull did to you," Cooper said softly. "And he said the hardest thing he ever had to do was bring you to his office that day in Waco."

Ben felt ill. Damn. He had only been in Miami a month, and already everything had caught up with him.

"I guess what I'm trying to say is that people come to the racetrack for all kinds of reasons. Most are running from something or somebody—wives, ex-husbands, the law," Cooper said, putting down the knife and fork. "But it seems to me that you walked away from a lot in Texas. And probably left behind some folks who care a helluva lot about you. I guess you figured it was what you had to do.

"But don't be so quick to think you can just let go of all of that so easy. These city people don't know what heritage means like we do. Just because you stop wearing your cowboy hat, doesn't mean you stop being a Texas cowboy."

Later that night as Ben lay in bed, he thought about what Cooper had said to him. Although he hadn't been pleased that the trainer knew more about him than he liked, he appreciated Cooper's concern. Seemed that no matter where he went, he was fortunate enough to come across good people who cared about his welfare. And he could see how an outsider couldn't understand why he had left Texas. But he wasn't having any second thoughts that it had been what he had to do. If he had tried to stay any longer, he would have lost his mind.

And then there were Scott and Lisa. If any good had come out of all this, it was that they had found each other. Although his ego had been bruised by that turn of events, he really did want them to be happy together. He would always care about them; he just couldn't be there for them right now. He hoped they understood and that one day, they'd forgive him.

Lisa gratefully slipped her feet out of the red high heels. She sat down at the kitchen table and began sorting through the three-days worth of mail. It had been a long day at the gallery, and she was looking forward to a quiet evening with Scott. He should be back from the ranch anytime now, she thought. When the University of Texas people had taken over the Matthews Ranch two months ago, Pete Jenkins had decided it was time to retire. Scott had been the obvious and immediate choice to become the ranch foreman. Lisa hadn't even tried to talk him out of it, knowing it was his way of coping with Ben's leaving.

She would never forget how distraught Scott had been the day Ben left. When he had finally come back to her apartment that night, he had been heartbroken. But unlike Ben, he had allowed her to share his pain and to comfort him. It was the first night they had made love.

Since then, Scott had moved in with her while they decided what to do. He thought eventually they'd build a house on the ranch, but right now they were both too busy with their careers. Although neither one of them talked about Ben, she could always tell when he was on Scott's mind. And she missed him, too. She wondered if he was finding any peace in Miami. She hoped so, but she knew how much Ben disliked cities and worried he had gone there out of desperation. And that his pride wouldn't let him admit he had made a mistake. Then what would he do?

Lisa stared at the envelope in her hand. It was addressed to Scott; she recognized Ben's handwriting. Although postmarked Miami, Fla., there was no return address. Her first impulse was to rip it open; her second was to throw it away. But in the next moment, she knew she couldn't do either. She heard the front door being opened then closed.

"Hey, babe," Scott said as he entered the kitchen, immediately going to her and kissing her. "Man, have I had me a day. Those kids are wearing me out," he said on his way to the refrigerator. "Want some tea?"

"Hmm, yes, that would be nice," she answered as she folded her hands across the envelope.

"You wouldn't think a person could feel so old at twenty-seven, but that's how those kids make me feel," he said, putting a glass of tea down in front of her and seating himself across from her. "Seems like just yesterday I was going to UT."

Lisa watched as he gulped several swallows of the tea. "Oh, I'm sure those kids are complaining right now about how you're wearing them out."

Scott laughed, but as he gazed at the woman he loved, he sensed something wasn't right. He didn't think he could take something else going wrong in his life. "What's up?"

Lisa slid the envelope across the table to him. "This came today."

Scott stared down at it and knew immediately who it was from. He slowly put the glass down and picked up the envelope, handling it as though it might crumble at his touch.

Lisa watched as he opened it and then stared at the single page for what seemed like an eternity. "What does he say?"

Scott cleared his throat. "Just wanted you and Lisa to know that I'm fine. Consider this an early wedding present. Enjoy it. Take care, Ben," he read quietly. Then he pulled free what was taped to the bottom of the page and held it up for Lisa to see. "It's the key to his house."

It was when the third hat was ruined that Ben decided Thoroughbreds and cowboy hats just weren't compatible. It seemed he was always having to pick his hat up after some Thoroughbred had knocked it off with its head. In short order, Ben learned that Thoroughbreds loved to use their heads as sort of a weapon. He figured it must have something to do with their height as compared to the shorter Quarter horse. The ones who weren't spooked by his hat were always nudging it with their noses. Or he was always having to take it off in a hurry when one of them got all wild-eyed.

He lost the first one when it got trampled in the shedrow by a two-year-old colt who was sure that hat was a demon. The second had been backed over by a feed truck. Ben had been leading Mymomsluck, a big-boned grey mare, around the shedrow when she swung her head around at him as they turned the corner and knocked his hat off. A gust of wind caught it and carried it out of the barn onto the asphalt where the feed truck promptly flattened it. The third hat was drowned by Time For Bucks.

When Ben had come back to Miami, Time For Bucks remembered him right away and this time around, didn't blink an eye at his hat. In fact, the horse apparently decided that hat was his own personal toy. One day as Ben walked by, the big red horse snatched the hat off his head as quick as a snake and then retreated into his stall. Cooper and the crew had gotten quite a laugh watching Ben coax his hat away from that horse.

It was about nine on a Saturday morning when the drowning took place. Ben was trying to give Time For Bucks a bath after a workout; the groom was doing his best to control him with the lead shank. But the animal was in peak racing condition, and the brisk five-eighths work had just cranked him up more. He kept tossing and slinging his head while he danced on the asphalt between the barns.

Ben was concentrating on trying to sponge the horse without getting stepped on when, in an instant, Time For Bucks swiped his hat. And then he immediately dropped it into the bucket of steaming liniment rinse water. Ben and the groom watched as the hat soaked up the water, collapsed onto itself and then sank to the bottom of the bucket.

Ben looked at Time For Bucks and he could have sworn that horse was smiling. The groom started to laugh and then Ben did, too. More laughter came from the shedrow. The incident became known simply as 'the drowning.'

That afternoon Ben drove all over Miami. He must have gone

into a dozen sporting goods stores before he found a Dallas Cowboys baseball cap. To be on the safe side, he bought six of them.

The next morning, Time For Bucks sniffed the cap and then never showed interest in it again. Ben was sure the horse missed his cowboy hat more than he did.

It was a pleasant November afternoon, and Ben was amazed it was 85 degrees. Even in San Antonio by this time, the weather had begun to get cooler. But here he sat in a light blue, short-sleeved polo shirt, scanning past performance charts and soaking up the south Florida sunshine. It was his first Saturday afternoon off, and he would be able to sleep in tomorrow morning, too. Although he wasn't on Cooper's payroll, he insisted on working the same schedule as the rest of the crew. The bugler announced the field of horses coming onto the track for the fifth race.

"I can't believe you finally take a day off and you end up spending it at the racetrack," Cooper said, casting a shadow over Ben.

Ben grinned. "I couldn't think of anything better to do," he said as he eyed the slim, short-haired brunette woman with Cooper. He thought he remembered seeing her on the backside during training hours.

"Yep, you've become a real racetracker," Cooper said with a chuckle, then turning to the woman, added, "Barbara, this is that useless Texas cowboy I've been tellin' you about."

Ben rose to his feet. "Ben Matthews, ma'am."

"Barbara Miller," she returned, shaking his hand as she looked straight into his eyes. What she saw there made her think of someone else. "It's nice to finally meet you."

"Pick any winners, yet?" Cooper asked as they all sat down on the bench.

"As a matter of fact, I had the daily double," Ben returned, glancing at Barbara. He liked the way her short-cropped black hair framed her face and set off her dark eyes.

Cooper grinned. "Got anything in this one?"

Ben shook his head. "Nothing but a bunch of maiden claimers not worth a dime."

"Maybe you'll want to put a little money on Barbara's horse in the next race," Cooper said. "How about it, Barbara, is that horse of yours ready to win?"

Barbara shrugged. "I wish I knew, Dan," she said. "He's not been earning his keep lately, and my trainer can't seem to figure out what's his problem."

Ben flipped open his program. "Which one is yours?"

"That one," she answered, pointing at the number six horse on the program. "First And Ten."

"Hmm, he's 30-1," Ben said. "I do like betting longshots. Anybody can bet the favorites, but there's no challenge in that. What do you think, Dan?"

Cooper scanned First And Ten's past performance chart. "I think the horse needs a new trainer."

Barbara laughed. "I'll make a deal with you, Dan," she said. "If he doesn't win today, he'll be in your shedrow first thing in the morning."

"I'll have his stall all ready for him," Dan returned as Ben rose to his feet. "Where are you going?"

Ben smiled. "I've got a horse to bet on," he said, then turned and hurried to the betting windows.

Barbara was still beaming when she came out of the winner's circle. "I still can't believe he won," she said, rejoining Ben and Cooper.

"Yes, ma'am, he sure did," Ben said, grinning as he pulled four betting tickets from his shirt pocket. "I guess supper's on me."

Cooper snickered. "It's the least you can do, since you cost me another horse to train."

Barbara wrapped an arm around Cooper. "Better luck next time, Dan," she said, then added, "Thanks for the dinner offer,

Ben, but I need to get going. It's a long drive back and I want to check on First And Ten before I go."

Ben was disappointed. "You don't live in Miami?"

"No, I manage a training center, Southerly Park, about ninety minutes north of here," Barbara answered, reaching out to shake his hand. "You're welcome to come and visit anytime. But I might just put you to work."

"I think I could handle that," Ben said, smiling.

She smiled back at him. "I've really got to be going. You two behave yourselves."

Ben watched her hurrying through the grandstand. "Nice lady."

"Yeah, she is," Cooper said, studying his friend. "And she's also married."

Ben frowned. "Damn."

Scott ambled down the hall with another box to put into storage; Lisa was determined that they would be having Thanksgiving Day dinner in the house. As he walked past Ben's bedroom, he heard muffled sounds. Putting the box down, he slowly pushed the door all the way open. Lisa was sitting on the sheetless bed, holding something in her hands and crying softly.

"Hey, babe, what's wrong?" Scott asked gently, sitting down next to her. As he did so, he saw what she held in her trembling hands.

It was a picture of him, Chris, Lisa and Ben, standing side by side with their arms intertwined and all smiles. It had been taken right after Ben had won his fourth all-around title in Oklahoma City. It was the last time they had all been together like that.

"I found it on the floor by the dresser. It must have fallen out of something when Ben was packing," she sniffed. "I'm sorry."

"Sorry for what? For missing the way we used to be?"

She nodded. "I don't want you to think I'm not happy. I am." She paused, then tried again. "It's just..."

"That you miss Chris—and Ben. And it's okay to miss Chris, but not Ben, right?"

She could only manage to nod again as the tears streamed down her face.

"And you thought I didn't know that?" Scott asked as he hugged her tightly. "I know you've been being strong for me. I know you want me to believe you really love me now and not Ben in that way anymore. I believe it," he said, kissing her on the cheek.

"But you said it yourself. A part of you will always love Ben. I would be a fool not to know that. But I also know we're together now, and you missing Ben is not going to come between us. You know how much I miss him, and that doesn't make you love me any less."

She looked at him and they kissed. Then they sat there, holding each other and looking at that picture. And soon the memories of that time in their lives made them smile.

"Just give him a good looking over while he's galloping," Cooper said, looking up at Ben on the pony horse, Wishbone. "Maybe you'll be able to figure out why he keeps getting sore on us."

Ben nodded as he watched the exercise rider guide Tiger Road out of the shedrow and toward them. "Want him to breeze down the stretch a little?"

"See how he warms up, Randy," Cooper instructed the rider. "If he feels okay, set him down in the stretch. But keep it easy."

As usual, traffic to and from the track was controlled chaos. High-strung, wild-eyed Thoroughbreds were being ridden and led by pony horse or by hand. It was 9:30 a.m. and there was only a half hour left before the track closed for training and was readied for the afternoon racing.

Once on the track, Randy gradually stood up in the stirrups as he started slowly jogging Tiger Road. Ben reined Wishbone to the outside rail, keeping parallel with Tiger Road but out of the main flow of horses and riders. The rules of the track were that horses worked on the inside, galloped in the middle and pony horses kept to the outside. Ben studied Tiger Road as Randy let him settle into a nice easy gallop. The rangy, dark brown horse had a lot of class about him; his head was bowed into his chest as his powerful stride carried him and the rider easily over the track. Before he had gone sour, Tiger Road had been a stakes horse. A complete veterinarian checkup came up empty, but the horse just wasn't right.

They were turning into the stretch now, and Ben could see Randy starting to sit down on the saddle to breeze the horse. Tiger Road had been waiting for the cue, and he immediately accelerated. Or, at least, he tried to. It seemed to Ben like the horse ran into a brick wall. He reared up, pawing at the air as he twisted backwards and fell over with a thud on top of Randy. Ben had watched helplessly as the scene unfolded before him, trying to get across the track without colliding with the horses being steered around the spill.

Ben jumped off Wishbone before the horse even came to a full stop. Neither horse nor rider was moving. In an instant, Ben knew Tiger Road was dead; bright red blood trickled from his nostrils, and his eyes were glazed over. Dropping to his knees, he grabbed Randy's hand and the rider moaned.

"Don't try to move," Ben said calmly, seeing now that the rider's legs were pinned beneath the dead horse. "I hear the ambulance coming. Just hang on, Randy."

The rider squeezed his hand, and Ben shuddered as a haunting memory filled his mind. He was the one lying on the ground, and it was Chris who was holding his hand, telling him to hold on. And he remembered how much he had just wanted to drift into the blackness he was on the edge of. But Chris wouldn't let him go.

Someone touched Ben's arm, startling him back to the present and making him aware that half a dozen people were now on the scene.

"We'll take over now. You can let go," the paramedic said firmly as he pried Ben's hand away.

Ben rose to his feet and slowly backed away as the horse ambulance arrived. The driver, the track vet and Cooper all climbed out of the front seat.

"We need to get the horse off him," the paramedic said to no one in particular.

The horse ambulance driver, Cooper and two other horsemen each took a position, lifting the horse enough for the paramedics to free the rider. They strapped him to the stretcher and loaded him into the ambulance, its sirens wailing as it was driven off the track.

"Looks like he had a heart attack," the vet, squatting at the horse's head, said to Cooper. "Probably dead before he even hit the ground."

Cooper turned around to ask Ben something, but he wasn't there.

Word had spread quickly on the backside, and an unusual quiet had settled in like a sudden early morning fog. Riders and horses getting hurt was a reality that racetrackers didn't like to face. In the blink of an eye, it could be your horse's leg shattering at 35 miles an hour. You could be the rider being flung to the ground and maybe trampled by the traffic behind you. If racetrackers thought about how easily and how often that could happen, they couldn't be in the business. They learned to live with the inherent dangers of their profession—just like rodeo cowboys did.

Ben lugged the Western saddle into the tackroom and hoisted it up on the stand. When he turned around, Cooper was putting the phone down.

"Randy's going to be fine," he said and saw the relief in Ben's eyes. "Broke his left ankle and has a concussion. But all in all, he's damned lucky."

"Have you talked to Tiger Road's owner?"

"That's my next call," Cooper said with a sigh as he watched Ben head for the door. "Are you okay?"

"Actually, I was thinking of taking a couple of days off. Think I'm coming down with a cold or something. Would that be a problem?"

"No, I think that's a good idea. For someone who's not even on the payroll, you've been putting in some long days," Cooper said. "You're still going to have Thanksgiving dinner with me and Eleanor, right?"

Ben was already halfway into the shedrow. "I'll see how I'm feeling. I'll give you a call."

Stretched out on the unmade bed, Ben could feel the whiskey doing its job. He'd just finished half a fifth and figured he'd save the rest as his Thanksgiving dinner. He was having trouble keeping his eyes open, but he was still afraid to close them. Still afraid he'd be back in that arena in Vegas—pinned beneath that bull. And knowing even amid the pain as he tried to drag himself away, that his life would never be the same.

The problem with getting drunk was that sooner or later, you had to wake up. Ben did it very slowly, very reluctantly, as he tried to cling to every last bit of the whiskey's effects. When he finally opened his eyes, he was surprised how dark the room still was. Surely, he had slept through the night. Reaching over to the night stand, he turned on the lamp and squinted at the clock radio. The digital panel blinked 6 p.m. in bright yellow. 6 p.m.? He pushed himself up to a sitting position; apparently he had not only slept through the night, but also through most of Thanksgiving Day.

Ben came out of the bathroom, wearing the blue terrycloth bathrobe Lisa had given him for his last birthday. She had said it matched his eyes perfectly. Maybe he should exchange it for one in a nice bloodshot color. He was just about to pour himself a drink when someone knocked.

"I told Eleanor you probably weren't up to eating, but she insisted I bring over this food," Cooper said, holding a plastic container as he stood in the hallway.

"Maybe later," Ben said, turning away as the smell of the turkey and dressing made him queasy.

Cooper followed him to the table. "Don't guess you watched any of the football games, huh? The Cowboys beat the Redskins 35-7."

Ben poured them each a drink. "That's good."

"Harry Miller's horse, Star Warrior, won the Thanksgiving Day Handicap."

"Good for him."

"Randy's spill made you think about yours, didn't it?"

Ben drained the glass, refilled it, and took a swallow. "It just snuck up on me."

"How long has it been?"

"Two years next week."

"That's right. The National Finals are always the first week in December," Cooper said. "Doesn't seem like that long, huh?"

Ben stared down into the whiskey. "Seems like yesterday."

"Well, something like that takes awhile to settle," Cooper offered, wondering if he should say anything about Ben having to also deal with the grief of losing his family; he decided against it. "Are you having second thoughts about coming to Miami? Thinking about going back to Texas?"

"No, I came here for certain reasons—and that hasn't changed."

"If there's anything I can do..."

Ben sat back in the chair. "Well, do you think I'm ready to get a horse or two of my own?"

Cooper smiled. "You've been ready. I was just waiting for you to say something," he said. "There's a horse running tomorrow for a $25,000 tag that I've been watching. You interested?"

"I'm listening," Ben answered, and suddenly he was thinking of having some of that turkey.

7

Claiming a horse of his own had really lightened Ben's mood. Cooper chuckled as he watched him pacing up and down the grandstand area like an expectant father. The horses that would be running in the $50,000 handicap were just being warmed up on the backstretch, and post time was still ten minutes away. Cooper figured Ben would wear out the soles of his boots by then.

The horse Ben had claimed for $25,000 two weeks ago was Magic Beans. The five-year-old gelding had shown a lot of promise as a two-year-old, winning two stakes. Then each year after that he had dropped in class and changed owners four times. Cooper had seen him run as a two-year-old and had tried to buy him for a client then. But his owner wasn't interested in selling him. The horse had later shipped out of Florida and raced mostly in New York. He had finished out of the money his first race back in Florida and then had run fourth the day Ben claimed him.

Ben had liked the looks of the blood-bay gelding right away; he was short-coupled and muscular like a Quarter horse. It had been Ben's idea to just pony the horse for a week, give him a strong half-mile work, and then pony him to the race. He also decided to take the blinkers, shadow roll and tongue tie off the horse. Apparently, each new trainer had felt compelled to add a new piece of equipment.

Eyebrows were raised when Ben entered Magic Beans in the seven-furlong handicap; it was a considerable step up in class. Fortunately, the race came up with a short field, and the racing secretary had to use Magic Beans to fill it. The odds board now showed him at 75-1, prompting Ben and Cooper to place sizable bets on him.

"The horses are entering the starting gates," the announcer told the crowd of 10,000 on a balmy mid-December afternoon.

Cooper walked up to Ben. "How ya doin'?"

"Whatever made me think I could train Thoroughbreds?" Ben said nervously as he looked across the track where the last horse was going into the gates.

"And they're off!" the announcer exclaimed as the field of Thoroughbreds broke from the gates in a blur of color. "Going straight to the lead is Magic Beans!"

Ben craned his neck to see. The jockey, Mark Reed, had the horse on an easy three-quarter length lead as they came into the stretch turn. And Ben could tell he was fighting the rider and wanted to go.

"Now!" Ben heard himself say. As if the jockey had heard him, too, he uncocked his whip, tapping the horse once high across his right flank.

Magic Beans exploded away from the field. Reed hand-rode him to an impressive five-length win. Ben and Cooper were jumping up and down like kids at a playground.

The shedrow was finally quiet now. There had been a celebration when Magic Beans had returned triumphant from the drug-testing barn. Neighboring horsemen had dropped by for a beer and to give Ben a congratulatory pat on the back. Although he was listed as the horse's owner, he was still officially licensed only as an assistant trainer. But Cooper made it clear that Ben had readied the horse for the race.

Ben leaned against the stall webbing, watching Magic Beans munch his alfalfa hay.

"Feel as good as riding a bronc for the eight and a 90?" Cooper asked as he joined him.

Ben thought about that for a moment; he couldn't deny the high he was still on. "There's an old Merle Haggard song my father used to sing all the time," he answered and then did his best Haggard imitation, "It's not love, but it's not bad."

Cooper laughed and at the same time realized it was the first time that Ben had said anything about his family.

Ben grabbed the phone on the third ring; he had been on his way out the door and had debated whether to answer it.

"Hi, Ben, this is Barbara Miller."

He was pleasantly surprised. "Hello, Barbara. Are you calling to give me a hot tip on a horse named First And Ten?"

She laughed. "No, he came back a little sore and we're giving him some time off. But I was hoping I might talk you into doing a little work for me."

"What kind of work?"

"I keep a string of pony horses for our clients to use. But some don't get used as much and get a little rank. I was wondering if you could maybe come out and work them for me. I'd be willing to pay you."

Ben was interested, but Dan had said she was married. "Well, I don't know about paying me," he said. "But I'll be happy to come out and see what I can do."

Barbara had headed for the barn when she saw the royal blue and silver pickup truck drive through the main gate. He had made good time driving in from Miami. When she entered the barn, he was talking in Spanish with Rico, one of the grooms. She figured he must be from south Texas.

"Glad you decided to take me up on my offer," Barbara said as she approached them.

Ben turned on his heels to face her. "Thought it'd be nice to get out of the city for awhile," he said, smiling. "How long have you run this place?"

"About seven years. A lot of trainers come here to break and train the young horses and then ship in to the tracks," Barbara replied, leading him through the barn and outside to get a better view of the training center. "Sometimes running this place makes me crazy. But it pays the training bills for our racehorses."

"Well, it seems to me you're doing a great job," Ben said, taking note of the well-maintained training track and pastures. "I can see why trainers like to board here."

Barbara smiled. "Thank you. So, do you think you might be able to give me hand?"

Ben looked out across the pastures that were bordered by woods; he already felt comfortable here. "Yeah, it'll be nice not to have to ride in circles all the time."

On the way back to Miami, Ben popped the new George Strait cassette into the tape deck. How ironic. The first song was titled "All My Ex's Live In Texas." He was glad it was a lighthearted song and not a lost-love ballad. The only time he got to listen to Strait these days was in his truck; country western music wasn't exactly popular in Miami. Just another adjustment he had had to make in his new life.

If anyone had told him a year ago that he'd be living in a high-rise hotel and training Thoroughbred racehorses in Miami, he'd have thought they had eaten a ton of loco weed. This time last year, he he'd been back on a horse for four months; he and Scott had started light roping practice. Chris was finally going back to school after the holidays, and Lisa was back home for good. His mother was in the middle of her usual weeks-long Christmas preparations, and his father was pretending to just barely tolerate it all.

Ben took a deep breath. He didn't need to be doing this—

remembering what his life used to be. There wasn't much point to it.
All the remembering in the world wasn't going to bring that life back.

"Mr. Matthews, this came for you today," the front desk clerk
said, handing Ben the large manila envelope.

Ben stared down at it, reading the return address of Walter
Hancock's law firm. When he had called Hancock to wire him the
money to claim Magic Beans, the lawyer had said he'd be sending
the ranch's fiscal report before the end of December.

Once in his room, Ben dropped the package on the table and
headed for the shower. He'd had all the memories he could handle
for one day.

Cooper had thought Ben was preoccupied all morning, and
now as he watched the water bucket he was filling overflowing, he
knew he had been right. "Hey, you trying to flood the shedrow?"

Ben looked blankly at him for a moment until the water splashed
on his boots. Then he yanked the hose out of the bucket. "Sorry,"
he mumbled, walking over to shut off the faucet.

Cooper grinned at him. "Since Thanksgiving didn't work out,
how about joining us for Christmas. Our girls will be home from
college, and they've been anxious to meet someone else from Texas."

Turning away from Cooper, Ben busied himself with wrapping the hose around the keeper. "I'm thinking of puttin' holidays
on that same list as women. They're both things I don't need in
my life right now."

"Well, think about it. Eleanor always cooks enough food to
feed the backside. Women just love Christmas, don't they?"

Ben stared at the package from Hancock; it had laid on the
table for two days now. He drank the last of the whiskey and then
reached for it.

As he flipped through the ledger pages, it became increasingly clear that the ranch was doing just fine without him. The cattle and the horses had sold damned well at the fall sales. And even after expenses, he and UT had come away with a sizable profit on the year. He thought his father would be proud that the ranch was thriving. But he was ashamed that it was doing so without his involvement.

But Scott was doing a hell of a good job; Hancock had told him about Scott taking over when Pete Jenkins retired. He had almost called to congratulate him, then had thought better of it. He had walked away from the ranch—away from Scott and Lisa—and he needed to keep that distance. Giving them his house had been his way of saying he was sorry for hurting them. And it had been another way of letting go of what used to be his life.

It was when he went to slide the report back into the envelope that Ben noticed another smaller one was inside. His name was printed across it, and he was surprised when he recognized the handwriting. When he opened the envelope, a picture fell out. His heart stopped beating.

Ben just stared at that picture, making no attempt to pick it up from where it had fallen on the table. Oklahoma City. His fourth—and last—all-around title. All smiles and all together.

Slowly, Ben picked it up and something made him turn it over: *Thought you would want this. We love you and miss you. Please take care of yourself. Love, Lisa & Scott*

Ben blinked to clear his vision as he looked away from the words. Another picture had been taken that day. Slowly, Ben rose from the chair and strode to the large walk-in closet. Against the back wall were his saddle and a dozen stacked boxes. He knew exactly which box held what he wanted and carried it back with him to the table. Taking the lid off, he reached in.

In a simple wooden frame was the other picture that had been taken that day. It was him, Chris, his mother and father. And just like in the other one, everyone was smiling and had their arms around each other. He had picked that picture from his mother's fireplace mantle collection to take with him to Miami. With a trembling hand, he gently touched Chris and his parents with his fingertips. He was surprised how cold the glass felt.

What a celebration they'd had when they had gotten back to the ranch. It had become a Matthews tradition, since December was the one time of the year they were all together. With a new title won, he was off the road until after New Year's Day. Chris was on holiday break from school, Lisa was home from Europe for six weeks, and Scott always preferred to celebrate on the ranch rather than with his mother and stepfather in San Antonio.

It was sort of an open-ranch affair for weeks. Ranchers would come from miles around, bringing beef to barbecue and whiskey to drink. On Christmas Eve, everyone was treated to a feast and there was a ranch rodeo. On Christmas Day, the ranch gates were closed and the day was spent just with family. That, too, was a Matthews tradition.

The only time tradition had been broken was when he was recovering in the Las Vegas hospital. But even then, his mother had insisted they do their best to enjoy Christmas. And they had—because they were together. Then last year, everything had almost returned to the way it was before his accident. And everyone had been looking forward to the new year, to moving ahead with their lives together.

But that wasn't what had happened. What had happened twenty miles outside of Waco had shattered all those hopes, all those long-held Matthews traditions. And he had been left alone with his grief—and his guilt.

Ben pressed his hand against the frame's glass; it was still cold.

Ben cued the dappled grey gelding into a trot. The horse tugged on the bit, wanting to break into a gallop. "Now, you just relax and understand that you're going to do what I want," he said quietly to the horse.

As the horse trotted around the large pasture, Ben felt himself begin to relax. He hadn't realized how much he missed riding in open spaces. Since he had been in Miami, his riding had been confined to ponying on the racetrack and going in endless circles. He had begun to look forward to his days at Southerly Park.

He let the horse ease into a lope, catching a glimpse of the farm's main house. Although he had been coming to Southerly Park for a couple of weeks now, he still hadn't met Barbara's husband. In fact, the subject had never come up. Barbara would sometimes meet him at the barn, chat for a few minutes and then be gone. Maybe there was trouble between them. And maybe he just needed to stick with riding horses and not worry about things that were none of his business.

"So, you decide if you're going to have Christmas dinner with us?" Cooper asked Ben as they were having lunch in the track kitchen.

Ben swallowed the last of the greasy hamburger. "Yeah, I think I'd like to."

Cooper was somewhat surprised; he figured Ben would want to spend the day alone, thinking about his family. "Good. It'll be nice to have another man around for a change. Eleanor and the girls will be delighted."

"You know I've been going over to Southerly Park to ride. Think your daughters would like to go riding that morning?"

"Oh, I'm sure they'd love it."

Ben wasn't exactly sure when he had decided to spend Christmas with the Cooper family. He had intended to get through the day much like he had Thanksgiving. Ben folded up the racing newspaper and dropped it to the floor as he stretched out on the bed. Likely had something to do with remembering those past Christmases when he had gotten the picture from Lisa. It had hurt so much to look at those pictures.

He was afraid to remember too much, afraid that if he did,

the fiery nightmare would come back to haunt him. So maybe if he spent Christmas with the Coopers, it would keep the memories—and the nightmare—away.

Scott pulled Lisa closer to him; sometimes he still couldn't believe they were really together. But here they were, snuggled up against each other in the guest bedroom of her parents' new home in Dallas. The memories of past Christmases at the Matthews Ranch had been too painful for them to bear, and they had decided to come to Dallas. It was time that they started making new memories. Scott had been surprised—and relieved—at how easily Lisa's parents had accepted they were together now. They had always been crazy about Ben.

And with a pang of guilt, he worried how Ben was getting through his first Christmas without his family.

"Are you glad we came up here?" Lisa asked, rubbing her foot along his leg.

"Yeah. Your folks have been great to me."

"Why wouldn't they be? They've always thought the world of you," she said, raising herself up on an elbow. "Mother always used to tell me that if I had any sense, I'd settle down and marry someone like you."

"You're making that up."

"It's the truth." She sat up and tugged on his arm. "Come on, let's go ask her."

"Okay, okay. I believe you." He reached up and caressed her face. "I love you."

Lisa smiled. "I love you," she whispered, lowering her head and kissing him.

Scott hugged her tightly. He loved her with all his heart, and he'd be lost without her. He needed to make sure that never happened.

Ben had to admit that spending the day with the Cooper family had been a hell of a lot better than getting drunk alone. He turned up the volume on "Ocean Front Property," he really liked that Strait song. As planned, he had taken Cooper's daughters, Allison and Amanda, riding. And since they were from Texas, he wasn't surprised that they were pretty good riders. Barbara had come out to the barn to wish him a Merry Christmas and had ended up riding with them. But there still had been no mention or sign of her husband.

Eleanor Cooper had indeed cooked a feast. And although he had tried not to, he couldn't help but think of his mother's cooking. But he had let the memory come and go, willing himself to be grateful to be with the Coopers.

Then, when he had gotten ready to leave, they gave him the present. He was embarrassed; all he had brought them was a bottle of wine. But Cooper had insisted he accept it, saying he was tired of hearing him complain about not getting to listen to George Strait enough. He had grinned from ear to ear when he opened the box and saw the portable cassette tape player.

Ben reached over and turned off the lamp. It would be nice to fall asleep listening to Strait. Somehow it made him feel not so far away from Texas.

"Well, you look like you welcomed the New Year with plenty of help from Mr. Jack Daniel's," Barbara said, watching Ben move slower than usual as he saddled Peppy, a stout liver chestnut with a knack for running off with a rider.

Ben grimaced. "Shows, huh?" He tightened the girth; the night of partying still making his head pound. After the little blond he had picked up had left, he had showered and thought maybe riding would make him feel better.

"Let's just say that you look a little ragged. Was it too much booze or too much woman?"

He felt himself blushing. "That's my little secret. We Texas cowboys do have our pride—even when we're hung over as hell."

Barbara laughed. "When you're done, come on up to the house for lunch. I'd like you to meet my husband," she said, adding as she walked off, "I think you two will get along just fine."

Ben followed Barbara down the wide hallway, hearing the sounds of the televised football game. He realized he hadn't even watched any college games this year and didn't even know if the UT Longhorns were in a New Year's Day bowl game.

"Honey, this is Ben Matthews," Barbara said as they entered the family room. It was a large room, accented by floor to ceiling windows that provided a great view of the wooded pastures.

"Ah, yes, the cowboy I've been watching ride," Mike Miller said as he turned to face them.

Ben was going to ask him how he knew he was a cowboy, but the words never came as he stared at the sandy-haired, brown-eyed man in the wheelchair.

"Hi, I'm Mike. I see Barbara failed to tell you of my little predicament," he said matter-of-factly. "I guess she was afraid it'd scare you off."

"Honey..."

"No, that's okay," Ben said quickly, extending his hand. "Sorry. I didn't mean to stare. Glad to meet you, Mike. And I really appreciate being able to come here to ride."

Mike firmly shook Ben's hand. "Well, anyone who enjoys riding just for the hell of it like you do, should be able to do it as much as possible."

"What a great view," Ben said, ambling over to the sliding glass doors; he could see Mike's reflection in the glass and figured he must do some weight training to keep his upper body as muscular as it was.

Mike had noticed that Ben limped slightly. "Yeah, I've watched you do things with those pony horses that I don't think they even knew they could do. All the trainers are fighting over them now," he said. "How about a couple of beers, hon?"

"Sure," Barbara said, bending over to give him a quick kiss before she left.

"Who's playing?" Ben asked, glancing at the television.

"USC and Notre Dame in the Rose Bowl. But later, it'll be Texas and Florida in the Cotton Bowl," Mike said, then chuckled at Ben's raised-eyebrows reaction to mention of the Texas Longhorns. "Hmm, want to make a little wager on that one?"

"Watch him, Ben," Barbara warned as she returned with beers and sandwiches. "He loves to bet."

Ben grinned. "That's okay. So do I. Hook 'em, 'Horns," he said, using UT's slogan.

"I think I'll leave now before it gets ugly in here," Barbara said, leaving them alone.

The two men laughed as Ben pulled up a chair to the table, and Mike rolled himself up to it. For a few moments, there was only the sounds of the football game in the background.

"So, what happened to you?" Mike asked and then took a swallow of beer.

"What?"

"The scar on your face and the limp. What happened to you?"

Ben knew he was staring again. Maybe a man in a wheelchair figured he had nothing to lose by being direct. "Oh—uh—it was nothing."

Mike shook his head. "You're just saying that because I'm in this wheelchair. And you're thinking you're pretty damned lucky you got away with just a few scars and a limp," he said, then took another drink of the beer. "Okay, I'll go first. Five years ago, a drunk driver broadsided me. I still don't remember anything about that day except kissing Barbara bye that morning when I left for school. I used to coach high school football.

"As far as accidents go, it was all very neat and fairly painless. I just woke up in the hospital with a concussion and a broken back.

They told me I'd never walk again and sent me home. That's my story. Now, it's your turn."

Ben looked into Mike's warm brown eyes; there was something very familiar there. "A bull," he heard himself say quietly.

Mike's eyes widened. "A bull? Geez, you mean like a rodeo bull?"

Ben simply nodded.

"You really are a Texas cowboy. Hell, a real rodeo cowboy, and I bet you're damned good."

"Used to be," Ben answered, still looking directly at Mike. "Just like you used to be a football coach."

Mike smiled knowingly; yeah, this man knew about the pain of losing part of yourself. "Two points for you," he conceded. "But unlike mine, your accident was messy and painful, wasn't it? And you remember what happened, don't you?

"Yeah, you remember every minute, every detail of it. And you replay it in your head, over and over, trying to figure out what you did wrong."

Ben looked away for a moment, then leveled his gaze at Mike. "You're right, I do remember. But I know what I did wrong. And I have to live with that everyday—just like you have to live with being in that wheelchair."

Mike raised his beer bottle in a salute. "Okay, now that the pity issue is out of the way, how much are you willing to lose on those Longhorns of yours?"

Barbara watched her husband sleeping peacefully; she hadn't heard him laugh as much as he had that afternoon in a very long time. And he hadn't even minded that Ben won their $100 bet when the Longhorns beat the Gators 17-16. Mike had always hated to lose at anything.

From the day they had met at the University of Florida until his accident, he'd always been the most competitive person she had ever known. He thrived on competition and winning; on being the best, first as a football player and then later as a coach.

Losing was unacceptable. But the accident had taught him that sometimes you did lose, and denying it wasn't going to change the facts. And, for Mike, that meant accepting he was confined to a wheelchair for the rest of his life, that he had lost too much to ever be again who he was before the accident. But she saw the anger in his eyes. She saw the longing there for who he used to be.

She had seen the same look in Ben's eyes. She didn't know what had scarred him, but whatever it was had ripped away a part of him and, like Mike, he was trying to cope with the loss. Despite whatever ghosts were haunting Ben, there was a real strength about him. And that's what she hoped he would be able to share with Mike. These past months, her husband seemed to be slipping away from her; he seemed to be giving up. She didn't see that fire in his eyes as much anymore, and that worried her.

Maybe it wasn't right that she was using Ben. But she loved Mike and she was willing to do anything to save him—even if it meant using someone else's pain.

Every time Ben got on and off Wishbone for the next few days, he thought of Mike Miller in that wheelchair. He admired the man's courage in dealing with that kind of existence everyday. If that bull had done that to him, he wouldn't have wanted to go on living. The doctors had sent him home with a wheelchair; he'd never even sat in it.

Mike had been right. Seeing him in that wheelchair had made him feel damned lucky. Maybe he couldn't do everything he had been able to before that bull, but he could still walk and he could still ride. And suddenly, that seemed like more than enough.

"Hey, Ben, I have a proposition for you," Cooper said, walking up to where he was giving Wishbone a bath on the asphalt between the barns. "Would you be interested in buying Time For Bucks?"

Ben looked at Cooper over Wishbone's soapy back. "Say again?"

"Old man Grisham says it's time for him to get out of the business," Cooper explained. "He's seventy-five, and none of his kids are interested in horses. His wife wants him to take a cruise around the world."

"How much does he want for him?"

"A hundred grand."

Walking around to the horse's head, Ben stared at Cooper. "A $100,000?" he asked in disbelief and whistled softly when the trainer nodded. "Do you know how much rodeoing I had to do to make that much every year?"

Again Cooper nodded. "Yeah, I know. I never even made a quarter of that much. But Bucks is just four, and he's already made the old man almost $300,000. If he stays sound, he could run for at least three more years. And then you could sell him as a stud. With his pedigree and race record, you could get a million for him easy."

"So, why don't you buy him?"

"I have two daughters to put through college and a house mortgage," Cooper answered. "The horse will be easy to sell. I just know how much you like him and thought I'd give you first shot at him."

Ben started rinsing off Wishbone. "I did make my money right back on Magic Beans. Hmm, let me think about it and make a phone call to check on my finances."

Cooper grinned at him. "You're going to buy him, aren't ya?"

"It only seems right, since it was that race he won when Billy Joe and I were here that got me hooked," Ben answered. Then, with a smile, he added, "Tell old man Grisham he can go on that cruise."

Mike looked over the cards in his hand. "You really spent $100,000 on this horse?"

"Yep. But I plan to get a quick return on my investment,"

Ben replied confidently. "I'm going to run him in a $200,000 stakes race this weekend at Gulfstream and he's going to win. Why don't you and Barbara come out and get your picture taken in the winner's circle."

"The horses have always been Barbara's thing. Football was mine."

Ben dealt him two replacements for the cards he had tossed out of his hand. "You played football in college?"

"Yeah, outside linebacker at Florida."

"Why didn't you turn pro?"

"Not big enough. But that was okay. I got what I wanted out of playing and was ready to coach," Mike answered, turning a trick much to Ben's dismay. "So how about you, Mr. Rodeo Cowboy? Just how good were you?"

Ben shrugged, trying to concentrate on the cards. "I won my fair share."

"Hey, can the modest bit. You were better than just good, weren't you?"

Ben looked up at him from his cards. "Four-time world all-around champion."

"Geez. So that means you did more than just the bulls. Not that riding those crazy bulls wouldn't be enough."

"To qualify for the all-around, you have to compete in at least two events," Ben explained quietly. "I rode the saddle and bareback broncs—and the bulls. The broncs were always easy for me. The bulls were the real challenge. I always appreciated life a little more when the buzzer sounded on a bull ride."

Mike shook his head. "And I thought football players were crazy," he commented, eyeing Ben. "And you went back even after that bull busted you up, didn't you?"

Ben looked away; he was feeling uneasy. "Yeah. But it was a mistake. I should have just stayed away," he said quietly, putting the cards face down on the table and conceding the pot to Mike. "I need to be going. Think about coming to see Bucks run. I promise you, he's gonna win."

Mike watched Ben limp down the hallway and heard the kitchen back door slam shut. There had been a definite shift in Ben's mood right at the end of their conversation. He had seemed comfortable enough talking about his rodeo days, almost relieved. Ben had called going back to the rodeo a mistake. Had he gotten hurt again? Whatever had happened, it was still tormenting Ben. For just a moment, he had seen the pain in his eyes.

"Ben already leave?" Barbara asked her husband as she came up behind him, kissing him on the cheek.

"Yeah." Mike gathered up the cards. "He really is a good guy. Just seems a little sad sometimes."

Barbara sat down next to her husband. "He's probably homesick. I can't figure out why someone who has Texas written all over him like he does would move to Miami. Has he said why?"

"No. And unless you ask him a direct question, he doesn't volunteer much," Mike replied. "Say how would you feel about going to the races this weekend?"

Barbara stared at her husband; she had never been able to get him to go to the racetrack. "You always said you wouldn't feel comfortable there."

Mike smiled. "Can't a guy change his mind? Besides, Ben seems fairly sure his horse is going to win. Wouldn't hurt to make a little bet."

Getting to her feet, she leaned over and kissed him again. "Sounds like a great idea to me. I need to get supper going," she said as she headed for the kitchen, silently thanking Ben.

Ben and Cooper shipped the three horses from Canton to nearby Gardner Park on Saturday morning. Later that afternoon, Cooper was running Money Inthe Bank in a $25,000 claiming race, and Ben had decided to run Magic Beans in another $50,000 handicap. Time For Bucks' race was the feature event on Sunday.

Money Inthe Bank ran his typical consistent race and finished a close second. Two races later, Ben was pacing again as he waited for Magic Beans to go to the starting gate.

"Hey, cowboy, I hope you have another pair of boots," Mike called out to him as he rolled toward him; Barbara followed closely behind.

Ben smiled at them. "After this race and Bucks' tomorrow, I think I'll just buy my own western store."

"You really need to get over this lack of confidence problem you have," Mike said, and they all laughed as Cooper joined them.

The track announcer said, "They're in the gates," and a second later, the gates sprung open. And just like before, Magic Beans went to the lead and stayed there.

"It's picture time," Ben said, grinning at them.

"Why do I have a feeling he'll be real tough to live with after tomorrow?" Mike asked.

Cooper chuckled. "Because he will be." And again everyone laughed.

Mike and Barbara had decided to make a weekend of it and checked into Ben's hotel. That night they had supper with the Coopers and Ben. Barbara couldn't believe how alive Mike was again, carrying on with Ben and Dan. He had really gotten excited over Magic Beans' race, admitting he hadn't realized what he'd been missing.

"Hey, hon, how about we turn our horses over to Dan to train?" Mike asked suddenly.

Barbara's eyes brightened even more. "That's a great idea. I've been thinking of switching trainers anyhow."

If they thought Ben had been wound up the day before, they knew now he had just been warming up. He had been at the barn since 5 a.m. and hadn't left Time For Bucks' side until the horse left the saddling paddock.

"You got a rope, Dan? I think we need to tie him down," Mike suggested as they watched Ben striding up and down the grandstand.

Cooper laughed as he glanced at the tote board. Time For Bucks was holding at 10-1; he was in tough, as several stakes horses had shipped in from New York. After he had run second and third in his last two starts, Ben had commented he thought Bucks was bored with the same level of competition. Maybe a step up in class would renew his competitiveness. Cooper just hoped the horse could earn a check and Ben could begin recouping his investment.

"And they're off! It's My Truest Love going to the lead with Mr. Goodbar in second and Time For Bucks in third...As they head into the backstretch, it's those three still there with Slew's Trick moving up, followed by Golden Rule...Mr. Goodbar is on the move as they come into the stretch, My Truest Love is in second...And, oh my, Time For Bucks is moving like a freight train on the outside...Time For Bucks is now in the lead...It's Time For Bucks by three!"

Cooper shook his head in amazement amid all the jubilation. "Damn, Ben, I have never seen anyone with your kinda luck. Has everything always been so easy for you?"

Ben flashed his Texas cowboy smile at them as he turned and headed for the winner's circle. "Blessed by the gods," he whispered to himself.

8

Ben glanced down the road one more time and shook his head; he didn't know why he'd expected Billy Joe to be on time for once in his life. Damn. Where in the hell was he?

He had called him two weeks ago to check when he was making another pony horse selling trip. As it turned out, he was planning on coming to Miami in late January. In anticipation of setting up his own stable soon, Ben had figured it was time to start training a pony horse. His last words to Billy Joe were to make sure he didn't bring him a Texas scrub pony. He finished hosing down the shedrow and was walking over to shut off the faucet, when he heard the stock trailer rattling on the asphalt.

"What did you do, take a left turn and end up in Atlanta?" Ben asked, walking out to the rig.

Billy Joe waved his arms. "What's a guy supposed to do? Disappoint the ladies?"

"Wouldn't be the first time," Ben said, snickering.

"Hey, I like it," Billy Joe said, motioning to Ben's Dallas Cowboys' cap. "You look like the women in Miami are keeping you fit."

"I can't complain," Ben said as they moved to the rear of the trailer. "Let's see what 'cha got."

One by one, Billy Joe led the six Quarter horses down the ramp for Ben's inspection. Of those, he kind of liked one chunky bay and a paint.

"One more," Billy Joe said, scampering back into the trailer.

As the blazed-faced sorrel came toward him, Ben thought there was something very familiar about the horse. He eyed him carefully as Billy Joe walked him by and away from him. The muscular, copper-penny colored gelding had white-stockinged front legs; he was wide across the chest and rear, yet still had the rangy look of a young horse.

Billy Joe turned the horse around and walked him back to Ben, stopping him square in front of him. Ben put his hand out and let the horse sniff it. Moving just to the side, he crouched down and ran his hands down the horse's front legs. He straightened up and slowly slid his hands over the horse's body. It was when he came around the animal's rear and to his left side that he saw the small brand there on his haunches.

Ben looked up at Billy Joe in surprise.

"Scott said to tell you 'happy birthday'."

Ben didn't say anything. His birthday was in mid-February, but he most certainly had no plans to celebrate it. He moved his hand slowly over the brand, fingering the MR4 imprinted in the horse's hide. His father had added the 4 to the Matthews Ranch brand after Chris was born; it was a symbol of their family. The horse was Cherokee's full brother—a horse intended for Chris. Every year they alternated taking the foal from the mare they owned together, either selling the horse as a yearling or keeping it as a ranch and rodeo horse. Chris had decided to keep the blazed-faced sorrel and had planned to break him last summer.

Silently, Ben walked to the horse's head, took the lead rope from Billy Joe and led him into the barn.

Barbara admired the animal grazing in the Southerly Park paddock."So that's what a Texas-bred Quarter horse looks like. Very nice."

"Yep. They don't come bred any better than that horse," Ben said, leaning forward on the fence. "He comes from bloodlines that have produced ranch horses for more than thirty years. There's not anything you can't do from their backs—cutting, roping, rodeoing."

"You seem very familiar with the bloodline." She glanced at Ben; he had that sad look in his eyes again. "So, you obviously think he'll make a good pony horse, too."

Ben nodded. "Yeah. He's only three, so I think he'll adapt to the racetrack life all right. It's not like he's an older horse that's been used to ranching and rodeoing," he said. "Thought I'd give him a couple of days to settle in, break him here and then bring him to the track."

"Feel free to keep him here as long as you like. Think he'll be tough to break?"

Ben stepped back from the fence. "His brother bucked like hell for a week."

"What you're saying is there are a lot of similarities between training horses and coaching," Mike said as they headed for the wooden deck after supper.

"Yeah. Just like a coach tries to bring out a kid's potential, that's what a trainer is trying to do with a horse." Ben slid open the patio doors so Mike could roll himself through. "Whether it's a ranch horse or a racehorse, each has a certain amount of potential, depending on his breeding, conformation and personality. A racehorse trainer has to get the horse in the best physical and mental shape he can, run him where he belongs and hope for some luck."

"But a horse can't tell you if you're doing the right things, like a kid you're coaching can."

Ben sat down on the redwood bench. "Sure he can. You just have to know what to look for and to pay attention to the little things. If nothing else, his performance is going to tell you if you're doing the right or wrong things.

"When I claimed Magic Beans, the first thing I saw was a horse built for speed. But his past performance chart showed he was being raced too far and too often. Plus, all that equipment on him wasn't doing him a bit of good.

"But, mainly, his confidence was shot. He needed to race within his natural abilities so he could enjoy running again."

"Hmm, I never thought of the psychological aspects of training a racehorse," Mike said. He had a feeling most of Ben's knowledge came naturally. "What have you and Dan decided about our horses?"

Barbara joined them with iced tea for everyone. "Yes, when do we start winning races like you?" They all laughed.

"Your filly, Preoccupation, needs some time off and some groceries. Dan had the vet pull some blood and we should have those results back in a few days," Ben said. "I'd say she needs to be turned out for at least sixty days. I think she has some ability, but she's just not a filly that can hold up to a lot of training."

Mike took a sip of tea. "What about First And Ten?"

Ben grinned. "First And Ten's problem is his balls. He doesn't need them."

Mike almost choked on the tea while Barbara giggled. "You think he needs to be gelded?" she asked.

"Yeah, his mind ain't on running and unless you're wanting to go into the breeding business, the sooner you cut him, the better," Ben answered.

Mike winced. "Geez, that's cold-hearted."

"Honey, we need to make money, not babies, with these horses," Barbara said. "I wouldn't mind raising a baby from Preoccupation later, but I don't think we need a stud around here."

"Excuse me?" Mike protested.

"Oh, I should have said that one stud around here is enough," Barbara conceded, leaning over and kissing him. "You men and your egos," she added, then looked at Ben. "Cut his balls off."

"Yes, ma'am," Ben said, and then as Barbara left the room, added, "Remind me not to get her mad at me."

Mike chuckled. "She can be tough when she has to. It's one of the things I've always loved about her."

Ben put his empty glass down on the bench. "I really envy what you two have," he said. "How long had you been married when you had your accident?"

"About five years. We had moved here two years before." Mike paused, then added, "I would have never made it through everything without that woman. Of course, my family was super, too. But Barbara was remarkable.

"No matter how crazy I got—and believe me, there were times I was unbearable—she wouldn't give up on me or us. I never once thought she loved me any less, even if I couldn't love her in the same way anymore."

Ben figured now was as good a time as any to ask something he had been wondering. "Can—uh—I mean—can you...?"

"Have sex?" Mike finished the sentence. "No, not in the same way. But we are very intimate with each other. And in a strange way, we're closer now and more in love than we ever were when we had sex like rabbits.

"I guess what happened made us realize how much we really loved each other, and that wasn't going to change because I was in a wheelchair. In fact, what happened brought me and my family closer, too. I'm sure it was the same with you and your family."

Ben nodded slightly as he looked down. "Yeah." He got to his feet. "You two are coming to the barbecue at the barn tomorrow night, right?"

"We'll be there. And we'll try to make it for your new filly's race, too. What race is she in?"

"The seventh," Ben replied as he turned to leave. "See ya then."

Mike sat back in the wheelchair. There it was again—that subtle change in Ben's mood. Something had a hold of him and he was fighting it so much that you could feel it.

Ben's latest claim, a filly named Succinctly, had come back to win a $25,000 stakes race that afternoon. With the win, Cooper was now the leading trainer of the Gardner Park meet. There was much to celebrate, and it seemed everyone on the backside was taking advantage of the free food and booze at Cooper's barn.

"Are you sure you'll be all right? I just want to go over and visit with Eleanor a bit," Barbara said to her husband.

"Of course, I'm fine right here," Mike answered, having parked himself at the end of the shedrow where the beer coolers were. "You go ahead. Considering I'm where the beer is, I'm sure I'll have plenty of company."

Barbara gave him a quick kiss. "I'll tell Ben you're down here."

Mike took a swallow of the ice-cold beer as he studied the cast of characters scattered about the shedrow. There were trainers, owners, jockeys, exercise riders, grooms, blacksmiths and a couple of vets. What an eclectic group of people were drawn to the sport of Thoroughbred racing. Now here comes a real character, Mike thought to himself as the cowboy approached him.

"Hi, my name's Mike Miller. You're a friend of Ben's from Texas, right?"

"You bet 'cha. Billy Joe Parker," he drawled, shaking Mike's hand and then reaching for a beer. "The hat probably gave me away, huh?'

Mike laughed; he was beginning to appreciate the Texas cowboy sense of humor. "Did you and Ben rodeo together?"

Now it was Billy Joe's turn to laugh. "You might say that, except there was a big difference between how I did it and how Ben did it. I mostly hit the ground a lot and Ben mostly won a lot," he said, pausing to take a drink.

"Sure do miss having him around. Damned shame what happened to him. And the thing of it is, even after that bull nearly killed him, he came back. Woulda been a champion roper, too, if it hadn't been for what happened in Waco."

"Did he get hurt again?"

Billy Joe leaned against the wall and shook his head. "His family was killed in a truck wreck. They were on their way to see Ben in the rodeo."

Mike stared at Billy Joe; he didn't know what he had expected, but what he had been told had stunned him. "When did it happen?"

"Hmm, let's see. That was last April—no, late May. Yeah, the Waco rodeo was last May," Billy Joe said. "And you know, as much as Ben loved his folks, I think losing his little brother, Chris, was really what took the heart right out of him. He just walked away from the rodeo, the ranch, everything and everybody in Texas."

It was 2 a.m. when Ben finally gave up trying to sleep. His leg was still throbbing and he couldn't stop thinking about Chris. Three days ago, he had started breaking that blazed-faced sorrel and like Cherokee, he had an affinity for bucking. He hadn't thrown him yet, but he had jolted him pretty good. And twice he had banged him up against the high wooden wall of the round pen.

With a moan, Ben rolled over on the right side of the bed and sat there massaging his aching leg. There didn't seem to be any serious damage; a couple bruises, but it hadn't swelled up like when he had hurt it in Wyoming. Reaching over to the night stand, he grabbed the bottle of aspirin, shook out a handful and washed them down with the whiskey left over in the glass from last night. It was a combination he had discovered worked as well as anything a doctor could prescribe.

Ever since Billy Joe had brought him that damned horse, he hadn't slept through a whole night. He should have just put that horse back in Billy Joe's trailer and sent him back to Texas. It was supposed to be Chris who was breaking his horse, not him. Chris had been crazy about that blazed-faced sorrel and couldn't wait to get a saddle on him. *"You just wait and see, Ben. He's going to be even better than Cherokee."*

Damn Scott and Lisa. First, Lisa sends him that picture. And now Scott sends him Chris' horse. Damn. Why couldn't they just leave him alone? Just when he was feeling better—settling into his new life—they reached out and yanked him back to Texas. How was he ever going to put that life behind him if they kept reminding him of who he used to be?

Maybe he should call them and tell them to leave him the hell alone. No. That would only hurt them and he had hurt them enough. Maybe the best thing to do was nothing. If he didn't respond to their gestures, then maybe they would just give up on him. They would finally see he was out of their lives—and that it was the best thing for all of them. It was the only way they were going to survive what had happened in Waco.

Eight months. Had it really been eight months since Waco? And had he been in Miami for four months? It was all a blur. It seemed as though it had all happened yesterday. And, yet, he felt like he had been on the run forever. Sometimes he was so tired that he just wanted to stop and lie down. But he knew he couldn't. Because if he did—if he lay still and let Waco catch up with him—he might never get up again.

"Okay, I've waited long enough for you to tell me what's been on your mind the last few days," Barbara said, slipping under the blankets and cuddling up against her husband. "So, out with it. What's going on?"

Mike sighed; he should have known better than to try to keep something from his wife. "I found out why Ben left Texas," he quietly said, wrapping his arm around her. "His family was killed in a truck wreck last May."

Barbara propped herself up on her left elbow. "Oh, how awful. His whole family?"

"Yeah, his father, mother and younger brother. They were on their way to see Ben in a rodeo. Apparently, it happened not very far from the rodeo grounds."

"Did Ben tell you?"

"No. That friend of his from Texas, Billy Joe, did at the barbecue. And it's been on my mind ever since. I just don't know what to say to Ben. With our accidents, we were on common ground. But this is different."

"Maybe you should just wait till Ben says something about it."

"I'm not so sure he will," Mike said, looking at his wife. "In all our conversations, he's never once mentioned his family. I had a feeling there was something else bothering him besides his bull-riding accident, but he never gave me a clue."

"We really haven't known Ben that long. And everybody handles grief differently. Maybe he's just a very private person."

"Bullshit. You wouldn't have introduced him to me if you hadn't thought he was a person I could relate to."

Barbara smiled at him. "And here I thought I had slipped one past you."

Mike kissed her. "I think we've been together too long and been through too much to fool each other," he said lovingly, then sighed. "But I still don't know what to do about Ben."

"Maybe the best thing is just to keep doing what we have been and be his friends," she suggested. "He really seems to enjoy coming out here to ride and talking sports and stuff with you. I think you've already helped him a lot and you just don't know it."

Mike thought about that for a moment. "And he's helped me a lot, too. Just like you thought he would," he said, grinning at her.

"Smartass." She slapped him on the shoulder and then kissed him as he slipped his hand under her nightshirt.

Ben couldn't believe it. Magic Beans had lost his race, finishing a well-beaten third.

"Well, you can't win 'em all," Cooper consoled him as they walked down to the track where the horses were coming back to be unsaddled.

"I hope he's all right," Ben said as he waited for the jockey to pull the horse up in front of him. "What happened?"

Mark jumped off Magic Beans. "I don't know, Ben. He just

never got into the bit," he explained as he pulled the saddle off and went to weigh in.

Ben quickly checked the horse, making sure he hadn't injured himself. "I'll walk him back to the barn," he told the groom and led the horse away.

"Coming back to the barn, he was full of himself," Ben told Cooper an hour later as they sat in the tack room.

"I wouldn't worry about it. Don't be so hard on yourself," Cooper said. "You know how sometimes horses just don't want to do. Figure it's their way of gettin' even with us. Hell, you still picked up a nice check for third."

Ben was about to agree when loud noises interrupted him. He and Cooper hurried out of the tack room and down the shedrow. Bam! Magic Beans kicked the back wall of his stall again.

"Hey, cut that out," Ben scolded him. "Come here," he called to the horse and when he came to the front of the stall, Ben rubbed his ears. "See, I don't think he intended on losing either."

Cooper laughed. "Ask him if he knows who's going to win the feature race tomorrow," he said and even got Ben to laugh with him.

As Ben limped down the hallway, he could hear the clanging of the weight machine and Mike's grunts. "Anyone ever tell you that you have strong masochistic tendencies?" he asked, stopping just inside the doorway of the training room.

Mike slowly brought the arm press down toward his chest. "This from a man who derives pleasure from riding animals who want desperately to buck him off," he retorted, bringing himself to a sitting position.

"Okay, okay. So we're both crazy."

Mike grinned at him. "You want to bring me that towel?"

"Sure," Ben replied, but when he tried to move forward, his

left leg refused. "Damn." He felt his leg cramp up on him; he slid back and leaned against the wall.

"Hey, are you okay?" Mike asked as Ben brought his hands down to his left thigh.

"Yeah, I'll be fine. It's just I haven't been on a horse that bucked in a long time."

"Maybe you should let someone else break him."

"No," Ben said, looking down at his leg. "If he's going to be my horse—really be my horse—I have to break him."

"Must be one of those cowboy rules, huh?"

Ben chuckled. "Yeah, that's it."

"When was the last time you had that leg massaged?"

"Not since I got through with physical therapy."

"Geez, no wonder it's giving you trouble." Mike lifted himself from the weight bench and into the wheelchair. "There's shorts and a sweat shirt in the bathroom. Get changed and Dr. Mike will fix you right up."

Ben looked dubiously at him.

"Remember, I was a coach. I know more than a little bit about sports injuries and massage therapy. Now, get your butt in there and change."

Ten minutes later, Ben was stretched out on the padded bench, propped up on his elbows and watching Mike running his hands over his leg.

"Geez, there's nothing but one knot after another." Mike expertly worked his fingers into the damaged leg. "How many pins and plates do you have in here?"

Ben shrugged. "I don't know. I never asked."

"Did you get hung up on the bull?"

"No. He fell with me, rolled over on me and then tried to stomp the hell out of me. Hey, ouch."

"Sorry. Try to relax." Mike moved his hands up to the scarred thigh.

"Easy for you to say...ouch."

"Hmm, I think you'd better lay down."

"Why?"

"Because I'm going to pull on your hip and it's going to hurt."

"Thanks for the warning." Ben stretched out on the bench.

"Okay, here goes," Mike said as he pulled gently but firmly on the leg.

Ben heard his pinned together hip pop."Damn." he muttered, feeling the warmth of tears in his eyes. "Damn."

"Okay, just give it a few seconds and it'll be all right," Mike said soothingly as he kneaded the once-again tight thigh muscles. "That's it. Relax."

Just as Mike predicted, Ben could feel the pain ebbing. He let out a grateful sigh.

"You really should get this leg massaged on a regular basis. You'd feel a hell of a lot better," Mike advised, handing Ben a towel.

"And you should consider doing this for a living," Ben said matter-of-factly, wiping the perspiration from his face.

Mike looked at him in surprise; it was as though a door had been opened.

"I mean, think about it. You have the sports background and having gone through what you have, you could do some good for a lot of injured people," Ben offered. "They would know you understood what they were going through. And seeing you in that wheelchair would put everything in perspective real quick."

Barbara appeared in the doorway. "It's a good thing I'm not an insecure woman, or I might be a little concerned by what I'm seeing."

The two men looked at each other in confusion then both realized Mike's hand was still on Ben's thigh. Mike jerked it away and they all laughed.

"Just giving Ben one of my special massages," Mike explained.

"Hmm, I thought I was the only one who got those," Barbara said, tossing the towel to her husband. "So what happened to Magic Beans? How'd he lose?"

"I've been trying to figure that one out myself," Ben answered. "But it's like Dan said, can't win 'em all. We'll get 'em next time."

9

When Lisa walked into the barn, Scott was going over Cherokee with the soft brush. "If that horse gets any shinier, you're going to have to wear sunglasses to ride him," she said, zipping up her down jacket.

"Yeah, the kids are crazy about him. They're always brushing on him," Scott quietly answered. "Thought I'd get a ride in while I could."

"Want some company?"

Scott shrugged. "Suit yourself."

"You've been a grouch since breakfast. Who put a burr under your saddle?"

Scott dropped the brush into the grooming box. "I talked to Billy Joe last night at Jake's," he said as he placed first the blanket then the saddle on the horse's back.

"And?"

"And he said Ben is doing great in Miami," Scott answered, tightening the saddle girth. "Said he has a couple of racehorses and, of course, he's winning. They had a big barbecue to celebrate while he was there."

Lisa had to smile. "No matter where he goes or what he does, Ben is always the star of the show," she said. "Did Billy Joe bring back any message from him? Was he happy you sent him Chris' horse?"

Scott shook his head as he slipped the bridle on the horse's head. "Not a word," he said, turning to face her. "It's like he's just cut us out of his life."

"Honey..." Lisa moved toward him.

"Don't," Scott snapped as he stepped back against the horse. "Don't tell me it's going to be all right. Because I don't think anything will ever be all right again.

"Today is his birthday and I can't even call him. You tell me what's right about that."

Lisa sighed. "What did you expect when you sent him Chris' horse? Did you think it would make him so lonesome that he'd come home?"

Scott looked at her in amazement; this woman knew him inside and out. He felt the anger leaving him. "Yeah, maybe I did," he admitted as he petted Cherokee. "Last year at this time, Ben and I were at the Reno rodeo. It was the first time we won as a team. I was so excited. We were going to be world champions. I just knew it.

"Now, look at us. He's training horses in Miami and we're together and living on his ranch."

"Don't forget, you own part of it now, too."

"I'm not talking about who owns what," Scott countered. "I'm saying this is his home and we're his family. Ben should be here. It's like a picture with a big hole in it."

Lisa tentatively approached him, and this time, he let her; she put her arms around his waist. "I agree with you. But you can't make Ben come home. He's going to have to come to that decision on his own," she said gently, looking into his eyes. "And you're going to have to accept that it may be a long time before he does."

Scott hugged her. "But you do think he'll come back, don't you?"

"Like you said, this is where he belongs. He'll come home," Lisa said, knowing it was what he needed to hear and what she wanted to believe.

"Honey, come here," Mike called out to his wife from the deck. "You gotta see this."

Barbara walked out of the house and joined her husband. "What is it, Babe?"

Mike motioned across the pasture to where Ben was loping the sorrel bareback. "Remember when you were a kid, watching The Lone Ranger and Roy Rogers, and you wondered if cowboys were real? Well, they are."

"It's almost like he's from another place and time," Barbara commented. "He has to be missing Texas like crazy."

Mike just nodded as Ben turned the horse toward them and came trotting over. "Looks like he decided to stop bucking," Mike said once he was in hearing range.

Ben brought the horse right up to the deck. "For now," he said with a chuckle. "But he comes from a long line of horses who just flat out like to buck for the hell of it."

"What did you name him?" Barbara asked, rubbing the horse's muzzle.

"Reno," Ben answered. He had finally decided just that morning it was time to name him. Even now, it made him smile when he remembered how excited Scott had been when they had won at Reno.

"What's all this?" Ben asked as he and Mike entered the room, beers in hand.

Mike rolled the wheelchair up to the table where several stacks of books were lined up. "This is your fault," he explained. "I've decided to go back to school and get a degree in physical therapy."

"That's great, Mike. When do you start?"

"Not until the summer semester. But I thought I'd better catch up on some essential reading and get back into the learning mode," Mike said as he watched Ben put his beer down on the table and pick up the *Gray's Anatomy* book atop one of the stacks.

"I bought this for Chris when he was fifteen," Ben said softly, and then couldn't believe he had.

Ben suddenly felt like he was in a vacuum; he was afraid to take a breath. He just stood there, staring down at the book in his hand and waiting for Mike to ask him who Chris was.

"It's all right, Ben," Mike said gently. "I know about your family. Billy Joe told me at the barbecue."

The words seemed to help Ben breathe a little easier. He slowly sat down, still holding the book and still not looking at Mike. He thought he should be angry at Billy Joe, but instead he was somewhat relieved that Mike knew. And that surprised him.

"Was your brother interested in medicine?" Mike asked.

"Yeah, he was going to be a doctor."

"Ahh, the smart one in the family. He had enough sense to stay away from the broncs and bulls."

"Oh, Chris was a heck of a cowboy," Ben corrected him. "He could ride a bronc as good as anyone. But he hated the bulls. Never even tried to sit on one. Thought I was crazy to ride 'em." He paused as the memories came rushing back.

"He'd never watch me ride the bulls. He'd pace behind the chutes and wait to hear the buzzer." He took a breath, then continued. "Except that last ride. He told me later that he started to walk off like always. But something made him come back and climb up on the fence with everybody else."

Mike eyed his friend; he could feel how painful remembering was for him. "You don't have to say anymore."

Ben sighed. "Sometimes I would wonder which I hated more—that it had happened, or that Chris had seen it happen," he said, adding, "He put grad school off for a year so he could be with me while I recovered. I never liked that he did that. But I don't know if I would have gotten through it without him."

"I'm sure it made him feel good to be able to help his big brother," Mike offered. "I know you were there for him when he needed you."

Ben laid the book on the table; the familiar tightness in his chest had returned. "The last time I saw him—and Mother and Dad—was for his birthday in late April. I was back on the circuit and pretty much on the road all the time. That's why we planned to meet in Waco," he said and the words sliced through him.

For a few minutes, the two men sat in silence.

Ben spread his hands out on the table in front of him and stared at them. "Even though you don't like to think about it, you know—you expect—that your parents are going to die before you," he whispered. "But not your little brother. Your little brother is not supposed to die before you." He had to stop; his voice was quivering now.

For the first time since he had picked up the book, Ben looked at Mike. "He had just turned twenty-four. My little brother shouldn't have died at twenty-four." He barely managed to say the words as tears filled his eyes.

Mike searched desperately for words to comfort Ben, words that he knew didn't exist. He could only watch helplessly as Ben got to his feet and strode out of the room.

On the last minute, Cooper decided to check the hotel lounge; there had been no answer to his knocks on Ben's hotel room door. Squinting through the smoky haze, he saw Ben sitting alone at a table toward the back of the room.

"I see you and me had the same idea about how to spend the night," Cooper said as he joined Ben, putting an empty glass down on the table. "Figure with Eleanor visiting the girls, I'd better howl at the moon while I can."

Ben poured whiskey into Cooper's glass and then topped his own. "Yeah, like Eleanor keeps you on a tight rein."

"Now, Ben, that's our little secret," Cooper said, then sipped at the whiskey. "You look like Texas has gotta hold of you again."

"Yeah. You were right about it not being that easy to let go," Ben said. "But my father always said that the harder something is to do, the more a man needs to do it."

Cooper raised his glass. "Good advice from a good man," he said and the two men each took long swallows.

"The way Succinctly ran today, I'm beginning to wonder if I'm just fooling myself," Ben said. "Just because I know Quarter horses sure doesn't mean I can train Thoroughbreds."

"You're doin' fine, Ben. You're just having a little bit of bad racing luck," Cooper assured him. "And fillies are tough to train. Any trainer will tell you he'd rather a barnful of geldings instead of fillies any day."

"But you won with Mymomsluck today."

"Well, she's a hard-knockin' old racemare. She knows the routine. She just goes out there and does her job," Cooper replied. "Succinctly is only three and high strung to boot. You'll figure out her key.

"Come on, Ben, you're the best damned horseman I've ever been around. And you need to start thinking about gettin' your trainer's license."

Ben looked at him. "You trying to get rid of me, Dan?"

"Hell, no. I love havin' you around. You've brought me more good luck than I've had in years," Cooper said, laughing. "But you're a natural and there's not much more I can teach you. Hell, you've reminded me about some things I had forgotten—like this old cowboy became a trainer because I like foolin' with horses."

Ben refilled both their glasses. "To Texas cowboys, their horses and Jack Daniel's whiskey."

Cooper grinned at him. "Hell of a toast," he said and then they drained their glasses.

The flames were everywhere; the heat of the fire made his eyes water. He wanted to run away. But he couldn't. He could hear his father, mother and Chris calling his name, begging him to help them. But every time he took a step forward, a new wall of fire erupted in front of him. And still he could hear their screams.

"No!" Ben cried out as he finally broke free of the nightmare and sat up in bed. Tears streamed down his face and he clutched the blankets.

He made himself take deep breaths, trying to slow down his breathing. Damn. The nightmare was back. He had been thinking too much about Chris and his parents and Waco. He had even been foolish enough to talk about Chris—about losing his little brother—with Mike. He should have known better. He should have known the nightmare would come back to haunt him.

Ben threw the blankets off and swung his legs over the side of the bed. As he headed for the bathroom, he stripped off the sweat-soaked T-shirt and briefs. Climbing into the bathtub, he turned on the shower and let the ice-cold water beat down on him.

Barbara was surprised when she saw Ben's truck parked outside the barn; there was a two-horse trailer hitched to it. When she walked into the barn, she saw Ben leaning against the double door entrance at the east end of the shedrow.

"Hey, Ben, what are you doing here at this time of the morning?" Barbara asked as she joined him.

"Pretty sunrise," he said quietly.

Barbara took notice of the gold and crimson streaks in the early morning sky. "Yes, it is," she agreed, looking at him and knowing he had been up all night. "Are you okay?"

"Yeah. I'm going to take Reno to the track today. Thought we'd get in a nice ride before he has to start being a pony horse."

She thought there was a tone of finality in his voice. "Well, I hope you'll still bring him over to ride every now and then."

Ben kept staring at the sunrise. "He needs to get used to his new life," he said deliberately as he turned away.

Barbara watched him limp down the shedrow and disappear into the horse's stall. She couldn't shake the feeling that something had happened, that something was wrong.

Two hours later, Barbara watched from the kitchen window as Ben drove away. He hadn't even come up to the house to talk to Mike. Now she was certain something was wrong. Ever since Mike had told her about Ben's family being killed, she had felt guilty. But how could she have known Ben was dealing with more than his own accident? She had tried to pretend that she hadn't made a serious mistake, that somehow Mike would be able to help Ben deal with his grief. But now she had a sickening feeling that her plan was going to backfire on her. And they were all going to pay for her recklessness.

"Hey, cowboy, you been riding the range or whatever it is you guys do?" Mike asked as he rolled himself toward Ben, who was standing alone at a far corner of the grandstand.

Ben gave Mike a feeble smile; he hadn't talked to him in almost a week. "Just been busy," he said, making fleeting eye contact as he looked back across the track where the horses were warming up.

"How's Reno doing?"

"He's doing great. I wish my racehorses were doing as good."

"Hmm, you don't think Magic Beans is going to run well?"

Ben shrugged. "He's been training fine and has been on his toes since that last race. But I don't know what to expect."

Just as Ben finished expressing his doubts, the gates sprung open. Magic Beans didn't go to the lead and, instead, got trapped in the middle of the pack. He finished fourth.

"I'll try to come by as soon as I can," Ben said quickly to Mike as he hurried down to the track.

Mike wanted to go after him, wanted to tell him that he understood talking about his brother had been too painful to handle. But it wasn't the right place and time. He turned the wheelchair around and headed back toward Barbara.

Ben ran his hands up and down Magic Beans' front legs. Ice cold. Just like before and just like Succinctly's had been. And just like after the other race, Magic Beans had come back to the barn full of himself.

Ever since his luck had gone bad, Ben had made sure he paid attention to every little detail leading up to each horse's race. Enough work, but not too much. Right mix of feed and supplements. Don't wait until the last minute to have new shoes put on. Make sure the right equipment was on the horse. Watch when the horse is jogging, galloping, working, cooling out. Make note of anything—anything—that seems amiss.

His horses had gone to the paddock on race day prancing, dead fit and ready to win. But they hadn't.

The parking lot lights had been turned on. The last race had been run fifteen minutes ago, and slowly the grandstand had emptied. Ben leaned against his truck parked just outside the jockeys' paddock entrance. Finally, Mark and another jockey emerged.

"I need to talk to you, Mark," Ben said as they went by him.

"Oh, hi, Ben. I didn't see you there," Mark said, then turned to his friend. "You go on. I'll catch up with you guys later."

Ben waited until the other jockey was in his car. "Get in the truck."

Mark looked at Ben; he had always thought he was a fairly easy-going guy, but now his tone was harsh—angry. "Is there a problem? Are you mad about how Magic Beans ran?"

"Get in the truck," Ben repeated dryly.

This time the jockey did as he was told and it wasn't just because Ben towered over him; it was because of the look in his eyes. No one had to tell him this was one mad cowboy.

"Have you been pulling my horses, Mark?" Ben asked immediately once they were both in the truck.

"Hey, they can't win all the time."

Ben turned himself sideways, draping his left arm on the steering wheel while he let his right hand rest lightly on the jockey's shoulder. "Now, Mark, you and I both know that I could turn you upside down. I'd rather not do that, but we Texas cowboys tend to get what we want one way or the other.

"So I'm going to ask you just once more, have you been pulling my horses?"

The jockey rubbed his sweaty palms on his jeans; he knew Ben wasn't bluffing. "Yeah," he whispered, not looking at him.

Ben's fingers tightened around the steering wheel. "Is it a jockeys' deal or you just cashing big bets on your own?"

"It's not that at all. There are some really heavy players in on this," Mark said, feeling Ben's hand growing heavier on his shoulder. "All I'm getting is my jock's fee plus a bonus. They don't even tell me who's supposed to win."

"Just that my horse isn't supposed to, right?" Ben said, feeling the anger welling inside him. "Tell me who they are."

Mark shook his head. "I don't know," he said, looking at Ben. The man's cold, grey eyes sent a shiver through him. "I swear. I don't know."

"Well, someone has to tell you when the fix is on," Ben snapped.

"You're not going to like it."

"Tell me."

"It's Dan Cooper."

Ben felt like all of the air had just been sucked out of his lungs, just like coming off a bull wrong and landing on your back. "You're lying," he rasped.

Mark swallowed, trying to ease the dryness in his throat. "No, I'm not. Dan's the one who's been telling me when to pull, and he's the one who's been giving me my money."

Ben heard the words and part of him knew Mark was telling the truth. The jockey was in no position to be playing games with him.

"Are you going to go to the stewards?"

Ben turned away from him, now gripping the steering wheel with both hands. "Get out."

"What are you..."

"Get out!"

When Ben staggered into his hotel room hours later, the note that had been stuck in the doorjamb fluttered to the floor. Awkwardly, he bent over and picked it up.

"We came by for supper. Sorry we missed you. Catch up with you later. Barbara and Mike," Ben read the note out loud as he slammed the door behind him and headed for the bed.

He let the note drop to the floor as he struggled to take his boots off. Finally managing to do that, he stretched out on the bed. Supper? He wasn't interested in having supper with anyone. After he had talked to Mark, all he had wanted to do was beat the hell of someone. What was left of his common sense had told him he'd hurt Dan if he confronted him right away. So, instead, he had decided to get drunk. At least that always slowed him down. But tomorrow he'd have to know the truth, and he'd have to hear it from Dan. Tomorrow would come soon enough.

10

It was nearly noon when Ben walked up the shedrow in long, purposeful strides. He had waited to come to the barn when he was sure the crew had gone to lunch; he knew Dan would be filling out the horses' training charts.

Cooper looked up from the notebook as Ben entered the tack room. "Hey, I was gonna come check if some woman's husband had hog-tied you."

Ben closed the door behind him, leaning back against it as he folded his arms across this chest. "When did you first peg me for a sucker? Right away or after I told you I didn't need to be on your payroll?"

"What are you talking about?" Cooper asked. He had a bad feeling in his gut and the look in Ben's eyes wasn't easing it.

"Can the act. Mark told me what's been going on with my horses," Ben said, glaring at Dan. "Now, I want you to tell me."

Cooper fell back in the chair. "I'm sorry, Ben. I thought it'd be over soon and you'd never know."

"Don't tell me you're sorry. Tell me the truth."

Running his hand through his hair, Cooper sighed in relief; he had grown weary of the deception. "There was a time last year when I couldn't win anything. Hell, my horses weren't even hittin'

the board," he said, glancing at Ben but not looking him in the
eye.

"I started losing clients. I had bills to pay, a mortgage on the
house and the girls in college. We were going to lose everything."

Ben stared at him. "So you started fixing races?"

Cooper looked down in shame. "I was approached one night
in a bar. They told me they wanted to use my horses to cash some
big bets. All I had to do was enter them, and they'd take care of
the rest. And they did. I started winning again. Then after awhile,
they stopped contacting me, and I tried to forget about it."

"And then?"

"And then about two months ago, they came back. They told
me I owed them."

"Why my horses?"

Cooper shrugged. "You were winning. And since you were
new to the game, the stewards weren't likely to think anything
suspicious was going on."

"Just a little bit of bad racing luck, right?" Ben said sharply.
"Tell me who they are."

Now Cooper looked at him. "I can't do that."

Ben's arms dropped to his sides. "I think you can."

"These are dangerous men, Ben," Cooper said with genuine
concern in his voice. "They threatened to hurt Eleanor and the
girls if I didn't play along. First, they hurt people and if that doesn't
work, they kill 'em."

Ben could see the fear in Dan's eyes. "Damn." He stepped
away from the door. "So we're just supposed to let them get away
with this? There has to be something we can do."

"If we go the stewards, we'd likely end up losing our licenses
and they'd pay a hotshot lawyer to get them off," Cooper said, the
feeling of helplessness evident in his voice. "Believe me, I hate this
as much as you do. But they're smart and don't mess with the
same horses for too long. I think they'll soon move on."

Ben shook his head. "But they'll be back. We have to find a
way to get rid of them for good," he said. "What if I win the next

race I'm supposed to lose? Maybe that'll get them mad enough to come after me, and then we could set them up with the cops."

"Didn't you hear what I told you? These guys make people disappear all the time," Cooper insisted. "You might be willing to take the risk, but I have a family to worry about. I have to protect them the best I can—and if that means playing along with these goons, then that's what I have to do. And if I have to beg you to do the same, then I'm begging."

Cooper's plea cut through Ben. Yeah, he knew about doing anything for your family—even selling your soul if that's what it took to protect them. If he had been given the choice, he would have gladly paid that price in Waco.

Ben paced across the room in frustration. He suddenly stopped and turned back toward Dan. "Bucks' race tomorrow, is it fixed?"

Cooper could only manage a nod.

"I'll scratch him out of it."

"They'll just wait until you finally run him. He'll go off one of the favorites whenever you run him and they'll pick a longshot to set the race up for," Cooper said. "It's better just to go along with them now and get it over with. We can't risk getting them riled up. There's no tellin' what they'll do."

Ben could still see the fear in Dan's eyes. He made himself look away and left in angry silence.

The sight of Mike parked outside his hotel room made Ben want to get back on the elevator. After his talk with Dan, he had just wanted to come back to his room and shut out the world. But Mike and Barbara had been kind to him; they deserved better than him avoiding them.

"You look a little lost," Ben said, putting his anger away. "You take a wrong turn somewhere?"

Mike grinned at him. "Well, it was either hang out here or have Barbara drag me through every department store sale in Miami," he said. "I was hoping you hadn't had lunch yet."

"As a matter of fact, I haven't," Ben said, unlocking the door. "Come on in and we can order something up."

All during lunch, the two men made small talk. Mike lamented about how difficult studying again was and Ben pretended to still be perplexed why his horses were running off form.

Finally, Mike swallowed the last of the beer and put the empty bottle down on the table. "Ever since our last conversation, I've been worried about you," he said quietly. "And you staying away and avoiding us hasn't made me worry any less."

Ben pushed the plate away. "I'm sorry. I shouldn't have done that," he said. "It's just I thought I could handle talking about what happened. But I guess I can't."

"It will get easier," Mike offered. "But not if you keep punishing yourself. That is what you're doing, isn't it?" he asked, but Ben didn't answer as he looked away. "It's what you were talking about when you said it was a mistake you went back to the rodeo. Somehow you've convinced yourself what happened is your fault because they were killed coming to see you in a rodeo."

Ben looked at him. "It's the truth. That's what happened."

"It was an accident, Ben. It was no more your fault than my accident was mine just because I happened to be on the road at the same time as the drunk driver who hit me."

Ben thought about that for a moment. "It's not that simple," he said, pushing back the chair and getting to his feet.

"But it is." Mike watched him go to the window and gaze out across the way to the racetrack. "It's just that you'd rather be angry and blame yourself than deal with the grief."

There was no response from Ben.

"I know about being angry and about denial, Ben. And believe me, there's no safety there. But for almost two years I thought there was, and I thought being that way was going to help me walk out of this chair. It didn't."

Ben turned to face him. "I can't even begin to tell you how much I admire you and how you deal with living in that chair. You have more heart than anybody I know," he said warmly. "And I really appreciate your friendship."

"But?"

"You think I'm denying my family is gone. But that's not it at all," Ben said, reseating himself at the table. "I know they're gone. I know it every morning when I wake up and think of how I'm going to get through another day without them. And talking about it only makes it worse," he explained, thinking of the fiery nightmare.

"So you're just going to lock yourself up in this self-imposed prison?"

"Call it what you want. But it seems to be the only way I can get through each day," Ben answered. "Maybe one day I'll be able to handle it differently. But right now, I can't."

Mike could see the pain in Ben's eyes. And he knew he was telling him the truth—that if he tried to deal with the grief now, he wouldn't survive it.

"Since I've been in this chair, other than Barbara, there hasn't been anyone who I could relate to on my terms," Mike said. "Until you. And that's because you're a survivor just like me. So I know you're going to be all right. I just worry about the price you're going to pay trying to get through this alone."

Ben managed a small smile. "Just chalk it up to another one of those cowboy rules," he said and Mike couldn't help but laugh.

Ben sat alone at the far end of the grandstand. He hated this—hated that he had to play this game because those bastards had gotten their spurs into Dan. It was like figuring out the trick to a bronc or bull; once you did, the ride was easy. He was determined to find out who they were. Then they'd see what it was like to deal with someone who had nothing to lose.

"Do you see him?" Mike asked as Barbara scanned the Saturday afternoon crowd at Gardner Park.

"No. I don't understand. He's usually pacing up and down over there," she said as the horses broke from the gates.

Ben didn't even stand up as he listened to the race call. What was the point? He knew the outcome.

"Green Mountain goes to the lead... Twist And Shout, Mayday and Blue Boy are bunched in behind him...Green Mountain opens up a length as Mayday moves into second...Then it's Blue Boy and Twist And Shout and making a bold move on the inside is Time For Bucks..."

Now Ben stood up to get a better view. The horses were coming into the final turn and as they straightened up for the stretch run, he saw that Mark had Bucks trapped on the rail. There were two horses on the outside of him and three in front of him. Ben knew the jockey was going to just stay where he was and keep the horse out of contention.

He was about to sit back down when he saw something he had seen the very first time he had watched Bucks race. That big red horse pinned his ears flat back on his head and shifted gears, almost yanking Mark out of the saddle. And Ben knew the horse had made up his mind he was going to win even without the jockey's help. Ben started walking toward the track; his heart pounded as Bucks bore down on the leaders.

"There he is," Mike said as he spotted Ben. They began moving through the crowd.

Any elation Ben had initially felt had suddenly turned to panic. Bucks had quickly made up the distance between him and the frontrunners; he was on their rears, but no hole had opened up on the rail. And he wasn't slowing down.

"No," Ben muttered, hurrying now toward the finish line. "No, Bucks. Pull him up, Mark."

As though he had heard Ben, Mark suddenly stood up in the saddle in a desperate attempt to avoid disaster. It was too late. Bucks rammed into the leaders, horses and jockeys screaming as their bodies collided. Behind them, the other jockeys jerked their mounts to the outside as a collective gasp came from the stunned crowd.

The impact sent Bucks and Mark over the rail into the grassy infield. In a horrifying instant, the jockey lay sprawled out a few feet from the thrashing horse, who was trying to rise on shattered legs. On the track, one horse was up and hobbling on three legs;

his jockey lay face down in the dirt. The third horse had already trotted off in a dazed panic while his jockey was on his knees, blood flowing from a gash across his forehead. Horsemen were spilling onto the track to try to help; ambulance sirens wailed.

Ben sank to his knees at Bucks' head, putting his hands on him to try to calm him. The horse was still struggling, but Ben could see the shock settling into his glazed eyes. Ben looked over to where Mark was sitting up, clutching to his left arm as a paramedic knelt down to help him.

He looked back down at the horse; both his front legs had snapped at the cannon bone and jagged edges protruded through the flesh. Ben thought he was going to throw up. Someone touched his arm and he looked up to see the state's track vet.

"You want to put him down?" he asked, the lethal injection already in his hand.

Ben stared at him; he knew there wasn't anything else to do. Bucks' legs were shattered beyond repair. All they could do was mercifully end his misery. Ben nodded weakly.

"It's all right, Bucks," he whispered, stroking the horse's neck. "It's not going to hurt anymore," he promised, and in the next instant the horse was suddenly still.

The vet left to check on the other horses. Ben sat there on his haunches, feeling the anger welling in him. With a shudder, he rose and started walking across the infield to the backside.

Mike and Barbara watched helplessly from the grandstand. Unable to get past the security guards, they had numbly viewed the horror and realized what Ben had had to do as they saw him walk away.

"Come on," Barbara said, hurriedly steering Mike around. "Maybe we can catch him on the backside."

They didn't see Cooper as they sped past him. He, too, had been stunned by the tragic events. He had seen Ben run out on the track and had started to follow him. But then, he had stopped; he was probably the last person Ben would want to see. Wearily, he turned away as they loaded Bucks into the horse ambulance;

the jockeys were on their way to the hospital and the other horses had already been taken away. The order of finish for the ill-fated race was finally posted on the tote board. But no one seemed to care. Most of the racing fans were still shaking their heads and whispering about what had happened.

Cooper walked out of his Canton shedrow to the Millers' van. "He's not here. Did you check at Gardner?"

"By the time we got to the receiving barn, he was already gone," Barbara answered. "Other than his hotel, is there anywhere else he might go?"

"There are a couple of bars we hit every now and then. I'll check them out and call you later."

Mike leaned forward from where he sat on the passenger side. "Why didn't Mark take Bucks off the rail?"

Cooper shrugged. "Who knows why jockeys do anything?"

"Was Mark hurt badly?" Barbara asked.

"I don't know. I'm going to go call the hospital right now, and then I'll look for Ben."

An hour later, Cooper was still in the tack room. Mark had a broken collarbone; both of the other jockeys had concussions and one had a broken leg.

Despite what he had told Barbara and Mike, Cooper knew he didn't have to go look for Ben. All he had to do was wait here and Ben would come looking for him. He'd likely beat the hell out of him. And that was just fine with him; he figured he had it coming.

There was a sound in the shedrow. Cooper stepped out of the tack room, but it wasn't Ben he came face to face with.

Ben was halfway up the dimly lit shedrow when he heard the voices. Very quietly, he slid over into the shadows against the stalls and cautiously approached the tack room. A burly man had Dan backed up against the wall and was poking him in the chest.

"That jockey was trying to win the race," the man growled. "My boss did not think that was very funny."

"The horse was trying to win, you stupid sonofabitch," Cooper shot back.

"No more games," the man warned as he punched Cooper in his midsection and he folded over in pain.

In two strides, Ben was there. Grabbing the man by the collar, he yanked him off Cooper and then very quickly, very forcefully delivered three blows to the man's rib cage. He was gasping for air when Ben threw him against the wall, knocking the rest of the wind out of him. He twisted his left arm behind the man's back, then used the right arm as leverage with his own, and brought them both up under the man's chin, pressing against his windpipe. Ben shoved his right knee into the man's crotch and pushed his weight against it. It was a technique a San Antonio cop, who also happened to be a steer wrestler, had taught Ben a long time ago.

"You know what I do for fun?" Ben rasped, staring right into the glazed black eyes. "I ride bulls. And their balls are a hell of a lot bigger than yours. So I think I can bust yours with no trouble," he said, putting a little more pressure against the man's groin.

"You tell your boss that from now on he deals with me. You understand?"

The man could only manage to blink in response.

"That's good. Real good," Ben said. "Now when I turn you loose, you'd better get your ass outta here before I decide to have a little fun after all."

Very slowly, Ben eased away from the man and then spun him around, shoving him as he released him. The man staggered away, coughing as he stumbled to one knee and stayed there for a few moments as he tried to catch his breath. Ben watched warily as he awkwardly rose, and then walked haltingly away without looking back.

"Thanks, Ben," Cooper whispered.

Without a word, Ben turned and walked away.

11

Ben drove aimlessly around Miami for hours, listening to Strait and trying to clear his head. He needed to calm down. No matter how much satisfaction he had gotten by putting the fear in that thug, he knew he couldn't just go off half-cocked into this thing. One of the hardest—and best—lessons he'd had to learn was that you never got on a bull mad. The anger kept you from feeling the bull's moves. It was the mistake he had made in Vegas, and he had paid dearly for it.

He had a lot of thinking to do, and he needed to act quickly on some things before they started watching him. He knew now that he'd sent them an open invitation, they'd watch him for awhile before they made their move. That gave him a little time to take care of some business. It was almost midnight when he turned into the main gate at Southerly Park.

"Eat," Barbara ordered, putting the sandwich down in front of him.

Ben's first impulse was to push the plate away. Then his grumbling stomach reminded him he hadn't eaten since lunch with Mike almost two days ago.

"So what you're saying is that Dan got himself caught in a no-win situation with these guys," Mike said from across the table as he watched Ben now biting hungrily into the sandwich.

Ben nodded, then washed down the food with a swallow of beer. "Yeah, he was afraid for his family. With Mark, I figure it was a little bit of greed and a little bit of fear. These guys find the weak spots and then push hard to get what they want."

"Don't you think once the stewards look closely at the race film, they'll be a little suspicious about how Mark rode that race?" Barbara questioned.

"Yeah, even I thought it was a little strange how he kept Bucks on the rail and then stood up like he did," Mike added.

Ben sat back in the chair. "I plan to pay the stewards a visit and make sure they know what's been going on. And then I'm going to set these guys up."

Mike looked up from his coffee cup. "What are you talking about?"

"I have a plan. They're used to dealing with people by threatening who, and what, means something to them," Ben explained. "Well, they're fixin' to deal with someone who has nothing to lose. It's like Dan said, I'm the new kid in town. They don't know a damn thing about me. Texas might as well be a million miles away. Except for you two and Dan, no one else here knows anything about me."

"What exactly are you planning to do?" Barbara asked, her brow furrowed in concern.

Ben shifted in the chair; he knew they weren't going to like what he was going to tell them. "For your own sakes, the less you know the better. And for it to work, I'm going to need to stay away from you two for the time being."

"No weak spots to push on, huh?" Mike commented, eyeing Ben. "Are you sure you're not setting yourself up, instead of them? Why don't you just let the authorities handle it from here?"

"No. This is mine to do," Ben said deliberately. "Dan is my friend. Bucks was my horse." He paused, willing himself to stay calm. "For the first time since that damned bull, I feel like I finally have a little control over my life again. This time I can do something about what's happened."

"That's just it, Ben," Mike reasoned. "You've had so much to deal with. Why don't you give yourself a break and let someone else take care of this?"

Ben stared at him. "No."

Barbara could feel the tension between them. "Okay, okay. We're all tired. Why don't you spend the night here, Ben? Then in the morning we can all look at this with clear heads."

"I'm not going to change my mind. I'm going to do this," Ben insisted.

"Fine. But you're too tired to drive back tonight," Barbara said, taking hold of his arm. "Come on."

Mike remained silent as his wife led Ben to the guest bedroom. He knew it was pointless to argue with Ben anymore. And he was worried about his friend, worried how far he'd go to make these men pay for what they had done. He was afraid Ben might go over the edge he had been on for too long now.

When Barbara came back to the guest bedroom with the blanket, Ben was already sprawled out asleep on the bed. He had managed to pull off his boots, and his shirt was out of his jeans. It looked like that effort had drained him, for he had collapsed on the bed without even pulling back the bedspread.

Barbara draped the blanket over him. "I'm sorry about Bucks," she whispered in his ear as she bent over him and kissed him lightly on his scarred cheek. "Please be careful."

Ben reached for the doorknob while holding a full mug of steaming coffee in his other hand. Behind him, he heard the distinctive sound of the wheelchair rolling into the kitchen. Outside, the sun hadn't even broken the horizon yet.

"Off to play The Lone Ranger, huh?" Mike asked.

Ben turned to face him. "I'll be fine."

"All right, but just remember this isn't Texas and these guys don't play by your cowboy rules," Mike said quietly. "And you're wrong about not having anything to lose. You could lose your life.

"I realize that with all the hell you've been through, that probably doesn't mean much to you. But it means something to me, Barbara and the people who care about you in Texas. So keep that in mind while you're out there playing hero."

Cooper was surprised when he saw Ben saddling Reno outside the tack room. He wasn't surprised though when Ben ignored him, finished saddling the horse and left the barn to pony Succinctly.

Two hours later after Magic Beans had also been ponied, bathed, walked and returned to his stall, Ben was still silent. Cooper watched him pull the saddle off Reno and decided it was now or never.

"Ben, I don't know what to say," Cooper offered, standing in the tack room doorway.

After putting the saddle up on its stand, Ben turned on his heels. "It doesn't matter. Because there's not anything you could say that I want to hear," he said dryly. "I'm on my way to take my trainer's test, and then I'm going to get stalls at Hallandale Park. And that's all I have to say," he bluntly added, brushing shoulders with Cooper as he limped out into the shedrow.

Ben folded his hands behind his head on the pillow. He tried to concentrate on Strait singing "Am I Blue," but his mind was replaying everything that had happened in the last few days. And that afternoon, he had taken the first steps towards getting some satisfaction.

When he had finished taking the written portion of the trainer's test, he had added a note to the racing secretary that he wanted to

talk to the stewards. The racing secretary then had called in two of
the state racing stewards. They all listened intently as he told them
what had been going on, what had happened in Bucks' race, and
what he wanted to do about it. Now it was up to them to file a
report with the state racing commission, and someone from that
office would then get in touch with him.

On his way out, the racing secretary told Ben he had made a
perfect score on the trainer's test. He was now officially a trainer
and he could apply for stalls. But for the time being, he had to
play the waiting game. He had to wait for the bad guys and the
good guys to make the next moves. Damn. He hated waiting.

Patrick Sean Ryan, state investigator for the Florida Racing
Commission, looked up as his assistant walked into his office.

"Here you go, Ryan," Terri said, handing him the computer
disk. "Everything you'd ever want to know about Ben Matthews.
And I'd like to volunteer if you need help on this one. I think I'm
in love with this man."

"I thought you believed all men were scum, Terri?"

Terri laughed. "I may have just found the last perfect, decent
man in the world," she said. "So try not to screw him up, okay,
Ryan?"

He watched her sashay away, and for the hundredth time,
wondered why a beautiful woman like that had become a cop.
Ryan shook his head as he swiveled his chair around to face the
computer and popped the disk in the main drive.

"Okay, Mr. Ben Matthews, let's see what Terri finds so impressive about you," Ryan mumbled as the screen displayed the
information on the disk.

First there was the full-color computer image picture. Sure,
Terri was a sucker for a handsome face. But as Ryan scrolled up
through the dossier she had compiled on Matthews, he was beginning to wonder if this guy was for real. Third-generation
Texan...ranching family...excellent student all the way through

college...outstanding college rodeo cowboy...professional four-time world all-around cowboy...

What the hell was this guy doing training racehorses in Miami? And how had he gotten mixed up with a race-fixing ring? Then Ryan saw the newspaper microfiche clipping Terri had included:

CHAMPION COWBOY CRITICALLY
INJURED AT NATIONAL FINALS

> LAS VEGAS (AP)-Four-time
> World All-Around Champion
> Cowboy Ben Matthews was
> severely injured during the
> final round of the bull-riding
> event here last night. In a
> freak incident, the bull fell
> with Matthews, crushing him
> and then kicked him repeatedly
> before the rodeo clowns could
> distract the animal away from
> him.
>
> Matthews was rushed to Las
> Vegas Memorial Hospital, where
> he was reported in critical
> condition.

Ryan's cop mind clicked. A bull nearly killing you could change your outlook on life. Ryan looked at the date on the clipping: two years ago. Still, Miami was a long way from Texas. Terri had put in another entry under family background. Ryan read the screen: Parents-Thomas and Sara Matthews—(Deceased); Brother—Chris Matthews (Deceased). And there was another newspaper clipping.

RODEO STAR'S FAMILY
KILLED IN CAR WRECK

WACO (AP)-The family of Ben
Matthews, the four-time world
all-around champion cowboy, was
killed in a fiery wreck on I-35
late Saturday afternoon. Thomas,
52, Sara,50, and Chris,24,
Matthews were all killed when an
18-wheeler struck their truck on
the interstate twenty miles outside the city. There was an ex-
plosion on impact, which killed
the truck driver as well.

    Matthews, who was injured in
a bull-riding mishap at the National Finals a year and a half
ago, was competing in the Waco
State Finals Rodeo.

Ryan let out a breath. This man had had more than his share
of bad luck and tragedy. Once again he checked the date. Not
even a year ago yet. The screen was suddenly blank. Ben Matthews
had just disappeared after the Waco accident. Ryan sat back in the
chair as he ran his right hand through his short-cropped light red
hair. What are you doing in Miami, Ben Matthews? Maybe you
just finally cracked up? Running away from ghosts? But whatever
Matthews' reasons for being there, he had come forward to try to
make right what was wrong. That said something about the man.

Ryan backed the program up to the beginning. He wanted to
know Matthews very well before he went down to Miami. He'd
make his decision on the case after he met the man.

From the corner of his eye, Ben saw the old black man shuffling up the shedrow of his Hallandale barn. He kept tightening the screw eye to hang the stall webbing from.

"I hear you lookin' fer help," he said, coming to a wobbly standstill just outside the stall.

Ben eyed him, thinking how easy it would be for a Thoroughbred to drag the wiry old man wherever it wanted. "Think I have all the help I need."

"I'm a helluva groom. You'll be real sorry if you let me go work for someone else," he said, giving Ben a tooth-gaped grin.

Ben chuckled. "Is that so? Hmm, well, how would you feel about being my pony horse's groom?"

The old man scratched his head. "Let me see him."

Ben led him over to Reno's stall. "What do you think?"

"He's got chalky, white front feet. Can be a real problem if you don't know what 'cha doin'."

"And I suppose you do?"

The old man grinned at him again. "Those feet won't be no problem for me. I got a secret paint my daddy gave me."

"Okay, you've got yourself a job. What's your name?"

"J.B."

Ben was about to tell J.B. he could bunk down in the extra tack room when there was a commotion in the shedrow.

"Gawdamnit. Never heard of such a thing. Damn eighty degrees in March," the large man with the tan felt cowboy hat and Western cut jacket bellowed as he came toward Ben and J.B.; two smaller men in expensive suits trailed him at a safe distance. "Damn unnatural, that's what it is. You Ben Matthews?"

"Who wants to know?"

"Patrick S. Ryan," he announced, offering his hand. "Ryan Oil and Drilling. If there's oil in your ground, we'll find it and make both of us rich."

Ben tried not to wince as the large hand clamped down on his. "What can I do for you, Mr. Ryan? I don't think there's any oil here."

Ryan laughed. "No, but I hear you're the new hotshot trainer who can put a horse in the winner's circle faster than I can smell oil," he drawled. "I have a couple of high-priced two year olds up in Ocala. I was hoping you might have room for them in your stable. Finding a good, honest trainer ain't so easy these days."

Ben looked at the man a little more intently. "Sure. We could talk about it."

"All right. Meet you at eight at The Black Angus. Nothing like a good cut of beef," Ryan said with a wink. "Gotta run. Got a conference call in the limo in five minutes."

Ben watched the trio hurrying down the shedrow. Bending down, he peeked under the awning and in a few minutes saw the stretch limousine pulling away.

"What in God's heaven was that?" J.B. asked.

Straightening up, Ben shrugged. "Beats the hell outta me," he said, but he knew somebody had finally made a move.

"Hope I didn't scare you this morning," Ryan greeted as he joined Ben at the table, removing the cowboy hat and putting it down on the extra chair.

"No, actually I've known men like that," Ben said, taking a sip of the whiskey. "Just not here in Miami."

Ryan eyed the scar on Matthews' face, knowing it was a souvenir from that bull. "As I understand it, you've come across quite a few unusual characters here in Miami," he said.

"Yes, I have. Are you interested in making their acquaintance?" Ben asked, taking in just how large a man Ryan was and how he was definitely someone you'd want on your side.

"Very much so," Ryan answered. "Why don't you tell me how we might go about doing that."

They were about done with their steaks when Ben finished outlining his plan. "So what do you think?"

Ryan drank the last swallow of his second beer. "I think you've really put a lot of thought into figuring out how to nail these guys," he said, cutting up what remained of his rare steak. "But I don't want to chance that they might have a cop somewhere on the take and could run a background check on you.

"So we're going to give you a new life. From now on, you're Ben Matthews, bad-ass horse trader from Stillwater, Oklahoma. You like to gamble on the ponies, cards and just about anything else. Got a real weakness for whiskey and the ladies.

"Had a few run-ins with the law, but no convictions, since you wouldn't be able to have your trainer's license if you did. Yeah, race fixin' falls right in with your lifestyle."

Ben refilled his glass with whiskey. "I think I can be that guy without any trouble," he said. "There's just one little problem. Do I have to be from Oklahoma?"

Ryan grinned at him; he had expected Ben's reaction since there was a long history of dislike between Texans and Okies. "I'm from Tulsa. Went to the University of Oklahoma. Played linebacker for the Sooners. Boomer Sooner."

Ben couldn't help but laugh; the cop had a sense of humor. "Hook 'em, 'Horns."

After Ben left, Ryan remained at the table and scribbled in a pocket-sized notebook. Yes, indeed, Ben Matthews was for real and he'd be just fine for this operation. As a veteran cop of nearly twenty years, Ryan had looked into a lot of men's eyes; he had discovered it was where you found the truth. Matthews had never wavered. The man was as honest as he was determined. And Ryan had seen just enough anger in him to get the job done.

Despite that limp and whatever other damage that bull had done to him, Ryan had no doubts that Matthews could take care of himself if push came to shove. Once a bull rider, always a bull rider. He had known a few growing up in Oklahoma and they were a tough lot.

Matthews also seemed psychologically sound. He hadn't detected any signs that the man was mentally struggling over the loss of his family. It appeared to him that Matthews had succeeded in dealing with his grief and moved on with his life. But, still, Ryan couldn't deny something was nagging at him. Maybe it was because he remembered not even a year had gone by since the Matthews family had been killed. That really wasn't very long at all to have to come to terms with that kind of trauma. But then again, everyone dealt with grief differently.

Yeah. Matthews would do just fine. Even if he was from Texas.

Damn. All these months he had been struggling to create a new life for himself and then Ryan just hands him one. Ben poured more whiskey into the glass as he scanned the barroom. He wondered if they had followed him in here; he hoped so. He was anxious to get this show on the road.

While driving back to the hotel, he had realized it was pointless for him to try to sleep. Too wound up after meeting with Ryan, he had detoured to one of the bars he and Cooper frequented. The appropriately named Post Time Bar was a popular hangout with the racetrack crowd. Might as well start being Ben Matthews, no-account horse trader from Oklahoma. He cringed at the thought; he owed Ryan one for making him from Oklahoma.

"I told you to leave me alone," the woman sitting at the far end of the bar told the man as he pawed her. "Stop it."

Ben methodically rose from the table and walked up behind the man. "Excuse me. I think the lady wants you to leave her alone."

The man spun around."Why don't you—"

Whack. Ben punched him right smack in the nose. The man collapsed with a thud to the wooden floor, blood running from his broken nose. He didn't even try to get up; he was out cold.

"Ah, hell," Ben muttered then turned away; he had hoped for a decent brawl to take the edge off.

He had just settled back down into the chair when the hassled woman approached the table. Without a word, she bent down over him and kissed him hard and long on the mouth.

When she finally pulled away, Ben grinned at her. "A simple thank you would have done just fine."

The tall brunette smiled at him. "That was my simple thank you. If you'd let me, I'd really like to show my gratitude."

Ben thought about that for a moment; he'd always had a weakness for leggy brunettes. Hmm, what would Ben Matthews from Oklahoma do? Well, of course, he'd take the lady up on her offer. He was starting to like this guy more all the time.

On his way to the Gardner Park saddling paddock, Ben spotted Mike and Barbara. Damn. What were they doing? Didn't they believe him when he said they needed to stay away from him? He walked right past them without even the slightest acknowledgment, tightly gripping the halter and lead shank in his right hand.

Down on the track, the paddock judge walked over to where Cooper was talking to the jockey as he pulled the saddle off Mymomsluck. She had just finished second by a nose in a $35,000 claiming race.

"Dan, your mare has been claimed," the paddock judge told Cooper. "Please bring her to the paddock."

Cooper looked at him in surprise. Mymomsluck was his own horse, not a client's, and trainers rarely claimed other trainers' personal horses. Cooper followed behind the official into the paddock where the switch of owners would take place. He wasn't too surprised when he saw Ben standing there; he kept his distance.

Once the groom led the big, grey mare into the saddling stall, he slipped off the bridle as Ben put on the halter. Ben made sure he didn't make eye contact with Dan and silently led the mare past him.

Cooper stood there in the paddock, watching Ben and the mare walk toward the backside. He supposed Ben thought it only fair that he take the grey mare in response to losing Bucks. But he wondered if Ben would stop at just the grey mare. He hadn't forgotten how angry Ben had been that night when he scared the hell

out of that goon. He should probably consider himself lucky if all
Ben did was claim his horses. Cooper suddenly realized the horses
for the next race were coming into the paddock and hurried toward
the grandstand. Mike and Barbara met him at the paddock gate.

Ben was walking back to his truck after putting Mymomsluck
on a van to Hallandale when he saw the license plate. Gone from
the rear of his truck was the Texas plate. In its place was one that
read 'Oklahoma Is Ok'. That was two he owed Ryan.

"He's going to get himself killed," Cooper said worriedly after
Mike and Barbara told him what Ben was up to. "I told him these
guys play for keeps."

Mike ran a finger through the water spot the iced tea glass had
made on the restaurant table. "Well, we couldn't talk him out of
it. All we can do now is not compromise his plan and stay away
from him like he asked us to."

"Did he tell you his plan?"

"No," Barbara answered, "but I have a feeling claiming your
horse was part of it. One of the reasons he's doing this is because of
what these men put you through."

"And by claiming my horse, he makes it look like we're on the
outs and he gets them off my back, right?"

Mike nodded. "I'd say that's a fair guess."

"Damnit. I should be helping him. I started this mess."

"You have Eleanor and the girls to take care of," Barbara reminded him. "Maybe we can't help him directly, but he can't keep
us away from the racetrack. At least we can try to keep an eye on
him that way."

Over the next two weeks, Ben had claimed three more horses off
trainers. The word had spread quickly on the backside that Ben

Matthews had turned out to be something other than an easy-going cowboy. He had taken advantage of Dan Cooper's generosity and then betrayed him. His quick early success had made him arrogant and he had apparently decided he wasn't going to play by the race-trackers' rules. Intent on building a large stable, he had no qualms about where the horses came from; to hell with professional courtesy.

Ben started noticing trainers avoiding him. There had been angry words said and physical threats made by two trainers whose horses he had claimed. For the most part, his plan was working and the reactions were what he had expected. But what had surprised him was how increasingly lonely he felt.

The Post Time Bar was crowded as usual, and Ben knew a few of the trainers sitting at the bar. But other than a few cold glances, no one had even acknowledged him, much less offered an invitation to join them. Ben drained the glass and refilled it. He really did miss Mike, Barbara and Dan. That surprised him, too. He supposed he hadn't realized until now how close he had gotten to them. But that very fact was all the more reason to stay away from them. He couldn't give those bastards a chain to yank.

But he was growing impatient with the waiting game. And Ryan had warned him that they might not even make contact with him and just take their business elsewhere. Yet he was sure he had spotted one of them following him yesterday. Of course, Ryan had men keeping tabs on him, too, but this guy hadn't looked like a cop.

Ben drank the last of the whiskey and decided he had put in his obligatory bar time. Ryan had said it was important to establish a set routine for contact.

The man was peering through the window into his truck when Ben walked out into the parking lot. This was too good to pass up. Maybe it was time to send another message.

Ben pulled his right hand out of the ice bucket, flexing it several times before submerging it again. He supposed he had overdone it, but beating the hell out of that guy had definitely felt good. Maybe the boss man would take him a little more seriously now.

"My man said he almost felt sorry for the poor bastard," Ryan said to Ben two days later as they sat in his Hallandale tack room. "He was glad you didn't mistake him for one of the bad guys." Ben shrugged. "I was bored. And I thought this might get some action going."

"It might, but you need to be careful," Ryan cautioned. "This is a team effort and you won't be any good to me if you're dead."

Again Ben shrugged. "So where did you get the horses?" he asked, changing the subject. "After all, you can't just pick up colts by Mr. Prospector and Seattle Slew off the street."

"An Oklahoma buddy of mine, Bill Ketchum, has been in the Thoroughbred business a long time and he owns a farm in Ocala," Ryan explained. "I told him I needed a favor and I promised the horses would be in good hands. If anything happens to them, the state of Florida owes him a couple of million. And I figure I'll take it out of your Texas hide."

Ben grinned at him. "You Okies are prone to grand exaggerations, aren't ya?"

Putting his foot in the left stirrup, Ben eased himself up into the Western saddle that his father had given him as a college graduation present. It was the first time he had used the saddle since moving to Miami. He had been so occupied with setting up his stable at Hallandale that he had yet to pony a horse. But it was time to get back in the training routine, and he had debated whether to buy a new saddle. Then that morning, he had just hauled it out of the closet and brought it to the barn. He figured he'd give it a try on Reno's back and see how it felt. It felt like home.

12

Ben knew he should leave; he was getting real close to being drunk. And ever since meeting Mike, he had become very conscious of not driving when he had had too much whiskey. But he wasn't looking forward to going back alone to his hotel room. He scanned the barroom, hoping to spot the tall brunette.

"I just had to meet the crazy cowboy who made little boys out of Manuel and Jose," the short, dark-skinned man with a Spanish lilt to his voice said. He hovered over the table where Ben sat alone away from the barroom crowd.

Ben looked up at him and smiled. "Have a seat," he said casually, figuring the well-dressed man to be from South America.

The man accepted the invitation. "I understand you wish to do business directly with me. I can respect that."

"I don't give a damn what you respect," Ben said, still smiling. "All I care about is making money. Lots of money. And I didn't particularly like it when I found out other people were making money off my horses."

"We had previously done business with Mr. Cooper."

"Well, from here on, you do business with me."

"That is a possibility," the man said, picking an imaginary piece of lint off his sleeve. "But first, I would like you to answer a question for me. It seems everyone believes you to be from Texas, but some friends of mine tell me you are really from Oklahoma. Which is it, Mr. Matthews?"

Ben sat back in the chair; Ryan had been right to be cautious. "Funny thing about what people believe. I guess because Cooper is from Texas, everyone just assumed I was, too. Probably has something to do with people thinking all cowboys are from Texas."

"Speaking of Mr. Cooper, I see that you claimed one of his horses," the man said. "You have claimed several horses from other trainers as well. It would not seem to be a good way to treat your friends."

"The only friends I'm interested in having are the ones who can help me make money," Ben returned dryly. "If you put your horse in a claiming race, you have to be ready to lose it. I don't owe anyone anything. Business is business."

The South American stared at Ben. "Perhaps we can do business, Mr. Matthews."

"Fine. But let's get some things straight," Ben said, putting his elbows up on the table and leaning forward. "I like to gamble. So when it's not profitable for my horses to win, I want to know who is going to win. Understood?"

"That may not be possible."

"It is or we don't do business," Ben said with a smile. "And I think you know we could do very good business together. I would be in it for the money, not because you're threatening me. Wouldn't it be nice to work with someone who thinks like you do for a change?"

The man laughed. "You are an interesting man, Mr. Matthews. Very interesting, indeed," he said, getting to his feet. "I will think about our little talk and get back to you."

"Oh, there's one more thing," Ben said. "Don't send any more of your goons. I do business with you and only you."

Again, the man laughed. "I will be in touch very soon."

"Oh, Lordy, looka here who's comin'," J.B. said, holding Reno while Ben sponged the horse down.

Ben looked up to see Ryan approaching. "Go ahead and give
him a couple turns around the shedrow, J.B.," he said, and the old
man shuffled away, mumbling to himself.

"Ben, my boy, how are my million dollar babies doin'?" Ryan
asked loudly, slapping Ben hard on the back.

Staggering forward a few steps, Ben cast Ryan a corner-of-the-
eye glance. "Just fine, Mr. Ryan. Come on, I want to show you
something on the Mr. Prospector colt."

"Now I hope this isn't bad news," Ryan drawled, following
Ben down the shedrow and into the horse's stall.

Squatting down next to the horse's front legs, Ben ran his hand
down the right one. "Oh, it's nothing serious. He just popped a
little splint here."

"Hmm, I can see that," Ryan said. "Nice show you put on last
night," he added quietly.

"I'd like to just slow down with him and I think he'll be fine,"
Ben returned. "I hope your boys are on him."

"Absolutely. I absolutely agree with you," Ryan said as he
backed up against the stall wall. "Mr. Ramon Escobar is being
covered like Oklahoma red dirt on a Texas longhorn steer."

"I figure once the Hallandale meet starts next week, we'll be in
business," Ben said as he stood up and looked over the horse's back
at Ryan.

"Well, from here on, don't push it. I don't want Escobar
getting suspicious and deciding a dead cowboy is the best
cowboy."

Ben swished the whiskey around in the glass. Hell, it wouldn't
be long now and he'd be in the race-fixing business. Damn. This
wasn't exactly what he'd had in mind when he moved to Miami.
But it was definitely a change of lifestyle. He wondered if Scott
and Lisa would believe him when he told them this story one day.
Of course, he was assuming he was going to live to tell the story.
As far as everyone else was concerned, there seemed to be some

question about that. Ryan kept telling him not to push too hard. Mike had stopped just short of saying he had a death wish.

Mike had been right about his life not meaning much to him these past months. But he didn't think he was trying to get himself killed. What if it did happen? It would definitely solve his problems. No more grief. No more guilt. No more pain.

But what about Scott and Lisa? Would he want them to go through more of that, too? Would he want their last memories of him to be how he had left Texas and ignored them for months?

"Hello. This is the Matthews Ranch. Where you, too, can learn to be a rodeo cowboy and bust your butt at the same time."

The unfamiliar voice caught Ben off guard; he heard laughter in the background. "Uh—is Scott there?"

"Sure. Who's calling?"

"Tell him it's Ben."

"Okay, just a second. Hey, Scott, it's for you. Somebody named Ben."

Scott looked up at Lisa from across the dinner table. She smiled at him as he hurriedly pushed away from the table.

"I'll take it in the den," Scott said as he headed down the hallway, going straight to the phone on the desk. "Okay," he said and heard the kitchen phone being hung up. "Ben?"

"Yeah. Who answered the phone?"

"Oh, that was Tommy. He's one of the UT kids staying over with us for the weekend," Scott explained, sitting down in the leather swivel chair.

"Some sense of humor."

"Yeah. He keeps us on our toes. But he's a good kid. You'd like him."

"So, I guess the deal with UT is working out okay, huh?"

"It's great, Ben," Scott said excitedly. "We've got a good program. The kids work hard, but we have a lot of fun, too. We have a little rodeo every Saturday and there's never a dull moment.

The San Antonio paper is sending out a reporter and a photographer to do a story on us."

Ben chuckled. "Slow down, Scott. I get the picture."

"Guess I was rambling on. It's just there's so much to tell you," Scott said, fidgeting in the chair.

"You're doing a damn good job," Ben said quietly. After a slight pause, he added, "And thanks for sending me Chris' horse. I named him Reno."

Scott felt something catch in his throat.

"We were a hell of a roping team. We would have been world champs," Ben said. "You know that, don't you?"

Scott swallowed. "Yeah," he managed. "Ben..."

"I don't know, Scott," Ben said quickly, answering Scott's unspoken question of if he was ever coming home. "Believe me, I wish I did."

"Are you okay?"

"Yeah," Ben answered, trying to convince himself as much as Scott. "And I don't want you and Lisa to worry if you don't hear from me for awhile, okay?"

"Ben..."

"Please, Scott, I'm doing the best I can," Ben said, feeling his emotions getting the best of him. "I have to go now. Please don't worry."

Scott heard the click; somebody might as well have kicked him in the gut. *No, not yet. There's still so much to say.*

Tommy suddenly looked up from his plate. "Ben? As in Ben Matthews?"

Lisa nodded. "The one and only," she answered him and the other boys, who were now looking at her, too.

"Ah, damnit. I can't believe how stupid I am sometimes," Tommy wailed.

"I can," Lisa said, tousling his hair as she walked past him and toward the den.

Scott was still sitting in the chair. He had finally put the phone down, but didn't seem to have the energy to get up.

Lisa sat down on the arm of the couch across from him. "What did he say?"

"Not much."

"How did he sound?"

"Tired." He paused, then added, "He named him Reno."

"What?"

"He named Chris' horse Reno."

Sliding off the couch arm, Lisa went to him. She leaned over and kissed him lightly on the lips, then walked away. As she headed for the bedroom, she couldn't help but feel hopeful. Maybe now she and Scott could go on with their lives.

Ben gulped down the glassful of whiskey. Damn. He never should have made that phone call. All it had done was stir up all the pain he had finally gotten some relief from these past few weeks.

Ben Matthews from Oklahoma didn't have to deal with that pain; he didn't have to feel like he owed any explanations to anybody. He just lived from day to day; no past and no future to worry about. His only concern was how much money he was going to make with this race-fixing scam. And not get killed doing it. That's what he needed to focus on. Nothing—and no one—else but that.

Damn. The walls were closing in on him. He needed to get out of this room.

The quiet, scarred cowboy had drifted off to sleep with his left arm draped across her breasts and his left leg intertwined with hers. The tall brunette gently moved his arm downward as she pulled the blanket over both of them. He hadn't told her his name or asked hers, but she knew who he was. She doubted there was a pro who worked the racetrack crowd who didn't know who Ben

Matthews was. After their first night together, when he had decked that scum who was bothering her, she couldn't help but brag to her friends about the identity of her latest client.

She ran her fingers through his wavy, black hair and kissed him on the forehead. It seemed odd to her that such a good-looking man was always alone. So who was Lisa? He had whispered the name two of the times they were together. Not that it bothered her, she was used to men calling her by their wives' or girlfriends' names. But whoever this Lisa was, he was obviously still in love with her.

"Secretariat is coming back," J.B. said, petting Magic Beans on the nose while he held him by the halter.

Ben looked up at him from where he sat in the stall's straw bedding, painting liniment on the horse's front legs. "What?"

J.B. gave him a look of exasperation. "I said, Secretariat is coming back. He told me so."

With a sigh, Ben started putting the leg wrap on the horse's left leg. His aspirin-whiskey morning tonic was beginning to wear off and he could feel a headache coming on. Maybe if he just ignored him, J.B. wouldn't say anything more. He didn't want to lose his temper with the old man, who had turned out to be a fairly good hand. Between J.B., the two Puerto Ricans who cleaned the stalls, and himself, the morning's training routine went smoothly. He and Ryan had agreed he needed to get by with a minimum crew; fewer people to worry about snooping around.

"You think I'm crazy just like everybody else does, don't you?"

Ben crawled over to the horse's right leg. "No, J.B., I don't think you're crazy. Just a little confused. Secretariat is at stud in Kentucky and I don't think he'll be coming back to the races."

"Well, you and everybody else don't know what I know. Big Red himself told me he was coming back and fer me to watch fer him."

Ben shook his head as he brushed on the liniment. "He did, huh?"

"Yes, siree, he did that time when Eddie—and I mean Eddie Sweat, he was Big Red's groom—let me rub on him when he was here at Hallandale," J.B. insisted. "I tell you, that big red hoss was something special. He was magic."

Ben slowly got to his feet. "You sure won't get an argument from me or anyone else about that. Secretariat will always be remembered as one of the greatest racehorses of all time," he said, patting Magic Beans on the neck. "But his racing days are long over and he's not coming back."

"Hmph, you'll see," J.B. said, turning away from the stall door. "And you better just be ready to help me with him when he does come back."

Ben leaned up against Magic Beans, burying his face in the horse's mane. "Please, would somebody put me out of my misery," he muttered, hearing the sound of a van pulling up outside his barn.

By the time Ben got down to the end of the shedrow, the van driver was lowering the rear door and a grey Mercedes Benz sedan was driving up. The car had tinted glass all the way around, and Ben was surprised when Escobar emerged from the backseat. The driver, who Ben was sure was the first goon he had roughed up, started to get out, too, but Escobar motioned him back in.

"Good morning, Mr. Matthews. I bring you some of my finest racehorses," Escobar said with a smile and a handshake. "I will rest easy knowing they are in your capable hands. I expect to be winning races very soon."

Ben smiled at him. "I'll do my best," he said, careful not to use the South American's name that he knew only because of Ryan. "I'm sure you brought all their necessary paperwork."

"Absolutely, Mr. Matthews," Escobar said, pulling a large envelope from inside his silk-lined suit jacket and handing it to Ben. "I am sure you will be very happy with their quality."

Ben watched as the six horses were led off the van, and he silently directed the handlers to the empty stalls at the far end of the shedrow. "If they run as good as they look, we'll both be very happy, Sir."

"Oh, please, call me Ramon. After all, we are business partners now."

After Escobar had left with a promise he'd be in touch soon, Ben carefully inspected each horse to make sure it matched the paperwork. He was positive the registration papers and racing records were forgeries. But they were damned good ones. The horses were all listed as owned by Tri-South Stables Inc.

Just as he finished checking out the last horse, Ben looked up toward the rafters of the barn. He knew there was a small remote camera there and that Ryan had likely observed Escobar's surprise appearance. Ben flashed a Texas cowboy smile. That ought to irritate Ryan.

"I was half expecting you to drive up in your limo, and then I would have had both of you in the shedrow," Ben said, laughing as he and Ryan sat at the bar.

"Yeah, you believe the balls of that guy? He must really like you to come himself like that," Ryan said. "And what an original idea, bringing you horses to train."

Ben turned sideways on the barstool. "I don't know if it's scary or funny that the good guys and the bad guys came up with the same idea."

"I never said they were stupid," Ryan commented. "But they are greedy. And that's why we'll get 'em. This whole setup is so sweet and Escobar will take a big bite."

"Hope you got everything on tape this morning?" Ben asked, trying not to grin.

"Sure did. Including you hamming it up for the camera," Ryan replied matter-of-factly. "You damn Texas cowboys are so cocky."

Ben raised his glass. "Well, you know what they say—if you've got it, flaunt it," he said, giving Ryan the same smile he had that morning to the camera. "Of course, you Okies wouldn't know about that."

Ben ambled up the tree-lined path toward the backside entrance to the Hallandale grandstand. One of the reasons he had decided to get stalls at Hallandale was because of the beauty of the track. There were actually trees and grass, not just asphalt and concrete. The saddling paddock was practically a park, complete with fountains, palm trees, flowers and benches. And the grandstand actually was grand with its rose-colored stone Spanish architecture whispering of another time and place.

Ben had purposely waited until he knew the horses for the third race were out of the paddock and on the track. He didn't want to risk any chance encounter with Mike, Barbara and Dan; First And Ten had shipped in from Canton to run in the third race.

After placing a sizable bet on First And Ten, Ben slowly made his way through the packed-house crowd. It was a beautiful spring day, and no doubt on this first day of April, there would be many fools who would lose their money betting on the ponies. Ben hoped First And Ten's race wasn't one fixed by Escobar. He would like the horse to win for his friends. Of course, at 50-1 he wouldn't mind the horse winning for him, too.

The horses broke from the gates. First And Ten ran the same kind of race he had the day Ben had cashed the big tickets on him. That had been way back in November, and gelding the horse had definitely improved his attitude. He crossed the finish line an easy five-length winner.

Ben couldn't help but smile as he saw Dan, then Mike and Barbara, heading for the winner's circle. And yet he felt a little sad that he wasn't with them. He turned away and went to cash his tickets. Remember, he told himself, money—not friends—was all that mattered to Ben Matthews from Oklahoma.

It was two days later when Escobar paid Ben another visit that it became evident they were all going to be making plenty of money soon.

"How did you get this so early?" Ben asked when Escobar handed him the overnight entry sheet for Friday's race card. "We don't usually see it until early afternoon."

Escobar smiled at him. "Just one of the many advantages of being partners with me, Mr. Matthews."

Scanning the sheet, Ben saw Magic Beans had drawn into the seventh race and Tango Dancer, one of the Tri-South Stable horses, was on the also eligible list for the eighth. "My horse is sittin' on a win," he said.

"Yes, indeed, and that is what will happen," Escobar said. "Also, there will be a scratch and my horse will get in the race. He, too, is—as you say—sitting on a win."

Now Ben was sure Escobar had someone on the take in the racing secretary's office, as well as several jockeys and at least one other trainer. "Any other little tidbits you'd like to share with me? Remember, I like to gamble and cash big bets."

Escobar nodded. "I remember. I understand you cashed a big bet on one of Cooper's horses on opening day."

Ben shrugged and was glad he hadn't risked talking to his friends. "I know the horse. Just because Cooper and I aren't friends anymore doesn't mean I should pass up a chance at some easy money."

"I like your sense of priorities, Mr. Matthews," Escobar said. "And because I like you, I will tell you the number four horse will win the third race and the number six horse will win the tenth."

Magic Beans was so ready to win after being pulled his previous two races that he won by three lengths at 25-1. As Escobar predicted, Tango Dancer did draw in and he, too, won at odds of 50-1. The other two horses Escobar had touted also won at more moderate odds. But they won.

Ben bet on all of them, using money from the special bank account Ryan had set up for him. Then he deposited the winnings, the marked cashed tickets and his share of the purse money back into the account.

"Well, looks like the party has begun," Ryan said, joining Ben at the table.

"Yeah."

Ryan gave him a sidelong glance. "What's eatin' you? I thought you would have been happy the show's finally on the road."

"I know my horse was ready to win, and it makes me mad that he did only because that scum thought the odds were good enough," Ben said, then drained the glass.

Ryan eyed him worriedly. "Now you knew the rules going in. You knew we were going to have to play his game for awhile. Hell, it was your idea. Don't let your Texas temper get you in trouble."

Ben watched the amber-colored whiskey filling up the glass then silently drank. He knew Ryan was right, but Magic Beans' race had made him think of Bucks. And how that magnificent animal had died trying to win a race Escobar had decided he wouldn't.

"Hey, Ben, you with me? Remember, the no-account horse trader from Oklahoma should be enjoying this. He made a lot of money today."

Bringing the glass back down to the table, Ben nodded. "Yeah, you're right. Did the recording system pick up everything between me and Escobar in the tack room?"

Ryan grinned. "Loud and clear. Every time Escobar walks into your shedrow, he's a star in the movies," he said, chuckling, then added, "I'm going to have to go back to Tallahassee for awhile. But my people will stay in place and back you up if you need any help. Just try to behave yourself, okay?"

Ben smiled at him. "I wouldn't think of doin' anything else. Besides, without you around to irritate, it'll be kinda boring."

13

By the third week in April, Ben was the leading trainer at Hallandale, and the special account had nearly three-quarters of a million dollars in it. Escobar was a happy man and as far as he could see, so was his partner. With Ryan gone, Ben's isolation was complete and he had slipped into his Oklahoma alter ego whole-heartedly. His nights were spent getting drunk, starting fights or playing in the high-stakes poker game that Escobar got him into. He also remained a regular customer of the tall brunette.

Thanks largely to his aspirin-whiskey tonic, he always made it to the barn in the morning. But his disposition kept everyone except J.B. at a distance.

It was the limp that made Barbara do a double take as she had glanced up from studying the racing newspaper. She squeezed Mike's arm and motioned slightly to where the two men were talking at the far end of the grandstand. After only catching glimpses of him whenever they were at the races, it was the first time in weeks they had seen Ben at a standstill. They didn't like what they saw.

He had at least a three-day old beard, was in sore need of a haircut, and had lost weight. He looked like he hadn't had a good night's sleep in a month. When he walked away from the short, dark-skinned man, his limp was more pronounced than ever.

"Ben, I know you're in there, so you might as well let me in," Barbara said after he didn't respond to her knocking. "I'm not going away."

A few moments later, he finally opened the door. "You shouldn't be here."

She walked past him and into the room. "We thought a woman coming to your door would draw less attention than a man in a wheelchair," Barbara explained as he shut the door.

"It doesn't matter. You still shouldn't have come." Ben sat back down at the table where he had been playing solitaire and drinking; Strait was singing in the background.

Walking over to the tape deck, Barbara ejected the cassette, then sat down across from him. "You look terrible," she said bluntly.

Ben glanced up at her. "Thanks. If that's what you came to tell me, you can go now."

"How much longer is this going to go on?"

"I don't know. It's not my call to make."

"And you're in it until the end, right?"

Ben only nodded in reply as he put down another card. Barbara reached out and covered his hand with hers.

"Mike and I are worried about you, Ben," she said quietly. "We miss you."

Her words and the feel of her hand on his made Ben uncomfortable. He had no need for this; it only confused things and made it harder to keep doing what he had to until Ryan grabbed Escobar.

"There's nothing to worry about," Ben said dryly, not looking at her as he pulled his hand away.

Barbara watched him flipping over the cards. She wasn't getting through to him. Mike was waiting in the van and she knew it was pointless to try to talk to him anymore. Silently, she rose from the table and walked to the door.

Just as she reached for the doorknob, she remembered something and turned halfway toward him. "Mike said to tell you that even The Lone Ranger had Tonto."

When there was no response from him, Barbara reluctantly left. She didn't know that what she had said made Ben smile ever so slightly.

Lisa closed the kitchen door behind her, walked to the table and put her briefcase down. That's when she saw the single red rose on the table. Smiling, she carefully picked it up and read the note attached to it. *Meet me in the dining room.*

Taking the rose with her, she hurried out of the kitchen and down the hallway to the little-used formal dining room. "Scott, what's going on?"

When there was no answer, she slowly pushed the slightly ajar door open. "Scott, what are you..." Her voice trailed off as she stared in amazement at the room.

It was aglow with candlelight and adorned with bouquets of red roses. The dining room table was set for two in fine china and crystal. Platters of food surrounded a sterling silver ice bucket with a bottle of champagne in it. Soft music from the stereo system completed the romantic setting.

Still speechless, Lisa looked at Scott. He grinned at her from across the table.

"Like it?" he asked, walking around the table toward her.

"I love it," she said, hugging him. "But what's the occasion? I know I didn't forget my own birthday."

Scott chuckled, cupping her face in his hands. "I just wanted you to know how much I love you," he said softly, then passionately kissed her.

When their lips parted, Lisa gazed into those kind eyes of his. And in that moment, she knew without a doubt that Scott truly did love her. Once again, she felt hope welling in her. Hope that the pain of the past year was behind them. Maybe tonight was the night he'd ask her to marry him.

"I have another surprise for you," Scott said, pulling a chair out from the table for her. "Have a seat, ma'am."

Lisa could feel her heart pounding; she laid the rose on the table. Turning away from her, Scott opened the hutch door and reached in. When he faced her again, he had a small jewelry box in his hand.

Disappointment washed over Lisa. The box was long and narrow; it wasn't the right shape to hold an engagement ring. Slowly, Scott opened it and she couldn't help but be mesmerized. The box held a stunning emerald and diamond necklace.

"It's beautiful," she said softly.

"I thought you'd like it," Scott said, handing her the box.

"Would you please put it on me?"

"My pleasure, ma'am." He carefully removed the necklace from the box and slipped behind her.

Lisa reached back and lifted her long, auburn hair as he placed the necklace around her neck. When she felt the clasp against the nape of her neck, she let her hair tumble down her back. Looking down, she gently fingered the necklace; the candlelight reflected softly off the emeralds and diamonds. It wasn't what she had hoped for, but it was beautiful.

"Thank you," she said as she rose to her feet to meet him as he came around to face her. "I love you, Scott Barnes."

Scott felt his heart soar. He took her in his arms and they kissed.

Ryan stared in concern at Ben, sitting across from him at the restaurant table. "Damnit, Texas, what have you been doing since I've been gone? You look like hell."

Ben took a long sip of the whiskey. "Our boy Escobar has been keeping me real busy."

"Yeah, I checked the account," Ryan said. "He's a greedy little s.o.b., and he's sure taking full advantage of the situation."

"It's what we wanted, right?"

"Absolutely."

"Then you should be able to nail his hide but good, right?"

"That's the plan," Ryan said, studying his friend. He now realized the toll the scam was exacting on Ben and made a quick decision. "In fact, I think we have more than enough evidence right now to put Escobar away for a long time."

Ben was suddenly uneasy. "What are you saying?"

"I think it's time to put an end to this little show. It's time to pick up Escobar."

Ben didn't know why, but he felt a twinge of panic. "Are you sure it's not too soon?"

"No, it's time."

"I want to be in on it," Ben said, looking straight at Ryan. "I want to be there when you pick him up."

Ryan met his gaze. "I don't think that's such a good idea, Texas," he said calmly. "It would be best if Escobar didn't know you helped set him up."

"Hell, Ryan, he's going to figure it out pretty quick anyhow."

"Maybe. But I'd just as soon not risk it."

Ben put his forearms up on the table and leaned forward. "The way I look at it, you wouldn't even have Escobar where you want him if it wasn't for me," he said quietly. "And what I want is the satisfaction of seeing that bastard's face when you take him down. I want Escobar to know that I set him up."

The two men, who had become friends, stared at each other. Finally, it was Ryan who broke the stalemate with a sigh of frustration.

"All right, Texas, maybe we can work something out."

"I'm listening."

Ryan ran a hand through his hair. "Here's the deal," he said. "You call Escobar and set up a meeting. Tell him you've got this great idea for a new scam that's gonna make both of you a ton of money."

"So far, so good," Ben said, relaxing back into the chair.

"Tell him to meet you up at the grandstand during the races," Ryan said. "I want to pick him up in full view of everyone, good and bad. It's a good way to send a message."

"Sounds good to me."

"But there's a catch."

"What?"

"When Escobar shows up, you stay out of sight."

"No."

"Listen to me, Texas," Ryan said sternly. "This way, you get to be there when we pull our little surprise on Escobar—and maybe I won't have to take you home in a pine box."

Ben glared at him, but this time, Ryan was unrelenting.

"You either take the deal or I'll just pick up Escobar without your help at all," Ryan threatened.

Ben thought about that for a moment. "All right, Okie, we'll do it your way," he conceded, then added with a small smile, "But just in case things get outta hand, I'd like something a little nicer than a pine box."

Ryan laughed. The cowboy hadn't lost his sense of humor.

J.B. looked up at Ben. "Are you sure you can handle feeding all by yourself this afternoon?"

"I'm pretty sure I can, J.B.," Ben said, draping an arm around his shoulders and gently directing him down the shedrow. "You haven't had any time off since you started working for me. Now I want you to go on and have a good time."

"But I just don't feel right leaving you by yourself," J.B. protested. "You gave them Puerto Rican boys off, too."

Ben reached in his front jeans' pocket and pulled out a money clip. "It'll be fine, J.B.," he said as he peeled away three one hundred dollar bills. "Here, you go buy that new pair of boots you've been wanting. Then catch a bus and go visit that cousin of yours that you're always talkin' about."

J.B. reluctantly took the money and stuffed it in his shirt pocket.

He looked at Ben one more time, then turned and shuffled away. Ben could hear him muttering to himself as he did. Ben looked up the shedrow, empty except for a couple of the horses hanging their heads out of the stall. He hurriedly limped toward the tack room; he still had a few things to take care of.

Ryan directed his men to spots around the grandstand. Just in case Escobar tried to bolt, he didn't want to chance him getting away. He glanced around, looking for Ben; he wasn't anywhere in sight. Good, he thought in relief. Maybe for once that stubborn cowboy would actually listen to him.

Ben heard the limousine pulling up to the barn. He quickened his stride.

"Go take care of that errand and then pick me up here in about an hour," Escobar told his driver.

The man nodded, then drove away. Escobar turned and smiled at Ben, who was standing there just outside the barn. Ben smiled back at him.

"By the look on your face, this plan of yours must really be something special," Escobar said as he and Ben began walking down the shedrow.

"I think you're going to be very pleased with it," Ben said as they reached the tack room.

Ben motioned for Escobar to enter and then quickly stepped in behind him. Reaching back, he locked the door.

"So tell me how you will make us both very rich," Escobar said as he turned to face Ben.

Ben swung at him, hitting him full force in his jaw. Stunned, Escobar staggered back a few steps and Ben hit him again in the face. Escobar dropped limply to the floor. Reaching down, Ben lifted him up by the lapels of his silk jacket, slammed him into the wall and held him there.

Escobar struggled to catch his breath, tasting the blood in his mouth and felt it running from his nose. He blinked to clear his blurred vision and found himself staring into Ben's cold, grey eyes.

"This is my plan," Ben said, his face only inches from Escobar's. "To make you feel what Dan Cooper felt like when you threatened his family. To make you hurt like my horse did when he broke his legs because of you."

Escobar swallowed the bile coming up his throat. And for the first time in his life, he was afraid.

Ryan paced up and down the grandstand. The horses for the last race were going into the starting gates and still no sign of Escobar—or Ben. Damnit. That Texas cowboy had no patience and if he was anywhere around, he would have shown himself by now. But in a sickening instant, Ryan knew Ben wasn't there because Escobar wasn't coming to the grandstand. In anger, Ryan signaled for his men to follow him.

Tires screeched on the asphalt, car doors slammed and men appeared in the shedrow. Ben made eye contact with Ryan, and the big man motioned for his men to stay back.

"What the hell have you done, Texas?" Ryan asked angrily as he strode toward Ben, who was standing just outside the last stall at the end of the shedrow.

Ben flashed him his Texas cowboy smile, then nodded to the stall. Ryan looked in and stared in disbelief at what he saw. Hanging upside down from a rope over a rafter was Escobar. His hands were tied behind his back; his face was bloodied, bruised and his right eye was swollen shut.

"Damnit, Texas. What a mess."

"Yeah, I know. It's not some of my best roping work, but it was the best I could do with what I had," Ben said, shaking his head. "Do you know how hard it is to find a good rope in Miami?"

It was two days later when the emptiness began to settle in on Ben. For months, he had focused on pretending to be someone else and making Escobar pay for what he had done. Now that it was over, he wasn't sure what to do next. He wasn't sure he could handle going back to being himself.

Ben was unsaddling Reno when Ryan came strolling up the shedrow. The big man stopped to say something to J.B., and the two of them laughed.

Ryan was still chuckling as he walked up to Ben. "You know, Texas, it wouldn't hurt you to shave once and awhile," he said, taking note that his friend still looked a little ragged.

"I don't know," Ben mused as he ran his hand across his chin. "I'm kinda gettin' used to it. And the women seem to like it, too."

Ryan snickered. "Then maybe I'll grow a beard," he said. "I just came by to tell you that I'm checking Escobar out of the hospital today. Of course, his arm—the one you broke in two places—will be in a cast for a couple of months."

Ben didn't respond to the comment. "What happens next?"

"He's going to be locked up until his trial," Ryan answered. "We'll send a van to confiscate his horses in a couple of days. Bill Ketchum said you can keep training his horses if you want to."

Ben nodded, trying to stifle the anxiety building within. He turned away and finished undoing the saddle girth.

"I'm probably spittin' in the wind here," Ryan said. "But it might be a good idea if you got the hell out of Dodge. We're gonna do our best to keep Escobar isolated, but he still might manage to arrange some payback."

Ben looked at him. "I'll be fine, Okie."

Ryan regarded him for a moment. "Yeah, I know," he said as he offered his hand. "We made a hell of a team, Texas."

"Yeah, I guess we did all right." Ben shook his hand. "Hook 'em 'Horns."

"Boomer Sooner," Ryan countered, then added as he turned away, "I'll be in touch."

Ben waited until Ryan was out of sight, then pulled the saddle off Reno and carried it into the tack room. When he turned back around after putting it down on the saddle rack, J.B. was leading the horse away. He pushed the door shut and sat down wearily in the chair, propping his feet up on the wooden desk.

As he leaned back in the chair, his gaze strayed up to the wall calendar hanging above the desk. April was a blur; the days and weeks had just flowed one into the other. April? Ben felt the panic gripping him as he stared at tomorrow's date. It was Chris' birthday.

14

Lisa took a sip of the wine and looked across the table at Scott. He had driven into San Antonio to meet her for dinner at their favorite restaurant. They had decided it was how they wanted to spend Chris' birthday.

"Remember the time Chris filled Ben's brand new snakeskin boots with whipped cream?" Lisa asked and saw Scott's eyes brighten at the memory.

"Yeah, you could hear Ben bellowing all the way to San Antonio when he slipped his foot in that boot," Scott recalled as they laughed. "And how about when he made a pinata out of Ben's favorite shirt and lucky hat?"

Lisa wiped away a tear of laughter from her eye. "I thought Ben was going to have a calf when we walked in the barn that morning and saw that thing hanging from the rafters." They both broke up laughing again.

After a few minutes, their laughter slowly subsided and Lisa saw the sadness come into Scott's eyes. She reached across the table and took his hand in hers. They sat there in silence with their memories of a special young man who had died much too soon.

Ben got through Chris' birthday the only way he knew how. For the first few drinks, he was mad at himself for resorting to getting drunk. But he didn't know what else to do. The race-fixing scam was over and Escobar was locked up. He just couldn't deal with remembering Chris' last birthday, with remembering the last time he had been with his family.

He was about half-drunk when the tall brunette showed up. A few drinks later, they headed to her place. It was the middle of the afternoon the next day when he woke up in her bed.

Even if it hadn't been too late to worry about the horses, he'd never made it to the barn. He spent the rest of the day throwing up what he was sure was all of his bodily fluids. By the time he made it back to his hotel, he had just enough strength left to shower and collapse into bed.

It had been a hell of a way to celebrate his kid brother's birthday. And he was ashamed that he hadn't had the courage to face the day sober.

"What's the matter with you?" J.B. asked as Ben cinched up Reno.

"What are you talkin' about?"

"Well, the way you been draggin' that leg of yours around, I figure there must be something wrong with you," J.B. said. "Maybe you puttin' in too much time with the women."

Ben shook his head. "Why don't you quit your jabbering and go get Succinctly ready for me to pony," he said, trying to sound mad. "Now, go on and get that horse."

Ben waited until J.B. had ducked into the filly's stall before he tried to mount Reno. It took him two attempts before he was able to get his left foot in the stirrup; he grimaced as he put his weight on his left leg. Once in the saddle, he shifted over to the right, and Reno moved in confusion beneath him.

"I know, you're wondering what the hell I'm doing up here,"

Ben said, patting the horse on the neck. "It's a long story. I'll tell you about it one day."

Damn. J.B. had been right. He had been limping worse than ever, and it wasn't getting any better. At first he thought it was just a couple of those bad days he got every now and then. But each day the leg hurt more; he was having to drink an aspirin-whiskey tonic in the afternoon as well as in the morning.

"Here's your hoss, massa," J.B. said, handing him the lead shank that was hooked to Succinctly's halter.

Ben scowled at the old black man and then urged Reno forward.

When Mike opened the kitchen door, he was a little surprised to find Ben leaning back against its frame.

"Hey, Tonto, think you could give this busted-up cowboy one of your massages?" Ben asked sheepishly.

Mike grinned. "What's it worth to you?"

"Hmm, how about a high-mileage pickup truck?"

"Yeah, that's just what I need," Mike said as he put the wheel-chair in reverse. "Get your sorry ass in here."

Mike ran his hands over Ben's slightly swollen leg. "Tell me what it feels like."

"It feels like it weighs a ton. I swear I can feel every piece of metal in there," Ben said, wincing as Mike's fingers dug into his knotted muscles.

"How long has it been swelling up like this?"

"Ah—ouch. The last couple of weeks."

"Weeks? Geez, you've been like this for weeks?" Mike said incredulously. "That day we saw you at Hallandale, I thought you were limping more than usual. That's one of the reasons Barbara went up to check on you."

"Where is Barbara?"

"She had to go to Ocala to pick up a client's horses."

"I owe her an apology. I wasn't very nice to her that day."

Mike shrugged. "Don't worry about it. She understood," he said. "So, can I assume since you're here that it's over? The bad guys have been caught?"

"The one that matters has."

"Why didn't they pick up all of them?"

"I didn't ask. Guess the cops figured without the head guy, the others will just fall by the wayside."

Mike reached over for a towel and handed it to Ben. "Do any of them suspect you were helping the cops?"

"Maybe. But I don't think it's anything to worry about," Ben replied. "Hey, why did you give me this towel?"

Mike grinned mischievously. "I thought you might want to bite down on it."

"Oh, hell, the hip pull," Ben said with a moan as he lay back down on the bench and covered his face with the towel.

"It has to be the humidity," Mike suddenly said as they sat in the hot tub on the back deck.

"What?" Ben asked, not bothering to open his eyes; he hadn't been this relaxed in months.

"It's the humidity that's making your leg hurt and swell up."

"We have humidity in Texas."

"Not like in Miami," Mike insisted. "Remember, this is a city built on water."

"Oh, great. So what you're telling me is that I now live in the most humid place in the world? And I can expect my leg to feel like crap for the next six months?"

"You got it, cowboy."

"You're such a good friend."

"I know."

Ben pushed the plate away as he swallowed the last bite of the roast beef sandwich. "When does school start?"

"Next week," Mike answered as he refilled their glasses with iced tea. "I'm really looking forward to it. It'll be good to feel productive again. I guess I hadn't realized what a routine I had settled into these last couple of years."

Ben took a drink of the tea. "Well, you've had a lot to deal with. You deserved a break from life."

Mike looked at him. "Yeah, I guess if anyone knows about that, you do, right?" Ben glanced away. "So, how are you doing?"

Ben's first impulse was to lie and tell Mike he was fine, but he knew his friend wouldn't buy it. "Not so good," he admitted, looking out the sliding glass doors to where the sun was setting. "It's been a year. A year..."

"And it still hurts like the day it happened," Mike said, finishing Ben's thought.

"Yeah," Ben said with a weary sigh. "And no matter what I do, it just keeps coming back."

"Miracle cure."

"What?"

Mike rolled himself slightly away from the table. "When I was in rehab therapy, I couldn't wait to get in this wheelchair," he explained. "I thought when I did, then I wouldn't have to admit I was paralyzed. But the therapist warned me that a wheelchair was no miracle cure.

"It could make me more mobile, but it could never take the place of my legs. And the sooner I accepted that reality, the better off I'd be. There was no miracle cure for me, Ben, and I don't think there's one for you, either."

Ben stared at him. "You think I've been looking for the easy way out of this?"

"Not exactly, considering how you keep punishing yourself for something that wasn't your fault," Mike replied. "But at the same time, you wouldn't mind if someone or something put you out of your misery."

"We've had this conversation before."

"Yeah, but I didn't like the way it ended."

"All right, go ahead. I'm listening."

"Since you've convinced yourself that a terrible accident was your fault, then take it a step further—and forgive yourself."

Ben looked away. "I can't."

"You're going to have to find a way to," Mike said matter-of-factly. " Did you ever really get over what that bull did to you?"

Ben swallowed; his throat was suddenly very dry. "No."

"Well, you're never going to get over losing your family, either," Mike said sadly. "You're just going to have to find a way to live with it."

Ben felt himself shudder; that smothering tightness was back. He knew what Mike had said was true. It was the truth that had made him run. And it was the truth that was haunting him now.

"I gotta go," Ben said as he stood up, and as he headed out of the room, added, "I'll talk to ya soon."

Mike watched his friend disappear down the hallway. "Damn stubborn Texas cowboy," he muttered.

Succinctly won her race on opening day at Canton by two widening lengths. But anyone watching Ben would have thought the filly had lost. He went through the motions of going down to the track and led her into the winner's circle. Then he handed the lead shank to the Puerto Rican groom and headed back to the grandstand. He had some time to kill before shipping the filly back to Hallandale.

Getting himself a beer, Ben sat down at one of the umbrella-covered tables. Ever since Bucks had died and the whole Escobar scam, racing had lost its thrill. He still enjoyed the training and had come to really appreciate Thoroughbreds, but he felt numb when the horses went into the starting gates. He wondered how many more Escobars were out there.

"Hey, Ben, we've missed you at the poker game," Ed Crawford said as he and Paul Wiley sat down without invitation.

"I've been a little under the weather," Ben said, eyeing the two trainers. "Besides, I figured you wouldn't mind having a little more money in your pockets."

Crawford chuckled. "Yeah, you did seem to win more than your share. Guess it's that Texas luck of yours."

"Oklahoma," Ben corrected him. "I'm from Oklahoma, remember?"

"Yeah, Ed. Ben's an Okie," Wiley spoke up. "And Texans and Okies don't much like each other, do they?"

Ben took a drink, licking the foam off his lips. "Not at all. So, you guys still playing same place, same time?"

Crawford nodded. "Since your horse just won, I know you got some extra cash just begging to be on that table."

"Yeah, maybe, but you'll never get your hands on it," Ben said with a laugh as the two men stood up.

"Can we expect you?" Wiley asked.

"I'll be there," Ben said and then watched the two saunter away, whispering to each other like two school boys.

There had never been anything subtle about Crawford and Wiley. They were as crooked as a Texas knotty pine. Ben took another swallow of beer and wondered why Ryan hadn't picked up those two. If anyone was going to be used by the next Escobar, it was going to be them. Which he realized now was precisely why Ryan had left them alone. Maybe he'd get some information at the poker game that would be useful to Ryan. And besides, Crawford was right, he always won more than his share.

"I don't suppose you'd let me buy you supper?"

Ben looked up at the sound of Dan Cooper's familiar voice.

"Yeah, that First And Ten is a whole different horse since we gelded him," Cooper said nervously as they waited for their food.

"It's okay, Dan. I'm not gonna hit you," Ben assured him. "I understand why you did what you did. It's just this whole mess has really gotten to me."

Cooper was relieved. "Yeah, I can see that."

"You and I know that the rodeo has its own ugly little secrets," Ben said, pausing while the waitress put the plates down in front of them. "But this stuff really makes me mad."

"Well, you did your part and put yourself on the line. That's a hell of a lot more than most people do." Cooper poured hot sauce over his steak. "So how come you were talking to Crawford and Wiley? You gotta know they're dirty."

Ben nodded as he finished chewing a bite of food. "Yeah. They're also chump poker players. So, if they want to lose their money, I'm willing to oblige."

"You watch your back with those two," Cooper warned. "You stepped on a lot of toes when you took on those goons. I'd be careful who I trust."

"That's easy. I don't trust anyone these days," Ben said, adding, "If you want Mymomsluck back, you can have her."

Cooper shook his head. "I'm quittin' training," he announced. "You were right. They'll just keep coming back now that they know how to get to me."

"I'm sorry, Dan."

"No, really, it's all right. Thanks to you, I feel better about myself than I have in a long time."

"What are you going to do?"

"I called up Jim Reynolds and he's going find me a place with his rodeo crew," Cooper said. "Eleanor and me are heading back to Texas."

Ben felt a twinge of homesickness. "That's great, Dan."

"How about you, Ben? Any closer to going home?"

"No, I think I'm still a million miles away."

"You'll get back there," Cooper said warmly, reaching for his drink. "Now how about our toast for good luck."

Ben raised his glass. "To Texas cowboys, their horses and Jack Daniel's whiskey."

"Here you go, Mr. Mike," J.B. said, handing him a cold soft drink. "Some kinda hot, huh?"

Mike gratefully accepted the can; even in the shade of the shedrow, the late morning heat was oppressive. "June in Miami couldn't be anything but hot," he said after he had gulped down some of the drink.

J.B. laughed. "You sure is right about that."

"Well, at least Preoccupation is getting cooled off," Mike said, motioning to where Barbara was holding the filly outside the barn while Ben bathed her.

"Mr. Ben sure has been in a better mood since you two brought your horses here," J.B. said, pausing to take a swig from the can. "But he sure is a tough one to figure out. One minute, he's sweet as molasses and the next–bam!–he's likely to take your head off if you even look at him. And I know that leg of his bothers him a lot more than he lets on."

Mike stared at the old man; J.B. was obviously more aware than anyone realized. "He doesn't mean to lose his temper. He just has a lot on his mind."

"Oh, I sure enough know that. Just that some days he don't know who he's madder at—the world or himself," J.B. said. "And that's when he gets himself in trouble. Like those no 'counts he's playing poker with. Sooner or later, they gonna get sick and tired of him takin' all their money. And you know, that Mr. Ben...well, he's damn cocky about it.

"And then there's the women and all that whiskey drinkin' he does. Lordy, it's tearing up his gut. That's two times I seen him throwin' up last week. 'Course, he said it was nothin'. I don't know how he's gonna help me with Secretariat the way he is."

Mike wondered if he looked as dumbfounded as he felt. The old man didn't miss much at all. "It's a good thing Ben has you to take care of him, J.B."

"Hmph, stubborn as that man is, it don't do no good to try to talk some sense into him."

"I can testify to that," Mike agreed as he reached down for

Barbara's purse at his feet. "Here, let me give you one of these and you call us collect anytime you think you need to." He handed J.B. a Southerly Park business card.

J.B. took the card, squinting to read the phone number. "I surely will, Mr. Mike. Maybe between you and me, we can keep that hard-headed cowboy from killin' himself."

"This better be good, Terri," Ryan said groggily as he let her in. "Hell, it's one a.m."

She glared at him. "The damn Feds are letting Escobar go."

"What?"

"He gave them some big dog in one of the drug cartels in Venezuela."

"Damnit!" Ryan bellowed, pacing across the living room. "This happens every damn time. We do all the dirty work and the damn Feds get the payoff," he snapped and suddenly pivoted to face Terri. "They didn't just cut him loose, did they?"

Terri shook her head. "No, they're going to escort him back to Venezuela, and he's not supposed to show his face in Miami ever again."

"Hell, we know how long that'll last."

"Yeah, and how much do you want to bet Mr. Escobar has made a few phone calls down to Miami while waiting on his travel plans?" Terri said. "He's had a long time to sit and think about Ben Matthews."

"I'll get changed. Call and tell them to get the plane ready," Ryan ordered as he hurried to the bedroom.

Ben glanced up at his rearview mirror again. Yeah, that car was still following him. And even in Miami, that was odd at 4 a.m. After he had cleaned up again at the poker game, he had just decided to come straight to the barn. As he turned into the Hallandale backside, he wasn't surprised the car behind him did the same. He parked his truck in the usual spot across the road from his barn and cautiously stepped out.

Ben hadn't taken more than two steps when he was surrounded. Even without the dim streetlights, he would have recognized Crawford and Wiley. With them were Escobar's two goons he had beaten up.

"Sorry, boys, I've had enough poker for one night," Ben said, quickly sizing up the situation. If he could take out the two big guys, Crawford and Riley would turn tail and run.

Crawford grinned at him. "Well, Ben, Mr. Escobar's friends would like to have a little talk with you."

"Oh, we've talked before," Ben said, deciding to go after the biggest one first. "But I guess we left some things unsaid, didn't we?" He swung as hard as he could at the thug.

Ben heard the man's nose break as his right fist landed hard. With an angry scream, the man staggered back and Ben hit him again with a left cross. As he went down, Ben turned toward Escobar's other man. But a sudden blow to his lower back knocked the breath out of him, and he fought to stay on his feet.

Crawford dropped the blackjack that he had hidden behind his back; he and Wiley grabbed Ben by his arms from behind and jerked him upright. Escobar's man punched him in the rib cage twice and Ben folded over in pain. Crawford and Wiley yanked back on his arms and straightened him up again. The big guy with the bloodied nose was coming at him now.

Ben winced. Damn. His father had always said that you ain't lived much if you don't get a few beatings before you die.

When Crawford and Wiley finally turned him loose, Ben felt himself falling in slow motion. Considering there wasn't a part of his body that didn't hurt, he was actually looking forward to hitting the ground and passing out. He made it to his knees before something stopped him. Damn. The big guy had a hold of him by his shirt collar and was lifting him up again. He threw him up against the front of his truck. The back of his head bounced off the hood, and Ben was sure he was going to throw up.

He felt the big hands letting him go as he slid downward. But his legs folded under him too fast; he twisted at an odd angle and his head crashed into the edge of the truck's front bumper. A thousand white-hot explosions went off in his right temple. He collapsed to the ground with a thump and, finally, the blackness came.

But then there was this terrible noise. He tried to move, but his body responded only with a dose of pain. The noise got louder. Then he realized what it was. It was the sound of a car engine being revved up. Damn. They were going to finish him off by running over him.

Fine. Let it end here. Let's finally finish what that damned bull started. Ben heard the tires screeching; it would soon be over. Then suddenly he was moving—or rather being pulled across the asphalt. Damn, that hurt. He felt the whoosh of the car speeding past him; just barely missing him, but missing him just the same. Then, mercifully, he felt nothing.

Ryan made out the last four digits of the car's license plate as he ran to where J.B. sat on the ground.

"Oh, Lordy, they done killed him," the old man cried, cradling Ben in his arms.

Kneeling down alongside them, Ryan put his fingers on Ben's neck and felt for a pulse. "He's still alive, J.B.," he said in relief, eyeing the damage. Blood trickled from Ben's nose and mouth, but what worried Ryan most was the deep gash across his right temple; he could only hope there were no internal injuries. "He's gonna be all right, J.B. I'm gonna take him to the hospital, okay?"

The old man looked at Ryan, as though deciding if he was going to let him do that. "You sure he's still alive?"

"Yeah, but I have to get him to the hospital right away," Ryan said quietly.

"Okay," J.B. said, lifting Ben's head from his lap.

"Come on, cowboy," Ryan said, pulling Ben up as gently as he could. Ben moaned. "Sorry. But Terri will have my ass in a sling if you die on me."

Ben had been trying to open his eyes for awhile now. But every time he even thought about it, his head throbbed. Sounds and voices drifted in and out; something cold pricked his arm. This was all very familiar to him. Maybe he was still in the Las Vegas hospital. Maybe it had all been one long, horrible nightmare. He'd never know if he didn't open his eyes.

He tried to ignore the pounding and concentrated on focusing his eyes. When the haziness cleared, it was Mike—not Chris—who was at his bedside, grinning at him. Sadness washed over him.

"I guess this is one time it's a good thing you're as hardheaded as you are," Mike said, relieved Ben had finally regained consciousness.

Ben took a breath and wished he hadn't. He grimaced as a familiar stabbing pain sliced up his right side. Damn. Busted up again.

"Take it easy," Mike said in concern, laying his hand on Ben's arm. "If you haven't figured it out, you've got some cracked ribs. So, try not to breathe."

Ben glanced sideways at him. "Funny," he whispered.

"Actually, you're damned lucky you're breathing at all. If it hadn't been for J.B., we'd still be scraping you up off the road."

Ben didn't respond and Mike realized he had drifted off again. Thanks to the serious blows to his head, the doctor had said they could expect that for a couple of days. Mike was just grateful Ben was alive. When J.B. had called them at dawn yesterday, Mike had been sure Ben had finally gotten his death wish. But, once again, Ben's Texas cowboy luck had saved him.

Crawford and Wiley were leaning up against the counter, talking with the assistant racing secretary when Ryan came up behind them and grabbed each by the back of their shirt collars with his beefy hands.

"Hey, boys, you're gonna take a little ride with me," Ryan

said, glaring at the assistant racing secretary. "And don't you even think of going anywhere. I'll be right back for you," he warned him as he hauled the two trainers out of the racetrack office.

It had been Crawford's car tag that Ryan had deciphered the last four numbers on as he had hurried to help J.B. with Ben. Escobar's two goons were already locked up. Ryan and Ben had known months ago that the assistant racing secretary was also on Escobar's payroll. But Ryan had left him in place to attract the next Escobar. But after what had happened to Ben, Ryan wasn't feeling so generous anymore.

The doctor scanned Ben's chart. "Considering everything, you're—"

Ben interrupted the doctor as he weakly raised his hand from the bed. "I know. I'm a very lucky man."

The doctor chuckled. "Obviously, you've been through this before. Out of curiosity, what happened that time?"

"Let's just say a bull and I had a little disagreement."

"Not unlike what you had with the men who did this to you, right?" the doctor said. "Well, I'd say you definitely fared better this time around. But you've got a lot of deep bruising and two cracked ribs. That's the good news.

"The bad news is you've suffered a severe concussion from the blows to your head. You can probably feel the lump back there, and this nasty little number here," he said as he gently pulled back the bandage on Ben's right temple, "is going to leave you with a new little scar for your collection."

Ben winced as the doctor fingered the head wound. "So when can I get outta here?"

"Oh, you're going to be with us for a week, maybe ten days, I'd say," the doctor replied, replacing the bandage.

"No way," Ben protested as he tried to sit up. "I'm not..." His voice trailed; those white-hot little explosions had returned. With a groan he let his head fall back on the pillow.

The doctor grinned. "Yes, you'll be with us for awhile," he said. "And there's one more thing. I don't know what you've been drinking. But by the looks of your stomach, it might as well have been battery acid. You've got yourself one hell of a bleeding ulcer."

Ben looked at him; the throbbing was subsiding. Damn. That explained all the throwing up he'd been doing lately.

"Unless you want to risk bleeding to death, I'd strongly suggest you lay off the booze for awhile and let your stomach heal," the doctor said, scribbling notes on the chart. "Other than that, you're a very lucky man, Mr. Matthews."

The next time Ben opened his eyes, J.B. was standing there at the foot of the bed. Ben smiled at him, but J.B. just shook his head.

"I told you I need you for when Secretariat comes back," J.B. fussed at him. "But if you want to die a stupid, drunk white man in Miami, then jest tell me and I won't be wasting no more time on you."

Ben started to say something, but before he could, J.B. just turned around and left.

"Guess he told you," Mike said as he rolled across the room. "And he makes a lot of sense, too."

"Ah, hell. I'm getting a little tired of everyone riding my ass and telling me what I should or shouldn't be doing," Ben said as he carefully propped himself up against the stacked pillows.

"Well, we can't hardly pass up the opportunity of having you flat on your back, now can we?" Mike needled him. "And if you'd just once listen, then maybe we'd leave you alone."

"Yeah, right," Ben said doubtfully as Barbara came into the room.

"Oh, your bruises are a nice shade of purple today," Barbara teased, bending over to kiss Ben on the cheek.

"I'm surrounded by smartasses."

"Takes one to know one," Barbara shot back, and they laughed.

Mike waited until Barbara had sat down in the chair across from him. "You really need to think about getting out of Miami, Ben," he said. "These guys might stay after you until they finish what they started."

Ben knew Mike was right. But where in the hell was he supposed to go? If he wasn't ready to go back to Texas before, he sure in the hell couldn't go back in the shape he was in now.

"Maybe you can come stay with us for awhile until you figure out what to do," Barbara offered, seeing the distress on Ben's face.

"No, I don't want you two to get hurt," Ben said adamantly.

"Well, maybe..." Mike started to make another suggestion, but Ryan suddenly filled up the doorway.

"Maybe I just happen to know that Bill Ketchum would love to have you up at his farm in Ocala," Ryan said, ambling into the room with a package in his hand. "Of course, once you were back on your feet, he'd expect you to do some training on the farm for him."

Ben eyed the big Okie; a smile tugged at the corners of his mouth. "Hmm, you know, Ryan, if word ever gets out that you actually helped a Texan..."

"Helped you? Hell, I saved your sorry Texas hide. And don't think I'll ever let you forget that, either," he said as they all laughed. "Here, this belongs to you."

Ben took the package Ryan handed him and tore away the paper. He smiled; it was his truck's Texas license plate.

15

Ben zipped his jacket all the way up, pushed his cowboy hat down, and turned Reno away from the March north wind. Damn. It wasn't supposed to be this cold in Florida. There had been a hard freeze overnight, and even now at noon it was still in the forties. It almost made him miss the humidity of Miami. Almost.

From his observation spot just off the training track's stretch turn, Ben watched the six riders jogging their mounts clockwise to warm them up. Then in pairs, they reversed their direction and began galloping the young horses.

The cold March morning had the horses feeling especially frisky, and the riders literally had their hands full keeping them in check. Ben smiled as he watched the just-turned two year olds prancing by him, their heads bowed into their chests with wisps of cold air escaping their flared nostrils.

The rider on the big bay colt gave Ben a thumbs up sign as he galloped past him. He had always liked that colt and had told Bill Ketchum he was the best of his two year olds. The big bay colt's attitude and natural athletic abilities reminded him of Bucks.

Looking out across the track, Ben scanned the hundreds of acres of Triple Diamond Farm. There was a certain beauty to this part of Florida, with its rolling hills and majestic oak trees. Although Ocala was only five hours north of Miami, it seemed a million miles away.

But Ben was still puzzled why Thoroughbred horsemen called their spreads farms and not ranches. You grew crops on farms and raised livestock on ranches.

With a shiver, Ben reined Reno toward the gap. "Let's get the hell out of this damned wind," he muttered as the horse trotted off the track and toward the barn.

J.B. and Bobby, the farm's assistant trainer, were waiting for them at the front of the concrete block barn, sliding the double doors shut once the horses and their riders were inside. Ben let Reno walk right up to the tack room door where the horse knew he always got unsaddled. As Ben dismounted, he made sure he shifted his weight to the right and eased his aching left leg out of the stirrup.

"Don't suppose it'd do me any good to tell you a doctor oughta look at that leg, huh?" J.B. asked, holding Reno by the reins.

Ben gave him a small smile. "It's just the cold weather, J.B. Don't worry about it," he said as he turned and limped away.

The old black man watched Ben until he ducked out the barn's side door. "Well, somebody has to worry about it. You sure enough won't," J.B. mumbled as he began unsaddling the horse. "You know, Reno, sometimes I think that hard-headed cowboy likes to hurt. I ain't never seen nobody that puts up with hurtin' like that man does."

Pulling off his boots, Ben leaned back in the recliner and warmed his feet in front of the fireplace. He wiggled his toes and smiled as Strait sang "Baby Blue" in the background. He reached over to the lamp table for the glass half-filled with Jack Daniel's. He knew he shouldn't be drinking, but right now he needed some relief from the icy aching in his left leg. And besides, a Texan couldn't go on indefinitely without his Jack Daniel's. He had poured only half a glass, promising himself he'd stop drinking if he felt even the slightest twinge in his gut.

Ben brought the glass up to his lips and sipped slowly. He savored the taste of the whiskey in his mouth, and the warmth of it as it slid down his throat. How could that doctor in Miami have compared this wonderful stuff to battery acid? He knew his over-indulgence had caused the bleeding ulcer, and he was determined not to go to that extreme again.

Damn. His leg was really hurting again. First the humidity in Miami and now an unusually cold winter in Ocala. But the cold made his leg hurt differently. The humidity had made it heavy and fill up with a dull throbbing. The cold clamped down on it like a vise that tightened up on him without warning, rattling him with those spasms of pain. Hell, it could be worse. He could be sitting in a wheelchair like Mike, not feeling anything in his legs. Now that thought always put things in perspective.

Ben drained the glass of the last drop of the whiskey and put it on the table. He closed his eyes as he rested his head back. A little whiskey, a little nap and he'd be just fine.

The phone rang persistently. Ben finally gave up trying to ignore it and reluctantly rose from the recliner. The fire was now nothing more than glowing embers, and when Ben glanced at the mantle clock, he realized he had slept through afternoon feeding.

"Yeah," Ben grumbled after he snatched the phone from the wall in the kitchen.

"Hey, Lone Ranger. You weren't engaged in some afternoon delight, were you?"

Ben chuckled at the sound of Mike's voice. "Don't I wish. No, I was trying to defrost. It's damned cold up here," he said, dropping into a chair.

"Yeah, I saw that on the weather. Nice and balmy seventy-five down here," Mike teased.

"I don't want to hear about it. Tell me how school's going."

"Great. But finals will be here before I know it."

"Ah, you'll ace 'em," Ben said. "You and Barbara need to start thinking about coming up for a visit. Ketchum said he was going to restock the lake as soon as the weather warms up. Then we can do some serious fishing."

"You got a deal, cowboy. Barbara sends her love and you take care of yourself, okay?"

"Yeah, Tonto, you and Barbara, too," Ben said, then hung up the phone.

He sat there, feeling the restlessness gnawing at him. When he had arrived at Triple Diamond seven months ago, he had concentrated first on physically recuperating, and then there had been the chaos of breaking the young horses. Now things were settling down and he was feeling uneasy again. There was a part of him that wanted to panic and bolt. But if he had learned anything in Miami, it was that he really couldn't outrun the truth. And now he could feel it catching up to him again.

"Hi, Ben."

Looking up from his lunch, Ben was surprised to see Mark Reed standing there next to his table at the Winner's Circle Restaurant.

Bobby waited for Ben to say something to the young man, whose slight build assured that he was a rider. But Ben didn't say a word, only glared at the obviously nervous man.

"I, uh , think I'll go over and talk to Dr. Peterson about that sore filly," Bobby said, getting to his feet and quickly walking away.

Mark slowly sat down in the vacated chair. "You probably won't believe me. But I'm really sorry about what happened to Bucks."

"Is that so?" Ben asked coldly.

"Yeah," Mark replied quietly. "I know what I did was wrong. I got greedy—and then I got scared." He paused for a moment, then added, "I realize that's probably hard for someone like you to understand."

Ben just kept staring at the visibly shaken rider. "You should have never started playing their games."

Mark nodded. "I know. I knew it when I sat up after the spill and saw you kneeling over Bucks," he admitted. "Then I knew you really cared about that horse. And that racing for you was really about the horses—not about just winning races and cashing bets.

"And when I was laid up, I thought about that. It made me remember a little horse-crazy kid who always wanted to be a jockey. And how I had let that little kid down."

Ben leaned back in the chair. "So why aren't you in Miami riding? What are you doing in Ocala?"

Mark shrugged. "After what happened to Bucks, I lost my heart for race riding. I thought maybe if I started all over, I'd get it back."

The rider's words sounded sincere and familiar to Ben. But Mark was wrong; he did know what it was like to make a mistake out of greed and fear. That bull had left him with plenty of scars to remind him of that.

Mark figured he had pushed his luck. He had said what he'd been wanting to say for a long time; he'd better leave before Ben forgot their size difference. Silently, he rose and walked away from the table.

"Hey, Mark," Ben called out to him. "Be at the barn at six in the morning."

As March gave way to April, the cold weather was quickly a bad memory. Both man and beast reveled in the pleasantly warm days. Ben was amazed how much better his leg felt; there were even days that his limp was barely noticeable. The two year olds continued to flourish, and on his last visit Ketchum had been delighted with their progress.

"Ol' Hopalong," J.B. said to Ben as he toted the bucketful of soapy water over to where the old black man stood holding Reno.

Ben looked at him. "Are you making fun of the way I walk, J.B.?" he asked, putting the bucket down next to the horse.

J.B. chuckled and shook his head. "No, Mr. Ben, you know I wouldn't do that. That was Secretariat's nickname when he was two years old."

"You're telling me that one of the greatest racehorses of all time was actually called Ol' Hopalong?" Ben questioned in disbelief as he began sponging Reno.

"Yes, siree, he was. Eddie told me that when he first got that horse to groom at Hallandale, he was fat and lazy. All he cared about was eatin'."

"Hmm, so when did they start calling him Big Red?" Ben asked, playing along; he'd gotten used to J.B.'s Secretariat stories and enjoyed hearing them.

"It wasn't until they shipped to Belmont Park that summer and Mr. Lucien Laurin just kept workin' him. One day he breezed him five-eighths and that big red hoss left 'em all staring at their stopwatches. From then on, nobody called him Ol' Hopalong anymore."

Ben laughed. "That's a great story, J.B."

"It sure enough is the truth, Mr. Ben. And I bet 'cha when I see Secretariat again, he's gonna be just as fat and sassy."

"I'm sure he will be." He had stopped trying to convince J.B. that Secretariat was not coming back in all his racing glory.

"I can't believe you actually do some work around here, Texas."

Ben peered around Reno to see Ryan grinning at him; he stood with his arm draped around J.B.'s shoulders. Ben was always amazed how such a big man could just suddenly appear.

"Yeah, some of us do actually have to work for a living," Ben said with a smirk. It was the third time the state cop had visited him at the farm. "But work is sorta a foreign concept to you Okies, ain't it?"

"Kinda like staying out of trouble is for you cocky Texas cowboys," Ryan shot back.

J.B. shook his head. "I swear you two are like spoiled kids who both want their way," he muttered, and the three men laughed.

"Come to take me up on the fishing offer?" Ben asked as he started rinsing Reno off.

"Don't I wish. Maybe next time," Ryan answered. "Just thought you'd like to know that Escobar got himself blown away in Miami a couple of days ago."

"What happened?"

"Oh, he decided to come back from Venezuela. But the new head honcho in Miami didn't much care for that, so he blew up Escobar's car—with Escobar in it."

"So much for the honor among thieves theory, huh?"

"Yeah," Ryan said, chuckling. "Well, I got things to do and people to see. You keep an eye on the cowboy, J.B."

"Ryan," Ben called, and the cop pivoted to face him. "In case I forgot to say so before, thanks."

Ryan frowned at him. "Now don't you start gettin' soft on me, Texas," he said with a wink and then walked away in those ground-eating strides of his.

"So, are you thinking of going back to Texas after you ship the two year olds out next month?" Mike asked casually as he cast his fishing line out again.

Ben shrugged. "Haven't given it that much thought. I've been concentrating on gettin' these babies to the racetrack in the best shape possible."

"Sure, Ben, whatever you say."

"Not buying it, huh?"

"Nope."

"Okay, I have been thinking about it. But funny thing is, I'm starting to think of Texas in a different way."

"How so?"

"Well, more like that used to be home when I was someone else," Ben explained, trying to sort through his feelings. "But now, after everything that's happened, maybe this is home. I really like this farm and Ocala. Hell, I'm wearing my cowboy hat again, and there's even a country western station on the radio."

Mike grinned at Ben's last comments, keeping his eyes on the bobber. "Oh, I'm sure you do feel more comfortable here than you did in Miami. But I don't know if that means this can take the place of Texas as home."

"Why not?" Ben snapped. "Aren't you the one who's always giving me a hard time about living by those cowboy rules? Well, maybe you were right and I'm trying to make a life without those damned rules."

"Wait a minute." Mike reeled in his line. "I never meant to make fun of those cowboy rules of yours. I was simply acknowledging their existence and trying to figure out what made you tick."

Ben looked at his friend. "Well, maybe I'm not a Texas cowboy anymore."

Mike laughed. "Ben, we could put you in a three-piece suit with a briefcase in your hand, and you'd still be a Texas cowboy."

"Funny. Don't you think a person can change?"

"Sure. And no doubt everything you've been through has changed you," Mike answered. "But you're talking about wiping out your heritage. Even if you could, I don't think that's what you really want to do."

Ben cast out his line again. "And I suppose you're gonna tell me what it is I really want to do, right?"

"Well, since you brought it up," Mike said with a grin, then turning serious, he added, "You want to stay here where it's nice and safe. Think about it, Ben. This is where you've finally found a little peace."

"Yeah. And what's wrong with that?"

"Nothing. And goodness knows, you deserve it."

"But?"

"But you're settling for a lot less than you could have."

"I'm a little confused," Ben said in exasperation. "Didn't you tell me there was no miracle cure? And that I would have to learn to live without what I lost?"

"Geez, you mean you were actually listening to me?" Mike teased, lightening the mood for a moment. "Yeah, I said those things and they still hold true. But that doesn't mean you have to live without what you still have.

"What about the ranch and the people there who care about you?"

Ben stared down into the water. "The ranch is doing fine without me. And the people—well, they've gone on with their lives. Like I said before, maybe I just don't belong there anymore."

"But you'll never know that for sure unless you go back," Mike insisted. "And that will be just one more thing you'll have to live with."

The two men sat in silence, the only sound the water lapping against the fishing pier. Ben reached over into the cooler between them and pulled out a can of beer. He popped the top and took a long swallow.

"Damn," Ben said quietly. "You think Barbara would get real upset if I just rolled you right into the lake?"

Mike gave him a 'you wouldn't dare, would you?' look, and then the two friends laughed.

"Matthews Ranch."

"Hi, Lisa. It's Ben."

"Oh, hi. How are you doing?" Lisa greeted, wondering why after all this time she was still uncomfortable when Ben called.

"Much better since the weather warmed up," Ben answered, wishing he could manage more than small talk with Lisa. "How's everything going there?"

Lisa cleared her throat. "Busy with spring branding and all. But the UT kids are a big help."

"And your gallery?"

"Doing just great," Lisa replied, trying to gather her courage. "Ben..."

"Yeah?"

"I-uh..." Lisa attempted, but the sound of the kitchen door opening distracted her. "Oh, here's Scott. You take care, Ben," she said quickly, relief washing over her. She handed the phone to Scott as she left the room.

"Is something wrong?" Lisa asked as she came back into the kitchen twenty minutes later. "Did Ben say something that upset you?"

Scott blew on the just poured coffee. "No, he sounded good. The best he's been in a long time."

"Then what's bothering you?" Lisa questioned, joining him at the table. "He's really made an effort to call regularly since he moved to Ocala. And we even know exactly where he is for the first time since he left."

Taking a sip, Scott shrugged. "Maybe it's that I can't believe he's been gone as long as he has." He paused, then added, "He never even mentions coming home anymore. And now I'm afraid to ask him because he might say never."

Lisa looked at him. "That's kind of how I feel about us getting married. I beginning to think it's never going to happen."

Scott looked at her in surprise. "One thing has nothing to do with the other."

"You're wrong. They have so much to do with each other that they're inseparable," Lisa returned wearily. "Despite the fact that Ben gave us this house as a peace offering, you apparently have decided to put your life—our lives—on hold until he comes home."

Scott rose from the table, walked to the sink and poured the coffee down the drain. "Well, considering what we did to his life, that only seems fair," he said as he turned to face her.

Lisa shook her head. "Scott, we did not chase Ben from here.

Everything—the bull, Waco—everything just caught up with him. Even if we hadn't been honest with each other and Ben about our feelings, he would have still left."

"Does believing that ease your guilty conscience?" Scott asked harshly.

The words stung Lisa, but she quickly composed herself. "Do you love me, Scott?"

Now it was Scott's turn to be taken aback. "You know I do."

"Well, maybe I'm starting to wonder about that. And maybe we both have a lot of thinking to do while I'm in Europe."

"Old habits die hard, don't they?"

"What are you talking about?"

"Whenever you didn't get your way with Ben, off you went to Europe," he answered. "Guess I should have known, sooner or later, you'd do the same with me."

Lisa sighed. "I've been planning this art-buying trip for months. I asked you over and over to come with me, but you said you couldn't leave the ranch."

"And you just happened to plan to go during our busiest time here," Scott returned sharply.

"I'm not going to argue with you about this when you won't even admit what the real problem is," Lisa said, getting to her feet. "I've got packing to do."

For the third time, Ben walked to the front door and even put his hand on the doorknob before turning away. No. He wasn't going to do it. He wasn't going to get drunk so he could get through Chris' birthday. Although the memories of having done that last year were hazy, the shame he still felt made him determined to stay sober. He strode into the kitchen. Maybe something to eat would calm him down.

Fifteen minutes later, Ben was staring at the sandwich he had only taken one bite out of. He had kept himself busy all day and had taken a long ride on Reno. He had even helped Bobby with some general farm maintenance work right up until dusk. But once he had come back to his cottage, the anxiety had grown as the night settled in. Glancing up at the phone, he thought of calling Mike. No. He couldn't go running to his friend every time he got a panic attack.

There was no point going around in circles. He had to deal with this head-on. If he kept running away, he'd never be able to go home.

Ben brought the box out of the closet, put it down on the bed and slowly took the lid off. There was his father's carving knife, his mother's knitting basket, his four gold all-around buckles, the picture Lisa had sent him in Miami. Hesitantly, he reached in and brought out the framed picture of him, Chris and their parents in Oklahoma City. When would their smiling faces not cause him such pain?

As he put the picture carefully back down into the box, he saw the partially visible envelope among the memories of another lifetime.

On his way to the screened porch, Ben stopped in the kitchen long enough to pour himself half a glass of whiskey. To hell with this being brave stuff. He finished filling the glass and then stepped out onto the porch. Sitting down in the well-worn recliner, he sipped at the whiskey and stared at the envelope with the Austin, Texas, postmark on it.

Ben,

Just wanted to say thanks for the great birthday presents! Although I won't be surprised if whipped cream magically appears in my new snake skin boots the next time I put them on!

With me going back to school and you and Scott hitting the road, we haven't seen much of each other these past months. I know you weren't very happy about me taking off from school to be home while you recuperated, but I want you to know how much it meant to me to do that. For the first time in my life, I got to do something for my big brother. You have always been there for me—and even under the circumstances—I'll always cherish that year we got to spend so much time together.

I have always been proud of you—but even more so after watching you come through what you have. Of course, I told you no bull was going to get the best of my big brother. After all, there's nothing you can't do—you were blessed by the gods!

See ya in Waco!

Love ya,
Chris

Ben didn't know when the tears had first started, only that now they were streaming down his face. The letter had come the day he and Scott had left for a three-week road trip that would eventually end up in Waco. He had checked the mailbox as they were driving out, stuffing the letter into his duffle bag. When they had stopped for the night, he had read it then and it had made him smile. He had put it back in his bag and that's where it had stayed until the day he packed for Miami. Unable to read it again then, he had put it in the box with his other keepsakes.

Maybe it would have been better if he had just thrown it away. Then the words that had once made him smile wouldn't be tearing him apart now. Damn. It hurt. He took a deep breath, trying to ease that damned tightness in his chest. Mike had said it would get easier. It wasn't. And if it still hurt this much here in Ocala two years later, what would it be like if he went back to Texas?

The thought made him shudder and he suddenly sat up. He wasn't going to sit here and let this pain overwhelm him. But then he realized it already had; he just didn't have the will to run anymore. In resignation, he slumped back down in the chair.

Hell, it didn't matter anymore. Because now he knew the truth. Chris' words had proven it to him once and for all. There was no way he was going home.

Sleeping had become a problem again. Ever since reading Chris' letter, Ben hadn't slept in his bed. He wasn't going to risk having that fiery nightmare grab a hold of him. He hadn't forgotten that the time he had it in Miami had been triggered by him talking about Chris with Mike. And even wide awake, as he had sat there clutching that letter, he could feel it haunting him.

The next day he had gone out and bought a dozen Louis L'Amour paperbacks, as well as several Thoroughbred books, including two on Secretariat. He spent the night reading until he dozed off in the recliner. Then later in the day, he'd make up for lost sleep with an afternoon nap. The routine had worked for more than a week now, and he was willing to do it for the rest of his life if it kept the fiery nightmare at bay.

Ben had settled in for a nap when he heard the faint knocking on the front door. He didn't open his eyes; maybe whoever it was would go away. There it was again and louder this time. Damn. He had just left the barn.

"All right, all right," Ben muttered, climbing out of the recliner. "This had better be important," he grumbled as he opened the door.

Ben just stood there in the doorway, stunned. He must have fallen asleep and he was having a wonderful dream.

Lisa saw the disbelief in his eyes. Slowly, she brought her right hand up and gently laid it on the scarred side of his face.

Ben sighed at her touch. She was real. Then she was in his arms and his heart ached. Damn. He had missed her. He held her as tightly as he could, afraid she might vanish as quickly as she had appeared.

He suddenly pulled away, but didn't let her go. "Is something wrong? Did something happen to Scott?"

"No, it's okay. Scott's fine," Lisa quickly assured him, looking into those incredible blue eyes of his. She had missed those eyes. "I just decided to make a slight detour on my way to Europe."

They had made small talk over coffee in the kitchen for half an hour now. Ben had let Lisa do most of the talking as he tried to keep from staring at her. Damn. She was as beautiful as ever. He had hesitantly checked her hands: no engagement ring, no wedding ring. It had crossed his mind that she was there to tell him she and Scott were married or to invite him to the wedding.

Ben was suddenly aware that Lisa had stopped talking. He figured now was as good a time as ever. "So why aren't you and Scott married yet?"

Lisa looked at him; he was as direct as ever. And she had taken too much of a risk coming here not to be the same. "Because of you," she answered quietly. "Because you're still the star and the show can't go on without the star."

Ben shook his head. "That might have been true a long time ago. But it's not anymore," he said. "Too much has happened. I'm not that person anymore."

"Oh, I know everything that's happened these past few years has changed you—and me and Scott," Lisa agreed, adding, "But no matter where you go or what happens to you, you'll always be *that* Ben Matthews to me, Scott, your rodeo friends, the UT kids and everybody else in Texas. It's what Scott calls the best of you."

Ben was humbled by her words; he didn't deserve them. "But you and Scott love each other. What I do or don't do shouldn't matter."

"But it does," Lisa said. "All this time, Scott has blamed himself for what happened between the three of us—and for you leaving the ranch. I've tried to convince him otherwise, but he won't listen. You're the only one he's going to believe, Ben."

Damn. He looked away from her. He had never realized what needless pain Scott had been putting himself and Lisa through. He had thought by giving them his house that he had let them know no one was to blame. And now Lisa was telling him that Scott had been carrying around that guilt all this time. Damn.

"The sad thing is that I know Scott loves me," Lisa continued as he remained silent. "But if you asked him to, he would leave me. I know that—and I don't know how much longer I can live with that before I'll have to leave him."

Ben looked back at her. "You'd regret it for the rest of your life," he warned.

She reached out and tentatively touched his hand on the table. "Then help me, Ben. Come home."

Lisa's plea knifed through him. He pulled his hand away as he rose from the chair and walked off into the living room.

Before he had turned away, Lisa had seen the pain cloud his eyes. If she had had any doubts before, she didn't now. Scott had been right; Ben was no closer to coming home than he had been a year ago. What was she going to do? How was he going to help her with Scott if he hadn't even forgiven himself? But she had to find a way to get through to him. She had too much to lose; she couldn't give up on the two men she loved.

"If you show me around this place, I'll buy supper," Lisa offered, standing in front of the couch where Ben sat.

"Now that's a deal I can't pass up."

Lisa took a sip of the tea while they waited for their food. "Ocala really is a pretty place. Not what you expect at all when you think of Florida," she said, hating to make chit-chat when there were so many more important things to say. "So how come they call them Thoroughbred farms instead of ranches?"

Ben chuckled. "I've tried to figure that one out myself. But no one seems to know the answer."

Just then when he moved, Lisa thought she saw something

along his right temple. She reached across the table and pushed his hair to the side. "What happened there?" She gently touched the faint scar.

"Oh, just a little mishap in Miami. Nothing serious," he said, glancing away as she brought her hand back down to the table.

"You never did tell us why you left Miami. You seemed to really like the racetrack."

"I did," Ben answered with a shrug. "But I just got tired of living in a big city. You know how I feel about big cities."

She smiled slightly. "Yeah, I know," she said quietly. "Other than Scott, I know you better than anyone else does. That's why I know you can't let Scott go on blaming himself."

"Lisa, please..." Ben began, then was grateful the waiter arrived with their food. "So how long are you going to be in Europe?"

"Until the first part of August," she answered, taking the hint not to press him. "I've got lots of art to look at and old friends to visit."

"Couldn't get Scott to go with you, huh?"

"Yeah, right. He's about as much a world traveler as you are. And, besides, there aren't any rodeos in Europe," she said, and they both laughed.

The minute they walked into the cottage, Ben went straight to the hallway closet and returned with bedding. "You take my bed and I'll sack out here on the couch," he said, unfolding the sheets and not looking at her.

Lisa sat down in the recliner; she wasn't going to be dismissed that easily. "The ranch has changed," she said, watching him preparing the couch to sleep on. "I know you still think of it as just the way you left it. But it's been almost two years and nothing stays the same. With the UT people and the kids, there's a different feel to it."

Ben sat down on the couch and looked at her. "What are you

trying to tell me, Lisa?" he asked; there was an edge to his voice. "That a little paint here and there and a bunch of kids running around will make it all right for me to go back? That just like that," he said, snapping his fingers, "everything will be perfect."

Lisa was surprised by the anger in his voice. "No. I'm not saying that at all," she said calmly. "I'm just saying you should give it a chance. You did a wonderful thing when you turned the ranch over to UT, and you should be there enjoying it. The kids ask about you all the time, and there's so much you could teach them."

She paused, waiting a few moments for him to respond; he only stared downward. "Yes, it is going to be hard to come back and face those painful memories. But you have a lifetime of wonderful memories of Chris and your folks. I know you want to remember those."

Ben couldn't bring himself to look at Lisa. He knew she was right. But he didn't know how to tell her that every time he thought of them, it still hurt. And that the good memories were behind a wall of pain he couldn't seem to find a way around.

Lisa watched him, sitting there lost in his thoughts. She wished he would talk to her, but at least he wasn't lashing out at her in anger or running away. Maybe there was hope after all. No sense in pushing him anymore tonight, she thought. It had been an emotional day for both of them and she didn't want to lose any ground she might have gained. She walked over to him and bent down to kiss him on the cheek. He remained silent as she turned for the bedroom.

The flames were everywhere; the heat of the fire made his eyes water. He wanted to run away. But he couldn't. He could hear his father, mother and Chris calling his name, begging him to help them. But every time he took a step forward, a new wall of fire erupted in front of him. And still he could hear their screams.

At first, Lisa thought it was Scott who was calling to her. But
then as she became fully awake in the unfamiliar bed, she realized
it was Ben who was crying out. Grateful she had fallen asleep with
the lamp on, she quickly climbed out of the bed and hurried toward the living room.

As she felt for the lamp on the table next to the couch, she
could hear Ben mumbling and tossing fitfully. "Ben, wake up,"
Lisa said as the light came on; she knelt down alongside the couch
and put her hand on his arm.

He suddenly came awake with such force that he knocked her
back to a sitting position on the floor. Shaken, she watched him
trying to catch his breath as he sat there trembling.

"It's okay," Lisa said, getting to her knees. "It was only a bad
dream," she added soothingly, reaching out for him.

"Don't..." Ben rasped as he huddled against the couch.

Lisa realized how afraid he was; she pulled her hand back as
she slowly got to her feet, then sat down on the far end of the
couch. "This has happened before, hasn't it?"

Ben didn't answer her; he didn't have to. The fear in his eyes
told her that the nightmare had been tormenting him for a long
time. Probably since Waco.

"Maybe it would help if you told me about it," she said gently. "Remember when we were kids—you, me, Chris and Scott—
how we'd sit under the oak tree and tell each other our scary
dreams?"

Ben glanced up at her. This wasn't a kid's dream about make-
believe monsters. This was a nightmare about what had happened
to his family. This was real. How could he put that into words?

Lisa could feel him struggling to regain his composure and
put the walls back up. He wasn't going to tell her about the nightmare; it was just too painful for him. He slid his legs over the side
of the couch and started to get up.

Instinctively, Lisa reached out and grabbed his hand. "Please,
Ben, don't shut me out again," she pleaded, now taking hold of his

arm as he made a weak attempt at pulling away. "I understand if you can't talk about it. Tell me how I can help you."

Ben could feel his resistance fading; he was so tired. He just wanted the pain to stop. He felt Lisa move closer to him and heard himself catch his breath.

Lisa slipped her around him; he was shaking again. "Please— just let me hold you."

Ben could feel the tears rolling down his face. It felt so good to have Lisa's arms around him. For the first time in a long time, he didn't feel so alone.

She hugged him tightly as he slowly collapsed into her arms. "It's going to be all right, Ben," Lisa said. She cried softly and wished with all of her heart for that to be true.

Lisa watched Ben sleeping from where she lay in the crook of his arm. She reached out and gently traced the scar on his face; he looked so peaceful now. As he had begun to fall asleep from exhaustion in her arms, she had managed to lead him into the bedroom. Afraid he'd have the nightmare again, she'd climbed into bed with him and had drifted off to sleep.

Now as the dawn's light filtered in through the curtains, she lay there thinking how much she cared about this man. And how sorry she was that he had been in so much pain for so long. And now she understood why he couldn't yet come home.

"Good morning," Lisa said as she saw his eyes flutter open.

Ben glanced at her and then lifted the covers. "Hmm, can't remember the last time I woke up in bed with you and still had all my clothes on."

She hit him on the arm. "Hey, remember that time I was over studying and your folks left to go to town?"

"Oh, yeah, we were in bed before they were out of the driveway."

Lisa laughed. "But we didn't know they'd had truck trouble and come back."

Ben chuckled. "You should have seen your face when Mother opened my bedroom door."

She hit him again. "Well, you were white as a ghost."

"We were damned lucky it wasn't Dad who opened that door—or we both would have been in the woodshed," Ben said as they laughed.

"Oh my, we must have been what—seventeen?"

"Seventeen. Thought we had the world figured out then, didn't we?" Ben said wistfully. "I did love you, Lisa." He propped himself up on his elbow, gazing down into her eyes. "I still do," he admitted. "I never meant to hurt you. And what I did to you when I came back from Wyoming..."

Lisa put her fingers on his lips. "It's forgiven and forgotten. Let it go."

He leaned forward and kissed her on the forehead; they held each other in silence. He had been a fool to let her go. And he knew they would never love each other that way again. She was committed to Scott now.

"Guess since you bought supper, breakfast is on me, right?" Ben asked as he slowly sat up.

"You betcha. And I'm really hungry," she said, grinning at him.

They had been standing there, holding each other in the doorway for several minutes now. "You'd better get going or you'll miss your plane," Ben said, reluctantly loosening his grip on her.

"Yeah, I know." She blinked back the tears. "I'll call you when I get back to the ranch in August," she added, slowly backing away from him.

"Okay," Ben said hoarsely, realizing how empty his arms suddenly felt.

She looked into those sad blue eyes of his. "Please remember that I love you."

Ben managed a small smile. "I will."

16

Ben watched the van pulling out of the circular drive in front of the training barn. The second group of two year olds was on its way to Ketchum's trainer at Belmont Park in New York. That left him with only ten late developers and half a dozen of Ketchum's older horses being rested up. The pace was definitely going to slow down for the summer.

"Thanks for putting in the good word with Ketchum for me," Mark said, leaning against his sports car. "I'm looking forward to riding some of those nice two year olds of his, especially that big bay colt."

Ben looked at him. "You just make sure you ride 'em to win— or you'll have me paying you a visit."

"You in New York City? Now that might almost be worth messing up for," Mark chuckled, then quickly added, "No, I promise, Ben, no more games. We don't get too many second chances in life, and I'm not going to blow this one."

Ben was halfway through the front door when the first wave of nausea washed over him. He stood there in the doorway a moment, waiting for it to pass. It did, but then came again stronger. Damn. He was going to be sick.

He drank the apple juice slowly, washing down the two pills. Once he had stopped throwing up, he had remembered he still had some of the ulcer medication the Miami doctor had prescribed. As he headed for the bedroom with the glass of juice, he realized he had been foolish to think the ulcer was cured. Damn. Back to half a glass of whiskey at a time.

Ben climbed into bed, sliding under the covers as he leaned back against the headboard. He was feeling a little feverish and had spit up blood. Of course, he shouldn't be surprised. He had spent the last week out all night, every night. Once Lisa had left, he had been overwhelmed by loneliness and couldn't stand the nights alone in the cottage.

Seeing Lisa again had been wonderful. But by coming to see him, she had made him face more of those unpleasant truths he couldn't seem to escape. It was really over between them. And he must have been clinging to a hope that if he ever did go home, they would get back together again. That would explain how empty he felt when he realized that wasn't going to happen.

When they had been together in bed that morning, he couldn't deny he had wanted to make love to her. But then he had seen the truth in her eyes; he had felt it when he held her. She truly did love Scott.

But he had believed her when she said she loved him, too. He had felt it when she had held him after the fiery nightmare. But it was a different kind of love that existed between them now. And he knew that even if he tried, he could never make *"I love you"* mean what it used to for him and Lisa.

Just one more thing to let go of, to learn to live without. Damn. All this letting go was killing him. It would be nice to find something, someone he could hold on to.

But if Lisa, who had known him all his life didn't want him anymore, what woman would? He wasn't exactly a prize these days. He was a has-been rodeo cowboy whose broken, abused body was already making him feel like an old man. And his mind was so messed up that he was afraid to sleep at night.

He understood why Lisa had decided Scott was the man she wanted to spend the rest of her life with. Scott and Chris had always been a lot alike. Both were sensitive and giving, willing to let people see their weaknesses—most certainly not traits he could claim. But Scott had always been quieter than Chris and content to be in the background. When his father had died, Scott had just quietly become a member of the Matthews family without anyone even discussing it. And now it was Scott who was running the ranch and who Lisa loved. Not at all what anyone could have anticipated happening.

But, then again, ever since that bull, all of their lives had taken unexpected twists and turns. He had always thought in terms of what that bull and Waco had done to his life. But Lisa had made him realize that she and Scott were victims, too. And he was sorry about that. But he just didn't share her conviction that he could go home and put everything right again.

Damn. He knew it was more than that. Hell, he was still afraid to go home. No matter how much Lisa believed the ranch had changed, he knew those painful memories were there waiting for him. And with them came the fiery nightmare. It had driven him from the ranch and haunted him all this time. He had to believe it would destroy him if he went back.

Mark had been right. You just didn't get too many second chances in life. And even when you did, sometimes the price was too high.

The flames were everywhere; the heat of the fire made his eyes water. He wanted to run away. But he couldn't. He could hear his father, mother and Chris calling his name, begging him to help them. He moved closer. He could still hear them, but their voices were growing faint. He had to help them or he was going to lose them forever. He reached out to them through the fiery wall...

Ben woke suddenly with a muffled cry, clutching his right arm against his chest. It felt like it was on fire. Leaning over, he turned on the bedside lamp and stared down at his limp arm. He hesitantly touched it with his left hand; it was all right. It hadn't been burned. That damned nightmare was so real. But this time it had been different. He'd never been able to get that close to the fire before. Not that it had accomplished anything. He still hadn't been able to save his family; he could still hear their screams.

"Sure, Ben, we can handle everything here," Bobby said as they sat in the tack room. "It'll do you good to get off the farm for a couple of days. And then when you get back, I'd like to go visit my folks in Pensacola."

"It's a deal," Ben said, getting to his feet. "I'm gonna talk to J.B. and then I'm outta here."

The old man was heading to Reno's stall when Ben stepped out of the tack room. "I hope you can stay outta trouble in Miami without me and Mr. Ryan lookin' out for you."

Ben chuckled as they ambled down the shedrow. "I promise I won't even go near the racetrack," he said. "I'm just gonna spend a few days with Mike and Barbara."

"No drinkin' and no women, huh?" J.B. asked skeptically, slipping under the door webbing into the horse's stall. "And how about gamblin' ?"

Ben put his hands up in surrender. "I promise. None of that."

"Hmph. You know I'll be able to tell when you get back," J.B. warned as he brushed Reno.

"Yeah, I know I can't fool ya," Ben said. "Just turn Reno out while I'm gone, and you do a lot of fishing."

The old man looked at him. "You will be back, won't you, Mr. Ben?"

The question surprised Ben. "Of course, I'm coming back,

J.B. I'm just going to visit Mike and Barbara. What makes you think I wouldn't come back?"

"I don't know," J.B. said with a shrug. "You been awful quiet lately. Like you are really somewhere else."

Ben shook his head; he was always amazed at how much the old man noticed. "Don't you worry, J.B. I promise I'll be back. You know I'm wouldn't go anywhere without you and Reno."

The old man smiled at him. "Okay, Mr. Ben. You tell Miss Barbara and Mr. Mike hello for me," he said. "And you behave yourself."

Scott was relieved at the sound of Lisa's voice through the static of the overseas connection. "You must be dead tired," he said, sitting down in the leather swivel chair in the den. "Is Paris how you remembered it?"

"Yes on both counts," Lisa answered, slipping off her shoes. "I meant to call sooner, but I've been going non-stop since I got here."

Scott cleared his throat. "Well, after the way I acted, I wouldn't have blamed you if you hadn't called at all."

"Now, Scott, you know I wouldn't do that to you," Lisa said. "It's not that I don't understand what you're feeling. It's just that we need to talk about it and not pretend the problem doesn't exist."

"I know. I'm sorry," he returned, adding quietly, "I love you, Lisa."

"I love you," she echoed.

Scott savored the words. "I guess sometimes everything just catches up with me. I shouldn't take it out on you."

"Just don't shut me out and we'll be fine," she said, then asked, "Have you heard from Ben?" She and Ben had decided to wait until she was back at the ranch to tell Scott about her visit.

"No, but it's really my turn to call him. Maybe I'll try to talk to him about coming home. Maybe a wedding will do the trick."

Lisa's heart skipped a beat, then she was sick to her stomach. "Scott, I want us to get married because we love each other and want to spend the rest of our lives together." She paused to take a breath. "Not as a way of getting Ben home."

"Oh, I'm sorry," Scott stammered, realizing now how it must have sounded. "I didn't mean it like that. Please, believe me, I didn't."

Lisa sighed. "This is too complicated to try to figure out on the phone across the ocean. We're just going to have to wait till I get back to the ranch."

"Whatever you think," Scott said. "I don't want to lose you. But I want Ben to come home, too. Is that too much to ask?"

Lisa couldn't answer him. "I'll call you in a couple of days," she said, adding, "I love you," as she hung up.

She sat there on the bed; she hadn't eaten all day and knew should order up some dinner. But she didn't have much of an appetite. The whole situation with Scott and Ben was really getting to her. Ever since she had left Ocala, she hadn't been able to get Ben off her mind. She had hoped calling Scott would put things back in perspective. It hadn't.

It was odd, but only now, two years later, did she fully understand how the loss of his family had devastated Ben. All that anger he had had when he left the ranch was gone, but the grief was still very much with him. And that horrible nightmare had been tormenting him all this time. As long as she lived, she would never forget his anguish when she had held him that night.

Two years ago, Ben hadn't even been able to cry in front of her and Scott. But the nightmare and trying to cope with his loss all this time had finally battered the walls down that night. And she'd never seen Ben look as vulnerable as the day she left him standing there in the doorway.

Part of her had wanted to stay with him. It was unsettling how easy it would have been to get lost again in those blue eyes of his. She supposed he would always have that power over her. When they had been together in bed, she'd thought of making love to him. But then she'd thought of Scott.

If only Ben had allowed her in before–had been able to share his pain before—they might still be together. But now it was too late, wasn't it? She loved Scott. But why did she have to keep reminding herself of that? Maybe it was because her feelings for the two men were spilling over, one onto the other. Maybe it was because she was angry that Ben still had so much control over their lives.

And despite the scars the last few years had left on Ben, she truly believed what she'd told him. The Ben Matthews she'd known and loved nearly all her life was still alive and well. She had to believe that—or there wasn't any hope for any of them.

The summer afternoon thunderstorm struck just as the chicken was barbecued. Grabbing up everything they could at once, the three of them had hurried into the living room from the deck. After the meal, they played a spirited poker game and Barbara cleaned Ben and Mike out.

"How come I feel like she's been setting us up for this for a long time?" Ben asked, watching Barbara count her winnings.

Mike snickered. "Because she has."

"Hmm, I wouldn't be surprised if you were gettin' a cut out of this," Ben suggested, looking over at Mike.

"Ha. Are you kidding? I have to beg for school lunch money."

Barbara laughed. "Poor little male egos got all bruised up," she teased as she began picking up the dishes that had been shoved to one side of the table.

"Guess I'd better help if we ever want a rematch and a chance to win back our money," Ben said, gathering up the silverware and glasses and following Barbara into the kitchen.

Ben had unloaded everything on the counter and was turning to go back to the living room when Barbara put her arms around him. She hugged him tightly and kissed him on the cheek.

He looked at her in surprise. "What was that for?"

238JoAnnGuidry

"Oh, I just thought you needed it," she said warmly as they stood face to face in a loose embrace. "And it's my way of saying thanks for all you've done for Mike."

Again Ben was taken aback. "What are you talking about? He's the one—the two of you are the ones who have helped me," he said sincerely. "Without ever asking anything of me, you two just accepted me the way I was. And, believe me, I know I didn't make it easy sometimes."

Barbara chuckled. "There were moments when I wanted to kick your butt," she admitted and he smiled; she hadn't seen that Texas cowboy smile of his in a long time.

Now it was Ben's turn to give her a kiss on the cheek; he heard the wheelchair coming up behind them. "And if you ever decide to ditch the guy in the wheelchair..."

"I should've known better than to trust a damned Texas cowboy," Mike said and they all laughed.

The rain had taken the edge off the hot, humid south Florida day. Ben and Mike had gone back out on the deck to enjoy the sunset; Barbara had opted to catch up on some reading.

"Sure you don't want me to work on your leg?" Mike asked, taking a sip of the lemonade.

"I told you it's fine. The humidity in Ocala isn't half as bad as here," Ben assured him. "And as much pleasure as it gives you, I'm not gonna let you pull the hell out of my hip."

"Geez, some friend you are."

The two men settled into the comfortable silence known only to good friends. An unusual June breeze drifted across the deck. Ben slid down in the lawn chair, closing his eyes as he rested his head back.

"Tell me about the ranch," Mike said quietly, glancing over at his friend.

Ben didn't move and he kept his eyes closed. "It's twenty

thousand acres of the prettiest Texas hill country there is. It's about thirty miles northwest of San Antonio."

"Did you say twenty thousand acres?"

"Yeah." Ben sat up in the chair. "Used to be bigger. But hard times over the years made it necessary to sell off some of it," he said. "My father made me promise that no matter what, I'd never sell the whole place.

"He'd say, 'Do you what you have to do, Son, but always keep the heart of the ranch.' To him, anything less than ten thousand acres and you might as well lock up the front gate."

Mike shook his head. "Geez, I never imagined it was that kind of ranch. You raise horses and cattle?"

"Yeah, we run a couple thousand head of Hereford cattle and raise the best damned Quarter horses in the whole southwest," Ben said proudly. "Matthews Ranch-bred Quarter horses can do it all, from ranching to rodeoing. And look good doing it, too."

"Reno is from your ranch, isn't he?"

Ben nodded. "He was supposed to be Chris' once in a lifetime horse. My horse, Cherokee, is his full brother. I left him at the ranch because I didn't think it was fair to take him away from the only life he had ever known."

That silence crept back. Mike was somewhat surprised at how easily Ben had talked about the ranch and his family.

"What are you waiting for, Ben?" Mike asked softly.

Ben gazed out across the pasture. "I don't know."

Ben was halfway back to Ocala, listening to Strait's newest tape when the realization struck him. He hadn't had the fiery nightmare. He had talked to Mike about the ranch, his father and Chris, but every night he was in Miami he had slept through till dawn.

He had just closed the cottage door behind him when he had to turn back around. "Hey, Bobby, what's up?" Ben asked, putting his duffle bag down.

"I know you just got back from Miami, but I was hoping you might check in on J.B.," Bobby said.

"Is he sick?"

"I don't think so. But he's been kinda quiet and hasn't come out of his room much since you've been gone."

Ben grabbed his truck keys on the fireplace mantle. "Thanks, Bobby. You go on home," he said, reaching down into the bag and bringing out a box. "I'll head over to the barn right now."

"J.B., Miss Barbara sent you some cookies," Ben said, rapping on the shut door before slowly opening it.

The old man looked up from the book that was opened across his lap; it was one of the Secretariat books Ben had given him.

"Told ya I'd be back," Ben said, sitting down next to J.B. on the bed as he opened the box.

J.B.'s eyes widened and he carefully picked out one of the homemade chocolate chip cookies. "Mmm, Miss Barbara sure can make a good cookie," he said, chewing slowly.

Ben nodded in agreement as he bit into one. "That's one of my favorite pictures of Secretariat," he said, pointing at the historic photo of the 1973 Belmont Stakes victory.

"I don't care what anybody says, that was the greatest race of all time," J.B. said. "Look at that jockey of his, Ronnie Turcotte. He's turned all the way around—lookin' back for the rest of the horses. But they ain't nowhere."

"Thirty lengths back, that's where they are," Ben chimed in.

"Thirty-one lengths," J.B. corrected him. "Big Red won the Belmont Stakes by thirty-one lengths in 2:24 flat. Them are both records that will be long after you and me is gone."

"Amen." Ben handed him another cookie.

J.B. took the cookie, but kept staring at that picture. "I'm startin' to think you were right, Mr. Ben," he said quietly. "I'm startin' to think that I ain't ever gonna see Secretariat again. After all, you are a smart man and you know about a lot of things."

Ben could feel the old man's despair. "Hey, remember, I'm the stupid white man whose hide you saved in Miami," he reminded him. "And besides, I didn't know a damned thing about Secretariat until I met you. I was just a kid when I saw him win the Triple Crown on television. But you were really around him and you've taught me more than any book ever could."

J.B. shrugged, taking a bite. "I guess I'm jest gettin' tired waitin' for him," he said, his voice weary. "And I know you got better things to do than sittin' around with an old man, waitin' on a hoss."

Ben draped his arm around J.B.'s shoulders. "Now didn't you promise me I'd get to help you with Secretariat?"

"Yes, but..."

"No buts. You made me a promise and I'm holding you to it. You and me are in this together."

J.B. smiled at him and popped the last piece of cookie into his mouth.

That evening as Ben sat in the recliner on the screened porch, he wished he'd realized earlier how important waiting for Secretariat was to J.B. Then he'd never just dismissed him with the facts when they'd first met. It was only when J.B. persisted and told him all those stories that he understood it was those memories that kept him going day to day.

No doubt the times J.B. had spent around Secretariat had been the best of his life. Nothing since then had taken the place of those memories. So J.B. clung to the hope that Secretariat would come back into his life. And no one had the right to begrudge him that hope.

In fact, it was somehow comforting that even if he didn't know what he was waiting for, at least J.B. did.

"I just turned him out," the stud groom said, leading them over to the fog-blanketed paddock. "Red!" he called out when they reached the gate. "Come on up here, Red. There's some people here to see you."

They heard him before they saw him, the steady trotting rhythm of horse's hooves on the soft ground. And then from the mist, he emerged. His red coat glistened from the early morning dampness, muscles rippling as he pranced up to them. Ben was sure he had stopped breathing. Even at nineteen, Secretariat was still perfection.

Ben watched in silent awe as J.B. reached out and patted that magnificent head, distinctly marked with an irregular star and thin stripe. And the horse, who had the most overwhelming presence Ben had ever felt, stretched his neck out farther across the fence.

A grinning J.B. slid his hand along the arched neck. "See, I told you, Mr. Ben. I knew he'd be fat and sassy when I saw him again."

Ben wanted to say something, but he couldn't. His breath hadn't come back to him yet, and he was having a hard enough time fighting back the tears. Slowly, he raised the camera and kept clicking until only four shots remained. Handing the camera to the stud groom, he went over to stand next to J.B. and Big Red.

As they drove back to Ocala from Lexington, Kentucky, Ben wondered why he hadn't thought of taking J.B. to see Secretariat before now. Hell, he knew why. Too occupied with his own problems. But he'd been really worried about the old man when he'd gotten back from Miami, and suddenly he'd known what he had to do.

"You know what, Mr. Ben?" J.B. said, shuffling through the pictures again. "I think this one here's my favorite," he announced, holding up one of them and Secretariat.

Ben glanced at it. "Yeah, I like that one, too."

"The minute I met you, I knew you was the one who was gonna help me with Big Red," J.B. said matter-of-factly. " 'Course, you kinda had me worried for awhile there. But I didn't give up on you. I knew you was the one."

Ben laughed. "Well, J.B., you were right all along about everything."

"And you know what else, Mr. Ben?"

"What?"

"You gonna be jest fine, Mr. Ben. You jest wait and see. You gonna be jest fine."

On his way to the walk-in closet, Ben dropped the department store bag on the bed. Bringing the box out, he put it down on the bed, too, and took off the lid. He reached in for the picture of him, Chris, Lisa and Scott, looked at it for a moment and then opened the bag. He slid the picture into the frame and then retrieved the already framed photo of him, Chris and their parents.

Ben strode into the living room and placed the two pictures, side by side, on the fireplace mantle.

17

Ben sat alone at a back table in the Winner's Circle, reading the newspaper and waiting on his breakfast. The headline jumped out at him; he could feel his heart thumping hard against his chest as he read the article.

CHAMPION BULL RIDER KILLED AT CHEYENNE

Cheyenne, Wyo.(AP) Lane Frost, the 1987 world champion bull rider, was killed yesterday at the Cheyenne Frontier Days Rodeo.

Frost, 25, was fatally injured during the bull riding competition. Details were unavailable as to the exact nature of Frost's fatal injuries.

Ben read and reread the small, one column sports brief thrown in with baseball, tennis and basketball news. He remembered Frost as a rising star when his all-around career had ended in Las Vegas. Frost had eventually won his gold buckle two years later, after his and Scott's team roping days had come to an abrupt halt in Waco.

Damn. He couldn't believe it. A man—a rodeo champion—had been killed, and all the paper gave him was two lousy paragraphs. He snatched the paper off the table and hurried out of the restaurant.

"Matthews Ranch," Scott greeted, then took a sip from the steaming mug of coffee.

"Tell me about Lane Frost."

Scott swallowed the mouthful of hot coffee; it made his throat ache as it slid downward. "Are you sure, Ben?" he asked hoarsely, surprised the news had reached Ocala.

"Yeah. Tell me."

With a sigh, Scott sat down at the kitchen table and put the mug down. "Rory Briggs—you know, the UT rodeo coach—was there with some of the kids. He called me last night and told me about it. The kids were really upset," he said, pausing to collect his thoughts.

"Frost made his ride okay. But when he came off, he landed on all fours in the mud. Everyone seems to think that kept him from getting up and out of there like he should have.

"The bull was headed over to the chute, so no one was paying him any attention. But then he just sorta turned around and looked over at Frost. Rory said it was like the damned animal couldn't figure out why that cowboy was still where he was.

"And real easy like, the bull trots on up behind Frost—like he was just curious and wanted to have a look. He got up right behind him, then it was like he changed his mind and turned back around." Scott stopped for a moment, hoping Ben would tell him he had heard enough; he didn't.

"He was one of those big, long-horned bulls. And when he

turned his head, a horn hit Frost in the back and knocked him back to the ground face first. The bull went on ahead to the chute, and it had looked like such an easy tap that no one thought Frost was seriously hurt. At worst, they thought he might've had the wind knocked out of him.

"Rory said Frost started to get up, raised his hand for help and then went down again. Then everyone knew he was in real trouble."

Ben cleared his dry throat. "Finish it."

"They think the horn broke a rib and it punctured his heart," Scott said quietly. "He was dead when they turned him over."

Silence. Ben could feel the tightness again in his chest, and he was sick to his stomach. One of his broken ribs had punctured his left lung; the doctor had told him it could just as easily have been his heart. Why Lane Frost and not him?

"Ben?"

"Yeah."

"Are you okay?"

"Yeah. I'll talk to ya later," Ben managed, then slowly hung up the phone.

He just stood there; numb, staring at the phone and hearing Scott's words replaying in his mind. *"...horn hit Frost in the back...broke a rib and it punctured his heart...he was dead when they turned him over."* Why Lane Frost and not him?

With a shudder, Ben turned away and walked to the kitchen cabinet. Retrieving the Jack Daniel's fifth, he poured a full glass and gulped it down. All of it at once. As he brought the glass down to the counter, the liquor was already setting his stomach on fire. He winced, but refilled the glass and drained it again.

The ulcer absorbed the second glass of liquor and sent him a painful warning. He gripped the edge of the counter until the spasm eased. This was crazy. What was he going to do? Stand here in the kitchen and drink himself to death? Damn. He needed to move, to get outside.

Hurrying through the living room, he grabbed his truck keys on the fireplace mantle. He paused, looking at the pictures on the mantle. Why his family and not him? Another jab of pain made him move, and he slammed the door shut behind him.

Ben was about to park the truck behind the barn when he realized the farm was not big enough for the kind of riding he needed to do. He could feel the panic gripping him tightly. Damn. He hit the steering wheel with a clenched right fist. Damn. Reaching over, he pushed the Strait tape into the cassette deck, turned up the volume and drove away.

"Triple Diamond Farm," Bobby answered.

"Hey, Bobby, it's Ben," he said. "Something came up. I'm going to have to be away for awhile."

"Sure, Ben," Bobby said. "Don't worry. I'll take care of everything."

"And tell J.B. not to worry," Ben added. "I'll be back as soon as I can."

He'd been on the outskirts of Pensacola when he'd pulled into the busy truck stop. After paying for the tankful of gas, he'd walked over to one of the six booths lined up outside the restaurant. There was another call he needed to make.

"Hello," Mike greeted, marking his place in the chapter he was reading.

"Hey, Tonto."

Mike put the book face down on the table. "What's up, Lone Ranger? And it's no use begging me to come up and work on your leg," he said jokingly. "No, you blew your chance."

"I-uh-I..."

"Ben, what's wrong?"

"I'll talk to ya soon as I can, okay?"

Mike didn't like the sound of his friend's voice. "Just tell me you're all right, Ben."

He shuffled his feet and grasped the phone tighter. "I'm all right," Ben said quietly. "Give Barbara my love."

Scott stomped on the brakes so hard that the mug tumbled off the dashboard; coffee splashed everywhere. He stared in disbelief at the royal blue and silver pickup truck parked outside the barn. Finally, he slid his foot off the brake and drove slowly forward, parking alongside the truck he hadn't seen in two years.

As Scott walked hurriedly into the barn, disappointment swept over him. No one was there. Maybe he had just imagined that truck. He turned around and went back outside. It was real; it was still there. Then Scott looked over to the corral; Cherokee was gone. He smiled. His first impulse was to saddle a horse and catch up with him. He knew he had ridden out to the oak tree. No. He could wait. All that mattered now was that Ben was home.

Something tickled his face; he tried to brush it away. It persisted. Ben opened his eyes and found himself staring at a horse's white-blazed face. Reno. Wait a minute—this was a bay horse, not a sorrel. The horse nudged him again as he quickly sat up.

"Cherokee, you ol' common-bred mule," Ben said fondly as he patted the horse's soft muzzle, then scrambled to his feet.

As far as he could see was Matthews Ranch land. Damn. He hadn't been dreaming. He'd driven straight through from Ocala to the ranch. Stiffly, Ben limped away from where he'd been sleeping under the oak tree. On the horizon, he could just make out a small herd of grazing red and white Hereford cattle.

He remembered sitting in the Winner's Circle, reading the article about Lane Frost. Then he'd called Scott because the article had said only that Frost had been killed, not how. And to a rodeo cowboy, the how was just as important. Maybe if you knew how, you wouldn't let it happen to you. Maybe if you knew how, the death would somehow make sense. Then maybe you could go ahead and make your next ride without thinking about it. Once a rodeo cowboy, always a rodeo cowboy.

The first light of dawn had barely crept in when he'd driven up to the barn. And somehow he wasn't surprised that Cherokee was up in the corral instead of turned out with the herd. When he had come out of the barn with the saddle and bridle, the horse had come up to him like he'd never been away.

Ben ambled over to the horse now and scratched him between the ears. "You'd be real proud of your little brother. He's a helluva pony horse," he said as Cherokee rubbed his head against him. "But I sure have missed you."

Sliding back along the horse, Ben reached in the saddlebag and brought out the canteen. He took a long swig before splashing some water on his face. From where the sun was in the sky, he figured it was mid-morning. He could still get in a couple of hours of riding before the late summer sun really bore down.

Scott saw him coming from way off. But he made himself wait there in front of the barn. Finally, Ben reined Cherokee to a stand-still a few feet from him. He dismounted in silence and just stood there, smiling at him.

Scott cleared his throat. "You're probably gonna get mad, but I'm gonna hug ya anyhow," he said, moving toward Ben and half-expecting him to step back.

Instead, Ben took a step forward. "I'd be real mad if ya didn't," he drawled and the two men embraced.

Ben ambled into the living room, taking in all the changes in his house. Or rather what used to be his house. He ran his hand through his still damp hair; the long shower and fresh clothes had him feeling like a human being again. Lisa had stored all his fur-nishings and redecorated. It was an odd sensation, standing in the living room of the house he had built with rodeo earnings—and yet knowing it really wasn't his anymore. And he had no inten-tions of taking it back. No. It belonged to Scott and Lisa now.

He walked over to the fireplace mantle, and there among some art pieces was a duplicate of the picture Lisa had sent him in Miami. Pictures on the mantle. His mother had left her mark on all of them.

Turning away, he made his way down the hallway to the kitchen. "Well, aren't we the happy little homemaker," Ben commented as Scott busily made sandwiches.

"With Lisa away, I've had to learn to fend for myself again," Scott said, handing Ben a plate with a triple-decker sandwich on it. "I see you found the boxes with the clothes you left behind."

"Yeah, you know Lisa. Everything was neatly labeled—Ben's blue shirts, Ben's brown shirts, Ben's work jeans, Ben's rodeo jeans." They both laughed.

"You should've seen the show she put on, packing for Europe," Scott said. "I've never seen such an organized person. I think she had a bag for every day of the week."

Ben chuckled. "I believe it," he said, remembering all the luggage in her rental car and feeling guilty for not telling Scott about her Ocala visit. "So, how are you and Lisa?" he asked, figuring it was a better subject than Frost.

Scott filled their glasses with iced tea as he joined Ben at the table. "She really wants to get married."

"And that's a problem?"

"Well, our situation is a little complicated, don't you think?"

"What's complicated? You love her. She loves you. Get married."

"But..."

"But hell what, Scott?" Ben asked deliberately. "What did you think? I'd show up one day and Lisa would leave you for me?"

Scott shrugged. "Yeah, I guess."

"Damn, Scott. Lisa and I are over. Hell, we were over long before we even knew it."

"But I know you two loved each other," Scott said. "And I guess I just can't get past that."

Ben sat back in the chair. "Yeah, we did love each other. But not the way you two do now. She wanted—and deserved—more than I could give her. And let me tell you something, even if I wanted to, I couldn't take Lisa away from you. She really does love you, Scott."

"How come you're so sure about that?"

"She came to see me on her way to Europe."

"What?"

"Yeah, she was really worried about the two of you," Ben explained. "She tried to talk me into coming home. She was afraid of losing you and said I was the only one you were going to listen to. So listen up," he ordered.

"What happened between the three of us wasn't your fault and it wasn't Lisa's. When I came back from Wyoming, I was like a horse on loco weed. And you two just happened to be in the wrong place at the wrong time. If I could change what I did to the two of you, I would. There's not a day that I don't regret it. But what's done is done. Now you and Lisa need to go on with your lives."

Scott looked at him, trying to absorb everything he had said. "And what about you? What about your life?"

Ben offered a weak smile. "I figure I've made it this far. It has to get easier from here on. But I won't lie to you. There's still a lot of stuff I'm sorting through. But I am sure about this—you and Lisa belong together."

Ben followed Scott through the new bunkhouse; he'd approved the blueprints when they were sent to him in Miami. In addition to the sleeping quarters, there was a large study room, six bathrooms, a kitchen and dining room.

"During the school year, we rotate out a group every other week," Scott said as they ambled through the facility. "Then during the spring and fall roundups, we use the juniors and seniors as much as we can. The rodeo team spends the weekends on the road."

"Sounds like you've got everything running smoothly. How's the team doing?"

"Finished second at nationals last year, and Rory thinks they might take it this year. No individual gold buckles, but there's a couple that'll get one or two before they're done," Scott said. "The ones that Rory took up to Cheyenne are the best of the lot. They wanted to stay here for the summer and since a couple are from broken homes, I didn't see any reason why not."

The mention of Cheyenne made Ben uneasy; he still wasn't up to talking about Frost. "Are they headed to another show?"

"No. Rory thought it'd be best just to come back here and let what happened to Frost settle a bit. They should be back by to-morrow," Scott said. He paused, then added, "You being here is going to really help them deal with it a lot easier."

"How do you figure that?"

"Because just like Frost, you're a hero to those kids. But you're alive and well—and here."

"I doubt those young bucks will be very impressed by the likes of an old-timer like me," Ben said skeptically.

"Well, I know better. You'll see," Scott persisted. "Now, come on. Let's see if we two old-timers can rustle up some supper."

Scott heard Ben coming out of the guest bedroom only half an hour after they'd turned in. After supper, Ben had kept the con-versation on ranch business. And that had been fine with him; he was still trying to deal with the fact that Ben had driven home on impulse—and hadn't said if he was coming back for good or not. As the night wore on, he noticed Ben growing anxious and yet he had had only one glass of Jack Daniel's the whole time they talked. He'd thought that was odd. Maybe Ben had lost his taste for the whiskey he'd practically been weaned on.

When Scott padded into the kitchen, the truck headlights shone through the window as Ben backed out then drove away. Scott knew where he was going. He'd seen Ben glancing over at his parents' house several times that afternoon. He just wished Ben would give himself a little time; he didn't have to deal with every-thing at once.

Ben leaned forward on the steering wheel, folding his hands on top of it. He wanted to go into the house. Or at least he thought he did. Damn. Not yet. He just wasn't ready to face what was waiting for him in that house.

Tommy groggily opened the kitchen back door, grateful for the aroma of fresh-brewed coffee. Closing the door behind him, he turned expecting to say good morning to Scott. Instead, he didn't say anything as he instantly recognized the tall, black-haired man with the scar down the left side of his face.

"Good morning," Ben said from where he stood in front of the stove. "You definitely look like you could use some good strong coffee."

Tommy silently watched him fill two mugs and then put them on the table.

"Oh, I'm Ben," he said, extending his right hand. "You guys must have gotten in late, huh?" he asked as he eyed the small, wiry, brown-haired, brown-eyed kid.

Tommy knew he was shaking hands with Ben Matthews, the four-time world all-around cowboy who owned the ranch and that he should at least try to say something. "Tommy Harper," he heard himself mumble.

Ben grinned. "Well, have a seat, Tommy. Maybe some coffee will get your brain working."

"It'd take a lot more than coffee to make that happen," Scott said with a chuckle as he walked into the kitchen. "Is everybody else still asleep?" he asked, pouring a mugful of coffee.

Tommy nodded, blowing on his steaming coffee. "Yeah. I was so tired when we got in, but then I just couldn't sleep."

Scott glanced over at Ben, who was looking at the subdued kid. "We're gonna go out and count cows shortly. You're welcomed to join us."

Tommy's face brightened. "I'll get the horses ready," he offered, hurrying out of the kitchen with mug in hand.

They had been riding for almost an hour now. Tommy still couldn't believe he was out counting cows with Ben Matthews. He had given up all hope that the man was going to come back to the ranch before he graduated. And here he was, riding with the four-time world all-around cowboy. He picked up snatches of Ben and Scott's reminiscing; he hadn't realized Scott had grown up on the ranch. He'd known the two men had been team roping partners, but it was obvious now just how close they were.

Of course, he knew about what had happened to the Matthews family. And though no one had ever said it out loud, everyone figured that was why Ben had been gone for two years. Maybe he was better off than he thought, being an only child and not particularly close to his divorced parents. He couldn't even imagine the kind of grief that had kept Ben away from the ranch for so long, and had made him stop rodeoing altogether. Champions just didn't walk away in the middle of the season, without good cause. But losing your family was definitely a justifiable reason.

"Ya see, Ben, this is what I'm talkin' about," Scott drawled, leaning forward on his saddlehorn. "Ya think these kids are paying attention, and they're just daydreamin' on ya."

Ben had reined Cherokee up alongside Marlboro. "Well, unless that horse of his can count, I'd say he'll starve tryin' to make a living as a cowboy."

"What the...?" Tommy muttered, suddenly realizing he was riding alone.

"By golly, I think he woke up," Scott teased as Tommy trotted his horse back to where they had stopped.

Tommy couldn't help but gloat when they rode up to the barn and his teammates realized who he was with. After Rory made quick introductions and the horses were taken care of, they headed back to Scott's house for supper. Tommy climbed in the truck with Ben and Scott, giving his friends a smartass grin as they drove away.

When supper was over and they were all just sitting around talking, Tommy waited but a minute or so before he followed Ben outside to the front porch.

"You mind some company?" Tommy asked as Ben propped his feet up on the wooden railing that framed the porch on all sides.

"Have a seat." Ben motioned to the empty chair alongside him. "Other than from the back of a horse, this is the best view of the ranch. It's why I built this house here."

Tommy scooted his chair closer up to the railing so he, too, could put his feet up. "Yeah. It must have been great growing up on this place."

Ben didn't answer right away; dozens of childhood memories were flashing through his mind. "It was," he said quietly. "But don't get me wrong. My father saw to it that his sons earned their keep. We didn't get any free rides. How about you? Where'd you grow up?"

"Dallas. My father has a law practice there. And my mother is somewhere in Switzerland on her third honeymoon."

"So how'd you get interested in being a rodeo cowboy?"

"Hell if I know," Tommy honestly answered. "But I don't ever remember not wanting to ride broncs and bulls. My dad swears my mother snuck a cowboy in on him, and if you knew my mother, it's not all that farfetched."

Ben liked how the kid didn't mince any words. "You and your father get along okay?"

Tommy shrugged. "He's all right. We just don't have a lot in common."

"But he's paying for your college education, right?"

"Yeah. We made a deal," Tommy replied. "As long as I got a degree, then it was up to me if I wanted to waste the rest of my life rodeoing."

Ben smiled slightly, thinking of his own father's insistence that he go to college before pursuing a pro rodeo career. "Well, that's a fair deal. There's plenty of time to rodeo."

"I don't know," Tommy said dubiously. "Look at Ty Murray. He's likely to win the all-around this year and he's only nineteen. I'm already twenty-one."

Ben shook his head in amazement at the mention of Murray; Scott had told him about the phenomenal kid who had the rodeo world buzzing. "Well, I don't think you're an old man yet, Tommy. Wait till you get to be my age, then we'll talk about feeling old."

Tommy chuckled. "Oh, I think you've got a few good years left in you," he said. "You were what—twenty-two when you won your first all-around?"

"Yeah, I was kinda in a hurry like you," Ben said, thinking how long ago that life seemed now. "I got my degree in three years and I was down the road."

"Man, I can't wait," Tommy said eagerly. "Was that first gold buckle the best one?"

The question caught Ben off guard. He had always thought of the first one as just that—the first of six and then hopefully, a record-breaking seven. Each one of his four gold buckles had just meant he was one closer to his dream. He realized now he had never taken the time to enjoy and appreciate each one individually.

"I guess that was a stupid question, huh?" Tommy asked when Ben didn't answer him. "I'm sure each one was better than the one before. I saw you win the fourth one in Oklahoma City."

Ben eyed him. "You must have been pretty young."

"I was sixteen and had just gotten my driver's license," Tommy recalled. "I begged and begged until Dad let me and some friends drive up to the Finals.

"You were unbelievable. I don't think there was a go-round you didn't score high in. You made it look so easy."

Ben shrugged. "I drew a lot of good stock. That makes a big difference," he said, getting to his feet; he didn't particularly like where the conversation was headed. "Let's go try to get a card game going."

For the second night, Ben sat in his truck and tried to will himself into that house. He lost track of time, finally giving up and driving away.

"So what do you think of them?" Rory asked after the six boys had each tried a horse.

"Not bad at all," Ben answered, watching from where they sat perched on the corral fence; the crew was running the bulls into the chutes. "You've done a nice job with them."

"I thought after what happened in Cheyenne that the best thing was to get 'em up on some stock," Rory said. "It sure worked out nice that you were here when we got back, Ben. Kinda took their minds off Frost. Any chance of you staying?"

Ben could feel Scott's stare on him; Briggs had just asked him what Scott had been wanting to since he had gotten there. "I'm not sure yet what I'm gonna do," he answered simply.

"Well, it'd be great having you around. These boys can be a handful," Rory added, tilting back his well-worn hat. "Wouldn't hurt my feelings a bit to have you show them a thing or two."

Ben watched Tommy climbing up on the chute. "We'll see."

As Tommy got set on the bull, Ben wondered if he'd be as good as he had been on the bronc. Tommy nodded and the gate sprung open. That kid was stuck to that bull like molasses on toast. Ben studied him closely; he had damned good form. His height had always been a disadvantage on the bulls, but Tommy's shorter, compact frame was well-suited for bull-riding.

And then it happened. Tommy spurred the bull—two quick rakes in the flanks. It was more than enough. The bull spun hard ninety degrees to the left and then reversed his action, ninety degrees to the right. Tommy flew off, hit the ground with a thud and rolled for a few feet before coming to a stop face down in the dirt. The crew chased the bull into the chute.

Ben was off the fence and in the middle of the arena before anyone else had even reacted. Grabbing Tommy by the back of his shirt, he jerked him to his feet and spun him around. He held him with both hands by his shirt collar now and waited a moment for the kid to get his breath back.

As Tommy's vision cleared, he realized he was face to face with Ben. And that only the toes of his boots were touching the ground. As he looked into those angry grey eyes, he was sure Ben was going to hit him.

"Don't ever...ever spur a bull here again," Ben warned, glaring at him. "It ain't worth the price."

From the fence, Scott watched as Ben turned Tommy loose; the kid staggered back a few steps before he regained his balance. Scott smiled. If that bull hadn't put the fear in Tommy, he was damned sure Ben had.

Without another word, Ben strode out of the arena. He walked over to the water trough, took off his hat and put his head under the pump's spout. Working the hand crank, he let the ice cold water trickle down on him. After a few minutes, he straightened up and pulled a handkerchief from his back pocket as he ambled over to the bench up against the barn.

Scott hopped down from the fence and joined him on the bench. They sat there side by side in silence for a few minutes.

"Remember that ol' bronc your father had?" Scott asked quietly.

"Hmph, how could I forget?" Ben said, running his right hand back through his wet hair.

"I remember how we used to sneak into his corral whenever your father was out working," Scott recalled. "He may have been old, but that bronc put you on the ground hard every time. You were what, twelve?"

Ben chuckled. "Yeah. And I was determined to ride that ol' bronc. But that horse and Dad had other ideas."

"I'll never forget the day you hit the ground right about the time your father rode up," Scott said, grinning at the memory. "He jerked you up off the ground just about like you did Tommy—and proceeded to give you one hell of a whippin'."

Ben was laughing now. "Yeah and as I recall, you sorta disappeared real quick like."

"I wasn't gonna risk him tearing into me just for the hell of it after he was done with you," Scott said as the two men laughed together.

Ben wiped his face with the handkerchief. "A little while after that, I asked Mother where that ol' bronc had come from. She told me Dad had had some of his best rides on that horse. But he had broken a few bones off him, too. Long after he was off the road, Dad heard that bronc was headed to the killers. He tracked down the stock contractor and bought him." Ben paused; the faces of his mother and father were suddenly all too clear. "Mother figured that ol' bronc reminded Dad of his best—and worst—days."

Scott glanced at Ben; he could feel how difficult it was for him even now to talk about his parents. "You never did try to ride that horse after that."

Ben shook his head. "One beatin' was plenty for me," he said. "And then after Mother told me that story, I somehow understood what that bronc meant to Dad. The day that horse died was one of the few times I remember seeing Dad cry."

Scott wondered for a moment if he should tell Ben about what his last comment had brought to mind; he didn't want to upset him, but he thought it was important he knew. "I saw your father cry once," he said. "When you got hurt, it was like the light just went out of his eyes. And while he was being strong for the rest of us, I could tell he didn't really believe you were gonna make it.

"And when Chris came in the waiting room that day and told us you had come out of the coma, your father just got up without saying a word and walked out. In a little bit, your mother followed him. Then when we headed for your room, we saw them down at the end of the hallway. Your mother was holding him—and he was bawling like a baby."

Ben leaned forward, clasping his hands in front of him as he rested his elbows on his knees. He was torn between wanting to hear the words and wanting to tell Scott to stop.

"I know your father wasn't much on words. But he did love

you, Ben," Scott said softly. "And he was so proud of you. Not because of all those gold buckles, either. But because he knew a man couldn't have asked for a better son."

Ben could feel his emotions getting the best of him. This was what he had been afraid would happen if he came back home. He suddenly got to his feet and hastily walked away.

Scott felt his heart breaking; he had probably just sent Ben running back to Florida.

Tommy poked his head in through the partially opened kitchen back door. "Is Ben here?"

Scott twisted around in the chair. "He's on the front porch," he answered, looking at the large purple bruise on Tommy's right cheek where he had hit the ground first. "You okay?"

"Yeah. Just ate a little dirt, that's all," Tommy drawled, holding the door ajar. "You think it'd be all right if I go talk to Ben? I don't want him mad at me."

"He wasn't mad at you. He was mad at what you did," Scott explained. "Yeah, go ahead and talk to him. But don't be surprised if you don't like what he has to say."

Tommy stood there for a moment. "I'll take my chances," he finally said, closing the door and heading for the front porch.

From the corner of his eye, Ben saw Tommy climb up on the porch and sit down quietly next to him. He kept staring ahead at the view.

"What I did was pretty stupid, huh?" Tommy asked.

"Yeah."

"Is that what happened when you got hurt? You spurred that bull at the Finals in Vegas?"

Damn. The kid knew how to ask the gut-busters. "Yeah," Ben answered. "And it was just as stupid when I did it."

Tommy moved to the edge of the chair, turning to face Ben.

"But you were trying to win the all-around—your fifth all-around. You were just doing whatever it took to win."

Ben thought about that for a minute. "No, I'd have won it on a straight ride," he admitted. "But I was mad at myself for it coming down to that last ride like it did. So I got cocky and greedy.

"I didn't want to just win—I wanted to win big. I wanted to make sure there was no doubt who the best damned all-around cowboy was." He paused, struck with how clearly he saw it all now.

"Well, I forgot one thing while I was trying to impress everybody with what a hell of a cowboy I was," he said, looking at Tommy. "That bull didn't give a damn that I was the four-time world all-around champion cowboy. All he cared about was gettin' me on the ground where he could hurt me. And that's what he did."

Tommy let Ben's words settle. He knew there was truth in them, but something was nagging at him. "But look at Lane Frost," he blurted out. "He had made his ride. That damned bull just came up behind him and popped him with a horn. No spurring. No bad wreck. But just like that, Frost was dead."

"Believe me, I've been trying to make some sense of it, too," Ben conceded. "If you compare the two wrecks, I'm the one who should be dead and Frost should be sittin' here talkin' to you. But maybe that's what you need to remember. Sometimes it just doesn't make sense. And being a rodeo cowboy is dangerous enough without thinking we can push our luck and not pay the price."

Tommy stared hard at Ben. "What if I'm willing to pay the price?"

"You're going to have to answer that question for yourself," Ben said, returning the stare. "Just don't think you'll get off easy. Don't be surprised that even long after your rodeo days are over, you're still paying the price. And that's when you'll know if it was worth it."

Dusk was just settling in. Scott was at the kitchen sink, washing the coffee cups that had piled up during the day. As he looked out the window, he saw Ben coming around the corner of the house. But instead of coming to the back door, he went to his truck. As he drove away, Scott hoped he'd find the answers he was looking for in that house.

Ben slowly unlocked the front door. After Tommy had left, he had sat there alone, trying to sift through all the emotions the kid's questions had stirred up. As the day's light had begun to fade, his thoughts were on his parents' house. Maybe it wouldn't seem so foreboding if he tried to go in before dark.

Making his way down the entryway, Ben hesitated for a moment. Maybe he wasn't ready for this. Damn. When would he ever be? He made himself move forward and, in reflex, flicked on the lights as he stepped into the living room. Everything was as he had left it when he had gone to Miami. Walking over to the couch, he pulled the canvas covering off; he duplicated the action with first his mother's rocking chair and then his father's recliner.

Going over to the fireplace, he bent down and opened the box he had packed the pictures in. One by one, he removed the newspaper each was wrapped in and put them back on the mantle. He didn't stop until the box was empty. Gazing at the pictures, he suddenly realized how connected they all were, each one forever preserving a moment in time that would never be again.

On unsteady legs, Ben moved away and slowly sat down in his father's recliner. He ran his hands across the well-worn arms. Bending over, he pulled off his boots and then pushed back until the foot rest popped up. With one last look around the room, he closed his eyes and waited for what he knew would come.

The flames were everywhere; the heat of the fire made his eyes water. He wanted to run away. But he couldn't. He could barely hear his father, mother and Chris calling his name. Their voices were so faint. He moved closer. He couldn't hear them anymore. They were leaving him. No, don't leave me. He ran through the fiery wall...

The fire was gone. There was a cool breeze blowing across the pasture. He turned around; he was under the oak tree. He listened for their voices. Silence. But they were here. He could feel them. They hadn't left him. Peace. Finally, peace.

"Ben," Scott whispered, gently touching him on the arm.

He woke with a sigh and slowly opened his eyes as he tried to figure out where he was. And then he knew. Ben sat up quickly, making the foot rest snap down.

Scott squeezed his arm. "It's okay," he said soothingly. "Here, I brought over coffee," he said, handing him one of the mugs as he sat down on the couch.

Ben wrapped his hands around the mug and took several swallows of the soothing, hot coffee. The heaviness he felt in his eyes told him he'd been crying in his sleep.

"Your mother loved those pictures," Scott said, looking up at the mantle as he sipped at the coffee. "Each new one had to have its special place up there."

Ben didn't say anything as he took another swallow from the cup and tried to clear his head. He knew he had had the fiery nightmare, but he had apparently slept through it this time. Then he remembered running through the wall of fire, not wanting his parents and Chris to leave him. He hadn't been able to save them; yet, he felt they were with him. And he felt more at peace with himself than he had in a very long time.

"Are you going to stay, Ben?" Scott asked quietly.

Ben stared at the pictures. "It still hurts, Scott," he said. "I suppose it always will. I'm just gonna have to learn to live with it." He paused and, after a moment, added, "And I think the best place for me to do that is here."

Lisa had had one of her gallery staff pick her up at the airport; she'd wanted to surprise Scott. Dropping her bags off at the house, she scampered into a ranch truck to go find him. She needed to hold him.

As she neared the main barn, she saw that most of the ranch hands and the kids were gathered at the corral. When she stepped out of the truck, she saw Scott on Marlboro in the middle of the arena, giving a roping demonstration. She waved at him, but he couldn't see her because of the men sitting up on the top railing of the corral. There was something very familiar about that cowboy leaning up against the gate next to Billy Joe. And then he turned around. It was Ben.

He flashed that damned cowboy smile of his; she felt her knees go weak as he started walking toward her. She wasn't sure if she wanted to run to him or away from him. She wasn't ready for him to be back. She needed some time alone with Scott.

But then Ben was there and she was in his arms. She didn't want it to, but it felt wonderful to have him holding her. She started to hug him tighter, but he abruptly pulled away and kissed her on the cheek as he did. And for a moment, he stared right into her eyes, right into her soul. With a wink, he gently released her and turned away.

Lisa stood there, watching him go back to the corral. And as the breath slowly came back into her body, she knew the truth. She loved Scott.

Hurrying to the corral, she could see Scott had gotten off the horse and was now coming toward her. He barely got the gate opened when she wrapped her arms around him. She didn't even mind the approving whistles and clapping from their cowboy audience as they passionately kissed.

"J.B., I really want you to come back to Texas with me," Ben pleaded as the old man shook his head.

"I know you do, Mr. Ben. But this where I belong," J.B. said matter-of-factly. "I belong here with these ol' racehorses."

"But who's gonna make sure I stay out of trouble?" Ben asked, trying another tactic.

J.B. grinned at him. "Oh, you be fine now that you going home," he said. "You be needin' to go home for a long time."

Ben sighed in resignation. "Okay. But I'm gonna leave Reno here with you. That way I'll have something to ride when I come to visit."

"That's a mighty fine idea, Mr. Ben. You know I'll take good care of him for you."

Ben slid his arm around the old man's shoulders, hugging him tightly. "Yeah, I know. 'Cause you're the best, J.B."

Mike steered himself to the kitchen table, taking the box that had just been delivered from his lap and putting it on one of the chairs to open it. He laughed as he brought out the two beige felt cowboy hats. Looking inside the box for a note, he instead found two first-class airline tickets to San Antonio. He smiled, blinking at the tears welling in his eyes. Ben was finally back where he belonged. The cowboy was home.

18

Ben grabbed the phone mid-ring. "Matthews Ranch."

"Hey, Texas," Ryan greeted without formality.

"Hey, Okie."

"I just thought I'd check up on ya and make sure I knew exactly where ya were," Ryan drawled. "Looks like we're gonna be neighbors soon. I'm starting up my own private investigation firm in Tulsa after the first of the year."

Ben chuckled. "I'll keep that in mind if I have to cross the line into that sorry country of yours."

"You do that. And you never know, we just might work together again. Stranger things have happened."

Ben was intrigued. "Well, Okie, if the need ever arises, you just call. And considering the way you holler, I know I'll hear ya."

Ryan laughed. "Boomer Sooner."

"Hook 'em 'Horns."

The plan had been to just be one of the crowd at the National Finals Rodeo in Las Vegas. But before Ben could get to the grandstands, cowboys he hadn't seen in years starting coming up to him. There were handshakes, slaps on the back and "good to see ya" greetings. Next thing he knew, Jim Reynolds walked up to him, shook his hand and stuck a VIP pass on his shirt pocket. Damn. So much for blending in with the crowd.

"It's great to see you, Ben," Reynolds said warmly. "You know Dan Cooper works for me now. He's around here somewhere, and he's gonna be one happy cowboy when he sets eyes on you."

Ben grinned sheepishly. "If we miss each other, I'll come by your office before I leave," he offered. "I'd better go find my seat."

Reynolds took him by the arm. "No way. You go watch on the fence by the chutes with the other cowboys," he insisted, pulling Ben in that direction. "That's where you belong."

The arena was eerily quiet now. The enthusiastic crowd had long gone; the cowboys had headed back to their hotel rooms to get ready for the ritual celebration. It had been a day a select few had become champions, while many others would tell of coming close.

Ben stood alone in the center of the arena where his life had been changed. He had wondered if the ghosts would haunt him here, but they were nowhere to be found. And he was glad he had witnessed Ty Murray become the youngest all-around champion cowboy ever. Damn. That kid was something special.

Bending down, he scooped up a handful of dirt and then let it sift through his fingers. It made him think of when he had spread J.B.'s ashes at Hallandale in October. The old black man had passed away quietly in his sleep—two days after Secretariat had died.

As the last of the dirt slid through his hand, Ben stood up and looked around the massive arena. He hoped Scott and Lisa were enjoying their honeymoon in Hawaii. As soon as they got back, they needed to start planning the traditional Matthews Ranch week-long Christmas celebration and rodeo. Mike and Barbara would be making their second trip to the ranch then.

And after the first of the year, he and Scott had a lot of hard work and rodeos ahead of them if they were going to end up here next December. He figured he owed Scott a team roping gold buckle.

Ben let Cherokee settle into that smooth, ground-covering fast walk of his. His father had always put a lot of stock in the way a horse walked. He'd say, *"Son, a good cow pony steps out like he owns the ground."*

Ben smiled, watching the horse's ears flick back and forth as he softly sang the words to "Amarillo By Morning."

Damn. He still couldn't sing like Strait.